ENTER THE EDGAR RICE BURROUGHS UNIVERSE

A century before the term "crossover" became a buzzword in popular culture, Edgar Rice Burroughs created the first expansive, fully cohesive literary universe. Coexisting in this vast cosmos was a pantheon of immortal heroes and heroines—Tarzan of the Apes®, Jane Porter™, John Carter®, Dejah Thoris®, Carson Napier™, and David Innes™ being only the best known among them. In Burroughs' 80-plus novels, their epic adventures transported them to the strange and exotic worlds of Barsoom®, Amtor™, Pellucidar®, Caspak™, and Va-nah™, as well as the lost civilizations of Earth and even realms beyond the farthest star. Now the Edgar Rice Burroughs Universe expands in an all-new series of canonical novels written by today's talented authors!

THE EDGE OF ALL WORLDS

CARSON OF VENUS®

EDGAR RICE BURROUGHS UNIVERSE™

The Edgar Rice Burroughs Universe is the interconnected and cohesive literary cosmos created by the Master of Adventure and continued in new canonical works authorized by Edgar Rice Burroughs, Inc., the corporation based in Tarzana, California, that was founded by Burroughs in 1923. Unravel the mysteries and explore the wonders of the Edgar Rice Burroughs Universe alongside the pantheon of heroes and heroines that inhabit it in both classic tales of adventure penned by Burroughs and brand-new epics from today's talented authors.

TARZAN® SERIES
Tarzan of the Apes
The Return of Tarzan
The Beasts of Tarzan
The Son of Tarzan
Tarzan and the Jewels of Opar
Jungle Tales of Tarzan
Tarzan the Untamed
Tarzan the Terrible
Tarzan and the Golden Lion
Tarzan and the Ant Men
Tarzan, Lord of the Jungle
Tarzan and the Lost Empire
Tarzan at the Earth's Core
Tarzan the Invincible
Tarzan Triumphant
Tarzan and the City of Gold
Tarzan and the Lion Man
Tarzan and the Leopard Men
Tarzan's Quest
Tarzan the Magnificent
Tarzan and the Forbidden City
Tarzan and the Foreign Legion
Tarzan and the Madman
Tarzan and the Castaways
Tarzan and the Tarzan Twins
Tarzan: The Lost Adventure (with Joe R. Lansdale)

BARSOOM® SERIES
A Princess of Mars
The Gods of Mars
The Warlord of Mars
Thuvia, Maid of Mars
The Chessmen of Mars
The Mastermind of Mars
A Fighting Man of Mars
Swords of Mars
Synthetic Men of Mars
Llana of Gathol
John Carter of Mars

PELLUCIDAR® SERIES
At the Earth's Core
Pellucidar
Tanar of Pellucidar
Tarzan at the Earth's Core
Back to the Stone Age
Land of Terror
Savage Pellucidar

AMTOR™ SERIES
Pirates of Venus
Lost on Venus
Carson of Venus
Escape on Venus
The Wizard of Venus

When a mysterious force catapults inventors Jason Gridley and Victory Harben from their home in Pellucidar, separating them from each other and flinging them across space and time, they embark on a grand tour of strange, wondrous worlds. As their search for one another leads them to the realms of Amtor, Barsoom, and other worlds even more distant and outlandish, Jason and Victory will meet heroes and heroines of unparalleled courage and ability: Carson Napier, Tarzan, John Carter, and more. With the help of their intrepid allies, Jason and Victory will uncover a plot both insidious and unthinkable—one that threatens to tear apart the very fabric of the universe…

SWORDS OF ETERNITY SUPER-ARC

Carson of Venus: The Edge of All Worlds
by Matt Betts

Tarzan: Battle for Pellucidar
by Win Scott Eckert

John Carter of Mars: Gods of the Forgotten
by Geary Gravel

Victory Harben: Fires of Halos
by Christopher Paul Carey

CLASSIC ERB UNIVERSE

Tarzan and the Valley of Gold
by Fritz Leiber

Tarzan and the Dark Heart of Time
by Philip José Farmer

EDGAR RICE BURROUGHS UNIVERSE™

THE EDGE OF ALL WORLDS

CARSON OF VENUS®

MATT BETTS

Includes the bonus novelette

PELLUCIDAR®
DARK OF THE SUN

BY
CHRISTOPHER PAUL CAREY

EDGAR RICE BURROUGHS, Inc.
Publishers
TARZANA   CALIFORNIA

ERB Universe Creative Director: Christopher Paul Carey

Special thanks to Win Scott Eckert; Geary Gravel; Blake Mann;
Janet Mann; James J. Sullos, Jr.; Jess Terrell; Cathy Wilbanks; and
Mike Wolfer for their valuable assistance in producing this book.

First paperback edition

Published by Edgar Rice Burroughs, Inc.
Tarzana, California
EdgarRiceBurroughs.com

ISBN-13: 978-1-945462-23-8

- 9 8 7 6 5 4 3 2 1 -

For my boys—keep dreaming, keep creating.

CONTENTS

FOREWORD
AN UNEXPECTED VISITOR

I N RETROSPECT, I am not sure I have had a stranger job interview. At the very least, this one was unique. I sat in the offices that once belonged to the renowned American author Edgar Rice Burroughs, across from the desk that he actually used, and stared at the dark wooden shelves lined with his books. That, in and of itself, would have been enough to make my trip here worthwhile. I was meeting with the company's director of publishing about an idea I had to write a new series based on *The Deputy Sheriff of Comanche County*, one of Mr. Burroughs' Western novels.

Shortly after our meeting began, my interviewer rose and apologized as he was summoned into the adjoining room for a brief consult with the company's president and vice president. I was left sitting in the marvelous office, trying my best not to pick up every little knickknack, wondering if it had belonged to the famous writer.

It had been an unusually cloudy day in Southern California when I'd entered the Tarzana offices, so I was grateful when a wide beam of sunshine suddenly streamed through the dark shutters behind me. I leaned back in my chair, taking a moment to appreciate the historic setting where I found myself.

I watched the motes of dust float slowly across the beam of light and considered crossing the room to examine the titles on the bookcase facing me. I wondered if any of the great author's reference books were still on those very shelves. With one last glance at the door, I moved around the desk. Even if none of his reading material were there, I figured I would at least get a look at some early editions of his books.

My path took me through the warm light, and as it fell on me, I could see more of the tiny specks of dust begin to spin around me. I stopped. A wave of heat washed over me and I turned to look at the source of the light. Surely even the California sun wasn't that intense.

There, next to the window, stood a fair-haired and athletic-looking young man garbed in the most unusual outfit. Bare-chested except for a leather harness, he wore a garment resembling something between a loincloth and a kilt. A strange pistol hung from a wide belt around his hips, and he wore tall boots with metal greaves. He looked at me with a confusion that must have mirrored my own.

"You are no one I know from Mr. Burroughs' company," he said.

"No." I pointed to the door. "They're all in the other room. I can get them for you." It occurred to me that maybe the man had slipped in when I wasn't paying attention. "Are you an actor here for some kind of promotional shoot?"

"No."

"Well, let me go get someone for you. They're just..."

"It doesn't work that way, sir."

Having no idea what he meant, I fumbled nervously through the stacks of paperwork on the desk before me, searching for a piece of scratch paper. "I'm not exactly sure what you mean," I said. "Do you want to leave a message?"

"I do, of a sort, but not the kind you mean."

"You could send them a text or an email?" I suggested, still confused.

The man shook his head. "I am Carson Napier. Mr. Burroughs and I used to have discussions, wherein he would listen to my stories and keep them in his marvelous memory, to later transcribe them. We had many an enlightening discussion about the state of the Earth and the happenings on Amtor over the years."

"Amtor? Like in the novels?"

"Yes, as in the planet Venus."

"Ahh. Venus. You definitely want to talk to Mr. Carey. I think he handles all the…ah…Amtor-related questions. Let me get him for you." I reached to guide the man to the door but was shocked when my hand seemed to pass right through his body. "What is happening?" I tried again with the same result.

"I'm not actually here in Mr. Burroughs' office. I'm projecting myself from Amtor. It's a form of telepathy whereby you can see me even though I'm nowhere near you." He reached out and passed his own hand through me. "And so you see, as I told you, it doesn't work that way. From this great distance, there are certain periods when I can connect with only one mind at a time. I cast my line across the heavens, and you were the one it ensnared."

"I don't understand," I said. "We're fishing now? Are there fish on Venus?"

He smiled. "All you need to know is that for now, because you were in this space instead of the one whom I meant to contact, you and I are linked. And I can communicate with you for a time, much as I could speak with Mr. Burroughs. Are you a writer, perhaps? That could explain why we are in psychological harmony, as I was with Ed. Maybe our connection can be useful after all."

"You want to tell me a story? Should I warm up my laptop, then?"

"I haven't the slightest notion what that means, but I will visit you again to relate my tale. It would be a delight if our discussions proved as edifying as those I had with Ed."

With that, Carson Napier disappeared from sight. I looked around the office to make sure he was actually gone and then tried the old cliché of pinching myself. It would have been embarrassing if I'd fallen asleep during my interview.

I was certainly awake.

A short while later, when the director returned to discuss my proposed series based on *The Deputy Sheriff of Comanche County*, I suggested I might just have a more interesting story for him. Oddly, he didn't question the validity of my tale about meeting this Carson Napier of Amtor, never batted an eye; he only asked when I could start writing the man's story.

In the months that followed, Carson appeared to me at my home office and told me of life on Amtor. Occasionally, we would walk out into the open fields, far away from the city lights, and talk about the stars and planets over our heads. He seemed more comfortable there, staring up at the open sky.

In his own time, Carson acquainted me with his adventures on Venus. He gave an abbreviated version of how he came to be on Venus after miscalculating his trajectory to Mars. He spoke of his initial landing in the tree-city of Kooaad, his first glimpse of his beloved Duare, and his horrendous ordeal in the Room of the Seven Doors. He told me of the political and social upheaval brought on by the authoritarian regimes of the Thorists and the Zanis. As we stared up at the stars by night and the clear blue sky by day, I learned of pirates, madmen, cannibals, and the City of the Dead. By the time he was finished, I felt certain either he was some sort of a madman himself, or I was for believing him.

While we found time to talk about the state of science on both Amtor and Earth, I decided not to mention our modern technology if he didn't ask about it. I was reluctant to try to explain email, laptops, or video chatting when I was unsure of how much time I would have with him.

I couldn't afford to waste a second of our time together; there was just too much to learn. He loved to speak of his life, his friends, and his family on Amtor.

As to the adventure at hand, he told it with enthusiasm, if not outright glee. Carson would even act out parts of his story, slashing the air as though he wielded a sword in his hand, pointing his finger like a pistol, and even falling to the ground to imitate an injury on more than one occasion. He would talk so quickly that I couldn't always write the words down fast enough and I had to ask him to repeat himself. A curious gleam came into his eye when he related the portions of his tale concerning the mysterious appearance by two individuals who by all rights should not have been found on Amtor. When I asked about the matter, he prompted me to inquire further at the offices in Tarzana.*

And so, here is the story of the latest adventure of Carson Napier, told to me in his own words. As Mr. Burroughs liked to say, I am but a conduit and the means to record the story for those interested to read it here on Earth, no different from a typewriter—or a laptop or a digital recorder, as the case may be. The story is all his.

MATT BETTS
San Margherita, Ohio
January 2020

---

* I did inquire and was enthralled to learn more details about the incredible backstory tied in with the events of Carson Napier's account. See page 215 of this book for the remarkable tale of Jason Gridley and Victory Harben, and the events that launch the Swords of Eternity super-arc spanning the first cycle of Edgar Rice Burroughs Universe novels.

AMTOR

DETAIL OF THE WESTERN HEMISPHERE OF THE PLANET AMTOR, AS DESCRIBED
BY CARSON NAPIER VIA GRIDLEY WAVE TRANSMISSIONS RECEIVED AT THE
OFFICES OF EDGAR RICE BURROUGHS, INC., TARZANA, CALIFORNIA.

1

AN ETHEREAL VISION

I N ALL THE YEARS since I had come to live on Amtor, I
could count on one hand the number of times I'd fallen
ill. There was an instance early in the failed peace talks
between my adopted nation of Korva and the Thorists where
their envoy poisoned my wine. While I had lived through
it, that episode could honestly be the worst I'd felt in years,
for I had been regularly taking a longevity serum since the
early days of my advent on Venus that, in addition to
slowing my aging, also blessed me with sterling health.

Nonetheless, now I found myself suddenly dizzy and weak
at the most inopportune time—I was soaring high above
rocky terrain, piloting an anotar, the Amtorian word for
aeroplane, as I transported a full complement of passengers
back to our home city of Sanara. With me was my dearest
Duare, along with our companions Ero Shan and Nalte from
the distant lands of Havatoo and Andoo. We were flying at
a high altitude with no way to quickly land safely, our destination still hours away. Duare, sitting next to me, noticed
my change in demeanor.

"Are you all right?" she asked.

I admitted I was not well and asked her to take the controls.
I was barely able to get the words out before my head began
to throb with incredible pain. I reached reflexively for my
temple. Then, just as I saw that Duare had, in fact, gripped
the control stick, the world went dark.

There, in the murk of my oblivion, I could feel heat on my

1

face, and I opened my eyes to the harsh glare of a sun that seemed out of place where it hung in the sky. I raised a hand to shield my eyes and scanned the horizon in each direction. A pale landscape with varying depths greeted my clearing vision. The ground looked cracked and dry, devoid of life. In the distance, I saw people walking—all of an alien race I did not recognize—flanked by great beasts of burden. I shouted, but they either couldn't hear or chose to ignore me.

"You there!" A voice came from behind me. It was a woman, about a hundred feet away, wrapped in a flowing, hooded gown of red and blue. The loose cuffs of the sleeves and leggings flapped in a wind that was much heavier than the air that reached me, revealing graceful hands and feet of a reddish-brown hue. Her clothing moved as if hit by a storm gale, flapping wildly about her body, but the hood that cloaked her face gave me no glimpse of whom she might be. I simply had no idea.

But I did know that I had merely fallen asleep in the anotar. This alien landscape was something that my mind had summoned from the depths of imagination to occupy the time until I awoke.

So I stepped toward the woman, intent on discovering her identity more out of some casual dream-state curiosity than any pressing desire. To my surprise, she took a step backward, placing her foot on the sandy ground just as I did mine. I stopped and stood straight, amused by her ability to keep herself stock-still save for one leg, which she moved to mirror my movement. Again, I took a small step forward and she imitated me in reverse, retreating exactly as far as I advanced.

I stepped back and she moved forward.

It was amusing for a moment or two, but soon my unconscious mind became impatient. Suddenly I was convinced that if I simply ran toward the woman, there was no way she could evade me by running that quickly backward. I charged, giving the matter no more consideration than it was due. It appeared my ploy had worked, for I was getting closer to her!

I say "appeared" because it was soon evident that, rather than attempting to run away, she was in fact drawing me closer to her. The bits of her garment that flowed freely in the wind stretched out to me like the probing tentacles of a great octopus. The fleecy appendages tangled around my arms and legs, and I was pulled into them, unable to stop the inexplicable force that dragged me toward her. Soon, the tendrils wrapped around my neck and head, and though I remained steadfast in my belief that it was only a dream, I was momentarily terrified when the darkness spread over my face and I was left in a void.

"Carson?" A familiar voice broke through the darkness. I opened my eyes to find Taman, the jong of Korva, standing alongside the anotar with Duare and my other traveling companions. In my state, I hadn't realized we had landed in Sanara, the capital of Korva, where Duare and I, along with our friends Ero Shan and Nalte, had made our home in the years since my last recorded adventure. On Amtor, the title of jong was similar to that of king and commanded the respect of the people. Taman had taken Duare and me under his care some years ago, bestowing upon me the rank of tanjong, or prince. He had become a good friend and a powerful ally.

"What's this? We were hours away from home," I said, confused. "How did we arrive so quickly?"

"You've been asleep for quite some time," Nalte whispered. "We sped here as quickly as we could, but we required a longer trip than usual to avoid a sudden windstorm, which caused our journey to become quite unpleasant. You slept through it all." Her voice wavered as she spoke. "I have not seen you like this in all our time together."

Taman put his hand on my shoulder and looked me up and down. "You seem none the worse for wear, but your companions tell me you've been ill. Shall I send for a physician?" He eyed me cautiously. Two of the royal guards behind him suddenly snapped to attention, waiting for their jong's orders.

I raised my hand to put the guards—and everyone else—at ease. "No, no. I'm sure I'm fine. I'll rest just as soon as we get to our chambers."

Taman seemed skeptical, but he relented. "That's probably best, but perhaps some nourishment might help as well. I came to greet you all and invite everyone to dine with me. If you feel so inclined, I would welcome your company."

"Yes, of course." It occurred to me that I was still slumped in the seat of the anotar, which didn't exactly offer the best evidence of my perfect health. I sat up, and my head spun, making it difficult to do anything, let alone extricate myself from the vehicle.

Ero Shan offered me a hand and I accepted. He supported my weight while I found my balance and stepped cautiously over the side. Aside from an already-fading headache, I felt better as soon as I took a few deep breaths. After I had composed myself and greeted the jong properly, we walked toward the stairs that led away from the landing platform. Ero Shan, at my side, touched my arm lightly and pointed toward the anotar.

I looked back and discovered that in my haste to assure the jong that I was fine, I had neglected to convince Duare. She was still sitting on the edge of the anotar, arms crossed and staring at me with a look composed of something between concern and annoyance. Either way, I did not wish her to worry over what could be nothing but exhaustion on my part. I thanked Ero Shan and returned to the anotar. The others went on ahead.

"You are honestly fine?" She pulled her long, dark hair away from her face, and the look in her eyes told me I'd best tell her the truth.

"It's just a bout of airsickness and fatigue," I said, for truly I believed it must have been.

"Just a bout? What if you had been alone in that anotar?

You might have crashed and killed yourself. Carson, I'm concerned about you."

I agreed that it might be something to investigate. "Let me rest here for a few days, and I promise you I'll see a doctor." I took her hand and waited for a response.

"I have your word, and that is good enough for now. Come, the jong is waiting."

Still clasping Duare's hand, I allowed her to lead me up the stairs to where a trio of the jong's ornately decorated gantors waited. The rest of our party had already mounted the elephant-sized beasts and were settling in when we arrived. I helped Duare onto the ladder and she climbed up to sit beside Taman. I joined her and within moments we were moving at a slow, but majestic pace through the streets of Sanara. The people we passed were kind enough not only to greet their jong, but also to offer pleasantries to myself and Duare. It seemed the citizens had fallen in love with Duare from the very moment we first arrived in the city and that spell has never been broken. It has always been one of the reasons I made Sanara my home and why I was eager to make it a better place for all who lived there.

Our procession continued through the avenues uninterrupted, advanced through the gates at Taman's palace, and stopped at the enormous courtyard that stretched before it. Here we all dismounted with the assistance of the palace staff and were led to the jong's private dining area. The servants were cordial and asked us for an account of our latest adventures, which we were happy to relay, if only in an abbreviated form. By the time we'd pulled ourselves away from their questions, our friends and several of Taman's advisors were already seated and drinking a dark wine, waiting patiently for us to join them. As we entered, the jong rose and smiled. "It has been too long since we all dined together. I have to say it is so good to have you back in Sanara. You must tell us all about your travels."

"Yes, Carson," a man named Lisant Or drawled. "You must

tell us all about…flying. I have to assume this latest adventure had you in one of your precious anotars?" Lisant Or was not one of our friends by any means, but rather the son of an important power broker in Korva, and therefore had insinuated himself into the jong's inner circle. His father owned a trading company that was instrumental in providing Element 105, a key component in the nation's manufacturing industry, not the least of which were anotars. That minor fact bought him some measure of celebrity in Sanara. Lisant Or was generally snide and petty whenever possible, privileged by his status. On that particular day it felt as though he were daring anyone to call him out for his sneering words.

I usually ignored him as best I could, but this time his words brought a pleasant thought to my mind. "Flying? You're not one who enjoys flying are you, Lisant Or? It's a shame. It's a freeing feeling." I took my place at the table and sipped the wine. "It can be terrifying sometimes, too. Leaving my home world of Earth all alone, breaking the atmosphere and crashing here on Amtor, was exhilarating and frightening and…"

Lisant Or laughed. "Yes, tell us again how you meant to land on another world beyond the surrounding flames but missed. I imagine that was a thrill." He emptied his glass and poured himself some more. It was true that my original target had been Mars and my calculations had failed to factor in the gravity of the Moon, knocking me off course almost as soon as I broke free of Earth's bonds. It was a miracle that I didn't die somewhere in space, and that I managed to fall under the gravitational influence of Venus. Jumping out of my craft and plummeting into the clouds and trees was certainly the most daring thing I'd done in my life, at least until I found myself on the surface of another world and my adventures on Amtor commenced. Nothing in the way that my interplanetary journey turned out was planned; it had all just happened, and it was indeed due in most part to my bad judgment. But I wouldn't trade my experiences on Venus for anything.

Before I could engage Lisant Or and address his tiresome banter, Duare, ever looking out for me, smiled at the jong and asked, "You wanted to hear of our latest adventure?"

Taman returned Duare's smile and asked us to proceed with our tale, while Lisant Or, careful to make sure the jong's gaze was not upon him, rolled his eyes and yawned.

"The whole affair started while we were on our way back from a diplomatic mission to Panga and Hangor…" I began. Duare and I went on to relate the story by turns, entertaining Taman and his courtiers with our account of the deadly serpentine vortos off the Maltorian coast, the fierce crablike tongzans and arachnoid targos of the treetops of Voo-ad, and the colossal, draconic joska of the Mountains of the Clouds. The jong was suitably impressed and actually clapped for us when we told of how we bested each challenge.*

It was a complete surprise for all of us when a burly soldier burst into the dining room and quashed our jovial mood.

"What is the meaning of this intrusion?" the jong demanded.

The soldier took off his helmet and bowed. "I am quite sorry, my jong. I humbly beg your forgiveness. The news could not wait. We have been apprised that the town of Jovita has been attacked and is in flames. Its people sent a rider to beg us for help."

Our enemies at that time were relatively few. There were always nomadic tribes of various minor factions that could wander into our territories, but none were quite so bold as to think they could attack one of our villages. An on-again, off-again war had been waged between Korva and the powerful technocratic city-state of Havatoo for years, but we had experienced no direct confrontation in recent months beyond the occasional minor skirmish, with neither nation willing to expend the resources to continue outright combat.

"Was it Havatoo?" I demanded.

---

* For the full account of Carson and Duare's previous adventure, see the comic book miniseries *Carson of Venus: The Eye of Amtor*, available from American Mythology Productions.

The soldier bowed. "I do not know. The rider from Jovita did not say."

"My liege, let us take you to your quarters," Lisant Or said, moving to the jong's side. "If one of our nearby towns is under attack, there may be a danger to Sanara as well. We must get you to safety."

Taman was having none of it. "Nonsense," he said. "Carson, can you get us to Jovita swiftly?"

"Absolutely," I said. Jovita was one of the closest settlements to Sanara, but it still lay nestled near a valley some half an hour away by air. "The anotar we arrived in should still be flight-ready out on the landing strip," I went on, "and my personal craft is waiting inside the hangar near that. We could take a few people with us, but not many." My anotar was designed to hold only a pilot and one passenger, though I knew we could squeeze in one more safely. The other anotar was a little more forgiving; meant to hold four in comfort, it might allow for another two or three passengers before the added weight would be a detriment to lift and velocity.

The jong said, "I will go with you and Duare."

"Very well," I replied. Unlike Lisant Or, I knew better than to suggest that the jong remain behind in safety. I spoke to the guard who had brought us the news. "Get to the barracks and rouse them to the task at hand. Ready a force to follow the jong to Jovita, but make sure a full contingent of soldiers stays here, in case this is the first move in a larger attack against Korva." The soldier ran and I told Ero Shan we would meet him and Nalte in Jovita.

After we arrived at my ship's berth, we climbed up into the anotar's cockpit and the jong slid in between Duare and me. Rising into the air, I maintained a safe speed until we cleared the outskirts of Sanara, at which point I pushed the anotar beyond its normal cruising velocity. Though Ero Shan and his group had a ready vehicle and a head start, our smaller, fleeter craft passed them mere moments after the city's lights disappeared behind us.

There are a variety of ways in which life can be more daunting on Amtor than on Earth. One of the most challenging aspects of the former is the locals' inability to properly map their planet. This was due partially to the fact that Venus was perpetually covered by two great cloud envelopes, blocking the sky day and night. Hence, the people of Amtor must rely on landmarks and other measures to navigate, since they can't count on simple things like stars and planets and, in fact, do not know that such astronomical bodies even exist. The general consensus I have found among all the peoples I've encountered on Amtor is not that their world is a round ball of rock and dirt surrounded by clouds, but that it is flat and floats on a bubbling, heaving sea of tumultuous lava. Consequently, their maps were a mix of misconception, bad science, and poor mathematics. I tried many times to correct them, and had brought my own earthly knowledge to influential scientists and leaders, but it was to no avail. They stuck with long-held beliefs such as the theory of the relativity of distance, which demonstrates that the actual and the apparent measurements of distance can be reconciled by multiplying each by the square root of minus one. The theory, of course, was only good for creating generations of lost and confused Amtorians.

The end result of all this was that I had worked out my own maps of Korva and the regions immediately surrounding it. Duare and I, as well as my friends Ero Shan and Nalte, used these for navigation. Once we traveled beyond the local area, however, we were as utterly lost on Amtor as the rest of its inhabitants. Fortunately, Jovita lay only a short distance from Sanara and was accurately marked on our maps.

"Do you suspect the Havatooans?" Duare asked Taman as the anotar speeded on its way.

The jong had been silent throughout the flight, staring off in thought. "I don't know. Why would they attack a town as insignificant as Jovita? And why now? There is nothing to gain by it."

"I was considering that as well," Duare said. "Jovita lies along a shallow stream, but it is by no means an important port or center of industry."

The jong nodded. "It has a sizable rural population, but it is spread out and mostly consists of farmers and herders."

"Could that be it?" I asked. "Could Jovita be considered a strategic site by our enemies as a provider of food to the country?" I knew the answer even before Taman replied.

"It is not that important," the jong said. "It contributes but little to our overall economy. No. There seems to be no strategy to it."

We'd been flying for nearly half an hour when smoke appeared on the horizon, thick, gray, and billowing wide toward the clouds. I opened the throttle wider and dropped low to the ground, hoping that if any attackers were still in the area, they wouldn't see us coming. The jong and Duare both gripped their seats as I swooped down and we skirted a copse of trees at high speed.

Now we were close enough to see the source of the smoke. "There, just ahead and to our right. Do you see it?" I brought the craft down and trundled it across a field just outside the small town. We could see buildings in flames and people running about in the streets. The town was in chaos.

I brought our craft to a halt and the three of us climbed out. We proceeded swiftly to the center of town, our weapons drawn, but we saw only townspeople desperately attending to the crisis that had struck their settlement out of nowhere. We guarded Taman as he moved into the town square looking for the local leaders to get a sense of what happened. At the jong's insistence, Duare and I stopped and helped when we found several people trying to move a collapsed wall.

"What's wrong?" Duare asked. We both knelt and grabbed a section of the debris and helped lift.

One of the villagers replied while she strained alongside us. "This is covering a well we might use to douse the flames. It's the only one on this side of the town hall."

A man beside us groaned under the weight of the debris, sweat forming on his brow either from exertion or the heat of the flames at his back. "We will lose this whole area of our town," he said, "unless we get the well cleared and working."

But it was soon evident that Duare and I had turned the tide and added the needed amount of muscle to the team's effort. The thick section rose slowly and together we tossed it aside. The others finished clearing the remaining debris away from the mouth of the well and fiddled with a crank-and-tube system inside.

Above us, Ero Shan and Nalte arrived in their anotar and began circling the ruined city. Within moments, a rope fell from the ship and Ero Shan proceeded to climb down it to a fiery rooftop. Duare and I watched with apprehension as he disappeared into the smoke, only to see him emerge seconds later with a woman and her child, their faces ashen with fear. Sweeping up both survivors in one arm, Ero Shan deftly managed to grab the dangling rope with his free hand, coiling the cable around his leg to secure his hold, as Nalte made another pass. After clearing the devastated structure, she flew in low at decreased speed and, as gently as possible, deposited Ero Shan and the survivors in the field near our craft. The additional half-dozen members of the royal staff they carried from Sanara were already on the ground to assist the people at the landing site. In no time the anotar took to the air again, Ero Shan once again dangling from the rope as both he and the ship entered the cloud of dark smoke rising from Jovita.

"Carson!" The jong waved us over to where he stood with a trio of villagers farther up the road. Duare and I left the well and ran to his side. "This merchant was trapped in his shop for some time. He says he can tell us what happened."

I greeted the man, whose left arm was swathed in a makeshift bandage of soot-stained cloth, and asked, "Are you injured badly?"

He waved a hand to dismiss my concern. "My arm has been looked after," he said. "I assure you I need nothing else.

I am Letson. My store is…" Letson turned to point to a pile of smoldering debris. "Was…over there. So I had a good view of the forest beyond the first hill." He pointed to the towering trees in the distance, where I noticed faint trails of vapor lingering in the air. "There's not much to tell, really. I was cleaning my cart when I heard a whistling sound that got louder and louder. I looked up and saw some dark objects streaking toward Jovita. They left behind those trails."

"How many objects?" the jong asked.

"Oh, there were only three at first, but I saw more coming behind them, so I tried to get inside. I shouted for everyone to run, but there was no time." A gloom hung over Letson heavier than the gray clouds above. "Those things started landing on the buildings and the streets, and they burst with fire immediately. When they broke open, they caused death and destruction like I have never seen. There was no way for anyone to know where to run. The things just blanketed the whole town." His already dour face seemed to sink further into melancholy. "Perhaps if I had acted faster, warned everyone of what I saw coming… If I'd done that, maybe…" Letson leaned against me and buried his face in my shoulder. "Maybe more Jovitans would still be alive."

"There was nothing you could do, Letson," Duare assured him. "This is not your fault."

The group of aides that had arrived with Ero Shan's anotar approached us. They were led by Lisant Or, who strode calmly past the flames and destruction, not bothering himself to stop and offer assistance, and barely turning his head to view the devastation. "What news, my jong? Who had the audacity to commit such a bold act against Korva?"

"We do not yet know." The jong looked clearly concerned for his people.

"Shall we follow the attackers?" I asked. "Those vapor trails in the sky should show us the right direction, but they're rapidly fading."

"Are you mad?" cried Lisant Or. "There are people here

who need your help. And you want to run away to try to seek revenge now? May I remind you that you are a decorated prince of Korva?"

"And that is exactly why I should seek out the villains who cause my people harm."

Duare touched my arm gently and gave me a knowing look. She was right. Engaging in a debate with Lisant Or would only waste valuable time.

At that point Ero Shan approached carrying what at first glance appeared to be a piece of wreckage. "I found this near one of the larger fires. I could not pick it up until I had doused it with water." He held up a twisted piece of metal and turned it so I could see all sides.

It was only about an arm's length long, but the curves and materials seemed somehow familiar.

"Are there more like that?" I asked.

"I don't know," he said. "I brought this one straightaway." He handed me the bent fragment of metal, and then returned to his anotar with Nalte. Soon the two were once more aloft.

"Look for more of these as you help the townsfolk," I said to the jong's party, holding up the hunk of metal. "But if any of the objects seem to be intact, clear the area and stay at a great distance. It could explode and kill many." The members of the group split up and moved into the village.

Nearby, the well was working again. A group of villagers had formed a line to pass buckets to pour water on one of the buildings, and others were dousing another structure with a hose. I ran down a narrow alley between two homes, shouting for the trapped or injured. At the end of that alley was another of the twisted black metal objects like Ero Shan had found. It was too hot to lift with my bare hands, so I nudged it over with my foot. This one was in much better shape than the last. In fact, only one side appeared to be damaged.

A startling realization dawned on me as I examined the object's untarnished side. It seemed impossible, yet the shape and dimensions of the shell appeared to make it a nearly perfect miniature version of the rocket ship I had flown from Earth to Amtor! I would have needed to check for exact measurements, but the ratios, the angles, the composition of the metal—they were all similar enough for me to be astonished at the likeness.

"What is it?" Duare asked from behind me.

"This is another of those shells that Ero Shan found." I held up the black casing so she could see. "Whoever attacked Jovita did so with these rockets. They look exactly like small versions of the craft that brought me to Amtor."

"Coincidence?"

"I suppose anything is possible, but I find it unlikely." The unspoken implication shook me deeply, and Duare's wide eyes revealed that she had reached the same conclusion.

As we continued to help the villagers, I could not keep my mind from the shells the attackers had used. After finding a great many of them in the rubble, I brought the most intact specimen to the jong. "We must track down this enemy before the trail goes cold. These weapons are like nothing I've seen any other country use in battle. And I've been shot at by most of them."

The jong shrugged. "They have done a lot of damage here, but as a weapon, isn't it fairly primitive? It is a projectile with some sort of explosive. It's only a step above throwing rocks." I understood the jong's slowness in grasping the great danger that threatened his country. In a world that had given rise to weapons that utilized the deadly and effective r-rays and t-rays, a propellant-fueled rocket might seem rather like a toy water pistol beside an elephant rifle. But I knew better from my knowledge of Earth history.

"If you know anyone who can throw rocks this devastating and from that far away, by all means, let's recruit them for your army, my jong." It was always dangerous to speak out of turn to a jong, even one who might be considered a friend. But the surprising resemblance between the missiles and my earthy rocket ship had disconcerted me, and I hoped Taman would give me some leeway. "Respectfully," I continued in a gentler tone, "I think you can see whoever did this is doing more than throwing rocks. These weapons devastated everything in the vicinity of impact, and they traveled a great distance. Whoever fired them must be tracked down and stopped immediately. I can do that easily in my anotar."

Again, it was Lisant Or who jumped at the chance to chastise me for wanting to leave. "One of the anotars is being used right now by your wiser friends. Yours could be required at any time. Surely you are not still thinking of abandoning your duties here? Moreover, you must leave your craft at the jong's disposal. His safety is of the utmost importance."

I was about to give the latter a piece of my mind or do something worse to him, when the jong raised his hand and cried, "Enough! I am not a feeble child who must be looked after by his nanny. I am the jong." Taman turned to me. "Carson, you will follow the trails in the sky, but you are to go alone, and you must return and report to me before taking any action on your own."

"Yes, my jong," I said and bowed.

Lisant Or narrowed his eyes but said nothing.

I took Duare's hand and, without further word, we headed for my anotar.

Along the way, Duare stopped. She found an old rag among the debris and used it to pick up a piece of exploded shell, which she examined intently. We continued on. When we were out of earshot of the others, we stopped again and I told Duare I did not like the idea of leaving her behind.

"And I like it even less that you are flying off on your own when you were so recently ill," she said. "But I know that you will return safely to me."

"How?" I asked.

"Because if you don't, I will kill you."

I drew Duare to me and kissed her. "I don't know what I'd do without you."

"Remember that," Duare said, with all the stern haughtiness

of the princess she was. Then she smiled slyly, handed me the shell fragment, and walked away.

I watched her return to the jong's party, which continued to work at the task at hand, moving rubble and helping with the fire brigade.

On the ground near where I stood lay another portion of a shell. I could still feel the heat emanating from the metal casing as I bent down to examine it, so I grabbed a stick to keep from burning myself. I poked at the metal, and turned it, trying to shake the feeling that it was in some manner born of my designs. I couldn't. The idea that I was responsible even in a tangential way for the surrounding chaos and destruction infuriated me.

I looked up as a shadow passed over me. Flying high above in their anotar, Nalte and Ero Shan were searching for more survivors.

Soon after I was in the cockpit of my own ship. I tossed the fragment of the shell onto the floor, fired up the anotar's vik-ro-powered engine, and lifted off into the cloud-enwrapped sky.

2
PURSUIT

THE ANOTAR RESPONDED to my slightest touch at the controls. It was as agile and powerful as the day I had finished building it, and despite all the advancements I'd helped devise for the Korvan military's newer models, this particular vehicle still seemed special. It had been constructed many years previous, during a time when no one else on Amtor besides my friend Ero Shan had a similar flying machine, at least to my knowledge. Air travel, space travel—both were foreign concepts to the inhabitants of Venus. While it was true that flight was natural to the winged humanoids known as klangan, the idea of building a craft with which one could traverse the skies had been unknown until my arrival on this world. Enormous tanks, submarines, longevity formulas, ray guns...these were all acceptable to the more advanced races of Amtor. Flying? Unheard of. The Korvans came around to my way of thinking eventually, and I spent a few years advising them on the construction of a fleet of anotars that was still flying after a decade. But even so, the fleet was small. Its ships could be counted on a single hand due to the periodic destruction of manufacturing sites during Korva's long-running conflict with Havatoo.

That thought brought me back to the strange piece of metal on my floor. I'd spent more than two decades on Venus, but never in all my travels on this world had I discussed with anyone the designs for the rocket ship that

17

had carried me to Amtor. Those designs had been created on an entirely different planet, so how did they end up here in the form of the missiles that had struck Jovita?

Before long a forest of colossal trees loomed ahead. I had found the general area where the trail in the sky had originated.

Perhaps I should explain that when I describe the immense size of the trees that make up this most common type of Amtorian forest, I do not mean to imply they are in any way comparable to the largest trees of Earth. The redwoods of California are but toothpicks alongside the colossi of Venus. Many of the trees before me soared five or even six thousand feet in the air, where their tops were lost in the gray shroud of the inner cloud envelope. Their gargantuan boles are of such vast girths that an entire palace might fit inside one at a height of a thousand feet, as is actually the case in the tree city of Kooaad on the distant island of Vepaja.

The colors of the trees are almost as breathtaking as their unimaginable heights, their lacquer-like bark arrayed in heliotrope, mauve, violet, and orchid hues. The foliage of these Amtorian behemoths is similarly colored and typically begins around two-thirds of the way up the trunk, which is devoid of leaf or limb from that point down to the base.

It was into such a forest that I flew my anotar, hoping to find some trace of the attackers. I directed my ship through the yawning spaces between the giant boles, surveying the forest floor far below for any sign of the rockets' origin. How long I flew I cannot say for sure, as the intensity of my concentration and the exotic landscape combined to put me into a sort of trance.

When at last I shook myself awake, it was with the realization that I had searched the area much longer than I'd intended. Ultimately, I concluded that if there had been anything noteworthy down there, I would have found a trace of it, though I really didn't know what I was searching for. Was it a group of soldiers carrying some new weapon? A vehicle of some sort? Whatever it was, there was no sign of it here. I sighed and wondered if maybe it would be best to return to Jovita and help with the rescue effort and cleanup of the city after all.

Just as I was about to turn my ship around, a flash of blue caught my eye in the thick grass that stretched between the trees. I skimmed low over the wide meadow, following a wave of moving grass. I trailed it, dodging the occasional saplings that grew amid the field's lavender grass. Soon, what I had assumed to be a single entity split into four, and as I chose one to chase down, it broke from the weeds and I was finally able to get a good look at my quarry: a basto, running for its life. The blue-skinned basto is an animal similar to the wild boar of Earth, but it is much larger and equipped with four great tusks and two deadly horns. Nonetheless, though the basto is a fierce fighter and terrifying to face one on one, it certainly couldn't fire a weapon at anyone.

My anotar passed over the basto. I had wasted still more time that could have been better spent elsewhere. I decided I would head back the way I had come and help deal with the crisis in Jovita.

Suddenly a bank of fog appeared before my anotar and I plunged headlong into it. I had believed it to be nothing more than a thin patch of mist that I would pass through swiftly, but soon I found I was mistaken. Utterly blind, I descended twenty-five feet, fifty feet, then a hundred, hoping to come out of the lower end of thick fog—and yet still I could see nothing. I looked at my altimeter, wondering whether I should risk descending even farther, when abruptly the fog cleared and I realized I had left the forest behind.

I had only a split second to consider my epiphany, for on the other side of the trees was an enormous metal vehicle blocking my path. Its exterior lights were so bright that I had trouble getting a good view of it. I wrenched the control stick, veering sharply to the right, but it was too late. My anotar clipped the corner of the thing, damaging my left aileron. I struggled to keep myself aloft, straining my aeroplane and my skills to the limit. I glanced back at the boxy vehicle I'd hit while I fought for control of my craft and noticed a small group of large creatures standing on top of it. None of them had moved away or evinced any concern at all about my craft, which had flown within just a few yards of their heads. Their large, pale orange forms barely registered with me as my anotar dipped away from them and back into the trees.

3
PEOPLE OF THE CLOUDS

I WASN'T DEAD. That much I could tell from the searing pain in my arm. But beyond that simple fact, and the crackling of an enormous fire nearby that had awakened me, I was completely unaware of my situation as I came to.

I tried to sit up and assess both my injuries and surroundings, but I could not. Something wet and heavy weighted down my whole body. Again I strained to sit up, but it was no use. Whatever covered me prevented me from moving my limbs. Free from the neck up, I struggled to lift my head, and with some effort, I found I was encased in a concoction of thick leaves and hard, gray mud. A foul stench told me that something else was mixed in, though I didn't want to speculate as to its origins.

"Ah!" someone nearby exclaimed. "You are awake. This is indeed fortuitous!"

I struggled for some freedom of movement, searching for the source of the voice. Whoever it was walked around near my head; I could hear the light crunching of leaves caused by the speaker's footsteps, but from my vantage I could not see the person. Failing to break free, I did my best to crane my aching neck and see who was speaking. Finally, my eyes alighted upon a shadowy figure kneeling between me and the fire. As my eyes adjusted, I saw that it was a person clad from toe to neck in thick brown furs from several different types of animals. A covering of furs and leather obscured the head. Beneath that hood, I could see dark leather goggles covering the eyes,

21

with a swatch of dark cloth over the mouth, leaving not a single inch of skin exposed to the air.

Cloud People. I had to assume that was who had found me. They were a race of humans who lived high in the mist-covered mountains of Anlap. They had few political or social ambitions on the world stage, and generally stayed away from the buzz and noise of the outsiders' tribulations, preferring instead to live an isolated life on the high, moisture-laden ridges and peaks. In their home environment, they could walk unfettered by the need for clothing, but elsewhere their extremely sensitive skin quickly dried and shriveled, leading ultimately to death. The tribes I had run into were friendly after a fashion.

I soon saw three more of them as my eyes further adjusted to the firelight. The others were standing at various positions around the clearing, most clad in the same fashion as the speaker. Their heads were covered by heavy furs with three holes arranged as necessary over the face to allow them to see and breathe.

"Your mud is the right consistency."

It came to me that I must have crashed my anotar. As the fog caused by my shock began to clear, I realized it was a woman talking to me. Her voice, muffled as it was, had sounded like a male's at first, thick and low.

"Thank you," I said. "Can I ask what this is holding me down?" Had I never met one of the Cloud People, my situation would have concerned me more than it did. There were long-standing rumors that they were cannibals who sustained their horrible predilections by trapping unwitting travelers traversing the mountains. Thankfully, my previous encounters with the Cloud People had taught me this was not the case. Still, it crossed my mind that not every tribe was necessarily the same; perhaps some might not turn up their noses at a meal of human flesh falling out of the sky onto their proverbial doorstep.

The woman poked me lightly with a stick and inspected the dripping mixture that oozed from the end of it. "You had many burns. Your body was layered with a salve, then covered with a special mixture to aid in its healing properties."

I wiggled my toes and fingers as best I could beneath the mound of debris. Moving my right arm immediately caused a jolt of heat to shoot up to my shoulder, and I cried out in pain.

"You also may have broken your wrist. We'll apply more salve to it later."

"What are Cloud People doing so far down from the mountains?" I drew a breath as my pain subsided.

"We are following the machine that you fought. It, and others, have destroyed the villages of our people throughout the region," she said. She stood and pointed to her companions in a grand gesture. "I lead the youngest of our tribe to destroy those that murdered our families. I am master tracker Vot, daughter of Mor, and I swear vengeance."

I tried to sit up at the young woman's declaration but was stuck tight to the ground. "Mor? You are the offspring of Mor? Years ago, my friends and I came upon him as he was being attacked by a tharban. We saved him. In return, he helped me to cross the mountains." I wanted to breathe a sigh of relief, but the slimy gunk on top of me made it hard to inhale too deeply.

"You are Carson?" Vot exclaimed. "My father told me that story so many times that I thought I might cry if he told it once again. You are a hero to my tribe."

"Is he…?" I hesitated to ask, but she knew the question that stuck in my throat.

"Yes," Vot replied. "He was murdered by the Linneauns along with the others. He and his warriors met the great war machine on the outskirts of the village. There was a discussion, a brief one, and then those shell-backed monsters killed our most skilled fighters within but moments. Then they fired their weapons on the village."

"Linneauns?" I'd never heard the name before, and it rang strangely in my ears, sounding quite unlike any Amtorian word I had ever before encountered. "They are the ones responsible? Who are they?"

"After killing our warriors, they called themselves that—Linneauns—and offered to spare the lives of anyone who would work in their factories."

I had many more questions, but one of the other Cloud People made a high whistling sound that drew Vot's attention. She held up a finger to silence me. When she spoke, her voice was but a whisper. "Tharbans have been skulking about for the last several hours. We built the fire high in the hope of warning them off, but they are bold. And getting closer."

The mixture of mud and leaves felt even heavier as I listened for anything that might be making its way toward us in the dense foliage just beyond our circle of light. I tried to squirm my way out of the mess, but it only seemed to make things worse. I was truly at the mercy of anyone and anything that might approach. I couldn't raise my arms to wield a sword or even strike with my fists, and my legs were bound such that I couldn't kick or even run away. Until someone let me up, I could do nothing but sweat my fate.

As if in fulfillment of Vot's warning and my own fears, a group of branches suddenly gave way with a snap and a fearsome tharban leaped snarling into the encampment. The sleek, muscular body gave it a terrifying presence akin to that of a huge jungle cat of Earth. The rows of teeth jutting from its wide jaws dripped with saliva as the beast reared up and roared. Its bristly red-and-white striped hair stood erect and I could see its bluish underbelly. Warriors shouted and ran in every direction, some to grab their weapons and others to flee.

Taut muscles propelled the monster past the guards standing on the camp's perimeter, and it landed not twenty feet away, where it fixed its terrible gaze upon me. I must have looked like an especially easy meal to the creature, bound and helpless as I was. In that moment, I could honestly say I agreed.

But before the tharban could charge at me, I saw something gleaming in the light of the campfire fly from Vot's outstretched arm. Suddenly a long, slim dagger was sticking out from the bristling hair on the creature's back. The great beast shook like a house cat that suddenly finds itself wet, dislodging the dagger and flinging it to the ground.

But now the mighty creature turned its frightful gaze from me and locked it upon the one who had done nothing more than enrage it by piercing it with the puny blade. Horrified, I shouted out curses at the beast, trying to draw its attention away from Vot, who had distracted the devilish thing and saved my life.

My efforts, however, were to no avail, for the tharban simply ignored the noisy man-thing, its mind made up to eliminate the greater threat. With a ferocious roar, it charged at Vot.

I wanted to close my eyes and look away, but I lay there bound and transfixed by the horrific scene playing out before me. And so it was that again I saw something in Vot's grasp gleam in the light of the campfire. What it was I did not know until a searing beam of energy pierced the night and burned a hole clear through the torso of the leaping tharban. The beast dropped dead at Vot's feet. In her hand I saw my pistol.

I sighed with relief, and the Cloud People regrouped from all the excitement. After dragging the creature away, a number of Vot's people fell to preparing the beast by skinning it.

When Vot and an assistant knelt and began removing the mound of twigs and leaves from my body, Vot said, "The meat of the tharban is distasteful, but it will sustain us as we pursue the Linneauns." She took great handfuls of the slimy mud mixture from me, rubbed some on a cut on her arm, and then tossed the rest into a nearby pack.

"Thank you for saving me again," I said. "That's twice in a day."

Vot scraped away the last of the mixture and I breathed easier with the weight off my chest, both literally and figuratively. I looked a mess, still covered in the remains of the gray mixture. Though I felt refreshed, I was puzzled by a thick, cumbersome wrap of wide leaves and paste that remained around my right hand and arm up to the elbow. "Can this come off as well?" It was green and smelled awful.

"The worst of your injuries were there. This concentrated covering will heal them in a few more hours if you allow the medicine to work."

I knew that it would limit my movements for some time and keep me from wielding anything, let alone a sword. I knocked on the wrap with my other hand, feeling that it had hardened to a consistency of wood. "A few hours?"

"At least. You should get some sleep. Rest will help you heal." Vot motioned to a pile of leaves and furs nearby.

As I tried in vain to fall asleep, it occurred to me that if I expected any help at all from my friends, I must find a way to signal them. Back on Earth, I had studied in India with a mystic named Chand Kabi who taught me, among other things, how to project a representation of myself across great distances. This image projection had come in handy during one of my previous adventures, so why not use it again now?

The area around the fire had quieted down considerably, with everyone else either sleeping or patrolling. I got up, sat down next to the fire, and crossed my legs, letting the flames warm me. I concentrated on my beloved Duare in the hope of guiding her and the others to me. A sharp dagger of pain pierced my brain the moment I tried to send my image out beyond the trees. Never before had I experienced pain of that sort while generating a projection. My teacher had taught me to work beyond physical distractions, so I kept trying, ignoring my discomfort. A picture of Duare formed in my head, and I called to her, but she did not react to my entreaties. I tried again, calmly describing where I was and what had happened to me. Normally, if we were in sympathy, I could talk to the target of my messages, almost as though I were standing there in person. But Duare did not respond. The attempt to establish contact with her felt like a scalpel slicing into the back of my head. Defeated, I ceased my efforts.

I was exhausted, so I returned to my bedding, pulled my furs about me, and fell instantly into a deep sleep.

Come morning, I awoke to find myself invigorated, if still filthy. The unguents had done their job to ease the pain and heal my wounds. My head was clear, and the pain had gone. As I took my leave of the Cloud People, they pointed me in the direction of my crash and bade me farewell with a package of tharban meat and a pouch of salve to aid in my journey.

A morning chill lay upon the forest, and I wished for the warmth of the furs in which my new friends clad themselves. In my haste, I had asked for nothing from them with which to keep myself warm.

I used my unfettered hand to rub my exposed skin, but it did little to stave off the cold. The woods were still a frightening place in the dim morning light. I imagined a family of tharbans lurking behind every tree, waiting to pounce the moment my guard was down. I kept my good hand on my gun whenever possible.

It was fortuitous that the edge of the forest and the remains of my poor anotar were not far. It lay half-buried in the mud just a few hundred yards from the trees. The starboard wing had been sheared off and lay nearby in a crumpled heap. The body of the vehicle was dented and scraped; the nose cone was crushed from the impact with the ground, the propeller useless. It was a hard moment for me, considering how much I had been through with it. It was the second such craft I had built on Amtor, the first having crashed near Hangor and been torn apart by the locals, but I had grown fond of it all the same. It had carried me faithfully through many dangers, and to see it in pieces made my heart ache. In the back of my mind, I had been holding out some hope that I could make repairs. Stick the wing back on with a little patient love and care, realign the body, and all would be right with the world. Unfortunately, that wasn't possible. I had no tools, no parts, no help, and only one good hand, and the vehicle was beyond being put back together with spit and high hopes.

I pulled a flask of water out of the anotar, a length of fabric from the seat to use as a bandage should I need to redress my arm, and, as I was not able to find my sword after the crash, a short, sharp piece of metal from the wing that I could use as an additional weapon if the need arose. I found a thin orange tunic meant to stave off rain in one of the compartments, and I pulled it on to help blunt the chilly temperature.

I took a moment to consider my options. Before crashing into the Linneauns' tank, or lantar as the people of Korva would call the tanklike vehicle, I had passed over some treacherous territory for one to traverse on foot—forests full of tharbans and targos as well as several rivers of unknown depth. It had certainly been treacherous with my anotar, so returning that way to my friends without it would be fraught with dangers even more daunting. Rather than face the things I'd already seen, I decided to press on into the unknown. It felt like the wiser of the two decisions at the time.

With one last look at what remained of my once-trusty aircraft, I followed the enormous tracks left in the ground by the great machine.

Were it not for these deep gouges in the soil, there would not have been much to see. The landscape consisted of small trees, bushes, rocks, and little else. When I finally saw a hill far off in the distance, it was with a sense of relief that something had at last broken up the monotony of the flat terrain. The lack of sizable features had also caused me some concern; if any creature came upon me, I'd have absolutely no place to hide.

I shifted my gaze from side to side as I walked so as not to be taken by surprise. I had proceeded only a short distance when a flicker of motion caused me to turn and focus on a small dot in the sky above the wide tread marks pressed into the soil behind me. Something was coming my way, gliding just above the path the lantar had taken, and moving quickly. With the land so barren around me, I had little choice for cover but to duck into one of the grooves left by the lantar's treads. These were deep and wide enough for me to lie down and conceal myself. At least I hoped they were.

My mind raced, wondering what could be on my trail. Klangan? Thorists? Could the army of Havatoo be nipping at my heels? I gripped my pistol and prepared to fight.

Within seconds, a craft silently raced over my head. It was an anotar! After it passed, I stood and saw that it was, in fact, the same craft Nalte and Ero Shan had flown to Jovita. With a shout of joy, I waved my arms at them. I ran after the low-flying craft, jumping and screaming to get their attention.

The anotar swung around and taxied in for a smooth landing on the grassy plain, coming to rest some hundred yards from where I stood. As I ran for the ship, Duare, Nalte, and Ero Shan climbed out of it and met me halfway. I embraced Duare, who was overjoyed to see me, though immediately concerned about my well-being.

"What did you do to your arm?" she asked, examining the cast of leaves and mud around it.

"More importantly, what did you do to your anotar?" Ero Shan demanded.

"I'm afraid I have the same answer for both questions." I relayed the tale of my flight through the forest and subsequent collision with the enormous machine, followed by my rescue by the Cloud People and their assistance.

"Well, we are thrilled to find you alive," Nalte said. "We feared the worst."

"Thank you. I admit I was a bit concerned when—"

"Serpents are the biggest danger, I would imagine, or maybe tharbans," Nalte said. "Serpents sometimes hang in trees and drop down on unsuspecting travelers. Oh, and with your injuries, I am surprised that ignats did not climb into your wounds and lay eggs." When she stepped away I could see her slight grin.

"Well, fortunately none of that happened," I said, though the wrap on my arm felt suddenly itchy.

"If it were not for your message, we might never have found you," Ero Shan said.

"You saw me?"

Duare nodded. "Yes. Your form and words were faint. But I heard your message."

I thought about that. What could be affecting my ability? Perhaps it was the same thing that was giving me the terrible pains in the first place? In any case, I hoped it would not be a factor if I needed to use the talent in the future.

I inquired about the situation back in Korva. Duare replied that no further attacks had been made, though the strike on Jovita had put the whole nation on alert.

Meanwhile, Ero Shan was eyeing the wrap around my arm. "Cloud People helped you? What brought them out so far?"

"Same thing that brought us here," I told him bleakly. "An attack by unknown enemies on their people."

Agreeing that it was best to move on and continue following the tread marks, we made our way to the anotar and were soon aloft, with Ero Shan at the controls.

"Carson?" Duare asked. "Are you sure that arm will be all right? I could try to rewrap it."

"It's nothing." I eyed the bulky wrap around my hand. "Vot told me I would be free to take the covering off by the end of the day. Should it still be inflamed or painful, they gave me a few leaves and a pouch full of their salve to apply once again." The rank smell hit my nose again, and suddenly the night couldn't come fast enough.

"Didn't you suggest this machine would be easy to find?" Nalte asked, after we had flown along the tracks for almost an hour. "If it is as enormous as you say, should not we have caught up with it by now?"

I admit I was as puzzled as Nalte. The Cloud People had said the vehicle was slow-moving when they'd surveilled it.

Presently, as Ero Shan directed our anotar over the hill I had seen from a distance, we became quite sure where it had gone.

Ahead of us lay the great ocean and the massive tracks led directly into it.

4
ATTACKED!

THE MACHINE WENT into the water?" Duare stood and stared off into the sea. "What manner of battle craft can attack on land and escape into the sea?"

"I don't know," I said truthfully. I had encountered various types of transport machines during my time on Amtor, particularly in Havatoo with its electric cars, and here on Anlap with its massive lantars. But other than my own anotar, whose pontoons would allow it to function as a seaplane when the need arose, I had never before seen evidence of amphibious or submersible vehicles.

Ero Shan brought us down to the ground and we disembarked, intent on examining at closer range the huge tracks left by the machine. We had not been mistaken in our scouting from above—as we waded out from the shore, we found the trail ran under the water and headed out to sea.

"Wonderful," Ero Shan said. "How do we follow such an enemy who can drive a lantar along the bottom of the sea?"

"Some of us could swim out and see what we find," Nalte said, "while another could fly out over the water to get an aerial view. Perhaps we can yet make some determination as to that great machine's whereabouts or direction."

Nalte was more optimistic than I, but she had the only plan so far. I was about to agree with her course of action when I noticed something strange just offshore: there appeared to be more rocks than when we first arrived.

"Look!" I cried, pointing toward what I had seen. As my

31

companions turned their attention to where I'd indicated, the rocks seemed to grow bigger.

"What are they?" Duare asked.

Ero Shan was similarly perplexed. "Could the tide be strong enough to move boulders from the depths?"

We did not have to wait long for an answer to the mystery. A greater portion of the objects broke the surface and it soon became apparent that some manner of living being was trudging through the tide toward us. I counted six of them. At first glance, it appeared the emerging creatures were actually encrusted in rock. Their backs were bumpy, rough, and jagged. Ocean grass clung everywhere to them, but as they pulled themselves fully from the surf, the seaweed slid free.

Now it became clear that their bodies were more complex than I had first conceived. The pale orange skin was not stone but rather scaled and banded like an armadillo's hide. Their thick backs rose higher than their heads like tortoise shells, protecting both their necks and their craniums. They stood seven to eight feet high, including their posterior shells. Segmentation on the creatures' arms gave them an advantage over humans—rather than being equipped with just an elbow and a wrist, the soldiers had another joint midway up the forearm that gave them added articulation.

The helmets that covered their heads confounded me. Though the shell I have mentioned protected their heads and necks from behind, their headgear was small and nearly conical, which made me wonder if the heads underneath the getup were a similar shape. Two large black bubbles had been constructed at the front of each helmet, where I guessed eyes were located underneath, and a wide, black strap ran below the chin.

Only one of the creatures—the one in the back—appeared to carry a weapon. This resembled a large rifle with a wide, five-foot-long barrel.

The creature bearing the weapon raised its free hand and pointed at us. "Surrender to the Linneaun vanguard," it said in the common tongue of Amtor, "and your lives shall be spared to work for the glory of Iralcus Iguiri."

The voice was deep and seemed to echo across the rocky beach. It sounded male to my ear, but it was hard to be sure through the helmet. And who knew whether the tenor of the thing's voice indicated gender?

The creatures confronting us certainly appeared to be the same size and general shape as the ones I'd glimpsed standing on the great machine just before I crashed my anotar, and they fit the description the Cloud People had given me of the Linneauns.

"Stay where you are," Ero Shan said to the soldiers. "We shall be slaves to no one, least of all your master." He held up a hand to the creatures, but they simply ignored him and continued to advance. Ero Shan looked to the rest of us for guidance on how to proceed.

As the creatures came at us, I think we were all a little in awe of them. That another species of intelligent beings existed upon Amtor was no great surprise to me, as I had encountered several in my travels. But the stunned expressions on the faces of my companions indicated the creatures were also entirely unknown to the average Amtorian. Whatever this threat was, it was something new to us all.

"Surrender immediately and you will be spared!" It was impossible to determine which of them had spoken this time. The voice issued from inside one of the helmets, but I couldn't guess which. "Otherwise, face immediate death by order of the mighty Iralcus Iguiri!"

It seemed there would be no reasoning with the creatures; they meant for us to become prisoners and workers for their war effort. But even so, I had to try.

"We are emissaries of Taman, jong of Korva," I said. "We surrender to no one. I am Carson Napier, tanjong of Korva, and I am empowered to speak on the jong's behalf. I ask to parley with your leaders. Your actions against Korva will have grave consequences. We would like to avoid further loss of life, whether that be to our people—" and here I paused, "or to yours."

The Linneauns stopped for a moment, and presently I again heard voices that were hard to pinpoint. The strange soldiers were speaking to each other, their buzzing voices low and curt, but I could not make out what they were saying.

For just a moment, I believed I might actually have succeeded in convincing them to turn and retreat into the sea. But then the Linneauns stopped their chattering and once again began marching toward us.

Duare stepped forward this time. "Stop!" She gripped the hilt of her sheathed sword to emphasize her words. "The Korvan empire is mighty, and strong are our allies. Think well on what you do next." The warriors continued without so much as a lost step. Duare made good on her threat and drew her blade from its scabbard, positioning herself directly in front of the closest of the creatures. The hairs on the back of my neck stood on end, as I knew it was a bluff: Duare had little training in the art of the sword, having grabbed the blade when we left the ship due to the shortage of guns among us.

Nearly in unison, Ero Shan whipped his sword from its scabbard and Nalte drew a mean-looking pistol from the holster on her hip. The creatures moved toward the others, but strangely none came for me. This baffled me, but I wasn't going to waste the opportunity it presented. I pulled my r-ray pistol and fired at the one closest to Duare. I was forced to use my weak hand because of the cast Vot had placed on my good one, but though my arm was shaky, my aim was true. The ray sizzled through the air and found the creature's shoulder. It was a shot that would have felled a gantor the size of a bus, but the Linneaun didn't even flinch.

Duare looked at me, as stunned as I that the hit had failed to lay low her assailant. She hefted her blade high and swung at the creature's midsection. The blade bounced off harmlessly, but Duare persisted, bringing the sword around for a second and third strike, though each blow had the same effect as the first.

Nalte and Ero Shan maneuvered themselves in position to fight one of the creatures together. Their weapons became a flurry of flashing metal and searing r-rays, pummeling the huge Linneaun from two directions at once. The attacker seemed to barely notice them or their attempts to injure it, until it raised one massive arm and took a swipe at them. Its movements seemed strangely agile for its size, and its append-age barely missed our companions.

The largest of our assailants remained in the back, overseeing its companions as they crowded toward my friends. The long, menacing gun I'd noticed earlier remained by its side.

Since the Linneauns still seemed to be ignoring me, I leaped at one that tried to flank Duare. I fired my pistol at it and then hacked at it with my short blade, trying to keep it away from her. It was here that the battle took a strange turn. Despite my attack falling short and merely cutting through the air a few feet from my opponent, the Linneaun recoiled. It raised its arms to protect itself from my advance.

Puzzled, I watched as my opponent backed away from me. I pressed my attack, and jumped forward, planting my blade firmly into the creature's arm. It left nothing but the barest scratch on its armorlike hide. The Linneaun continued to shield itself with both arms while it retreated before me.

To my left, I saw Duare's attacker landing blow after blow against her defenses, knocking her backward. Trying to take advantage of its narrow focus, I hurried to join the fight. Before I could, a booming voice startled me.

"You were told to avoid contact with the Carson Napier at all costs." It was the one with the weapon in the back of the fight. "Yet you engaged him in combat."

The Linneaun whom I'd cut just moments ago raised its arms again, this time to protect itself from someone other than me. "No. I was retreating from the Carson as ordered. He was too quick." This one's voice seemed louder than I'd expected as well. I wondered if their small helmets had some sort of amplification device inside.

"You disobeyed," the larger one said. The long, wide-barreled rifle it held suddenly rumbled to life, spewing fire and smoke into the air. Had I time to react, I might have run, pushed my companions out of the way, or thrown myself on the ground to avoid being shot with the weapon. But as it was, I could only watch as the Linneaun attacked. Its target, however, was not me or my friends. Instead, one of its own soldiers fell to the ground in a great cloud of red fog. The creature fell hard on its back. Planted firmly in the center of the soldier's chest jutted the back end of a projectile shell similar to the ones I'd seen in Jovita, resembling in miniature the torpedo-shaped rocket that had brought me to Venus. This one was even smaller, no larger than the size of a fist, and it had easily penetrated the thick chest that my weapons barely scratched. The creature's gaping wound smoldered with black smoke.

"Carson!" Duare was at my side. "We must retreat back to the anotar!" she shouted to both me and our companions.

I watched the rust-red fog rise from the dead Linneaun and wondered what it all meant, how it all connected to me and to my arrival on Amtor.

Again, Duare urged me to return to the anotar, but I took an extra second to consider charging at the Linneauns. If they weren't supposed to attack me, I could attack them. What would they do then?

"Salvage what you can and return," the leader ordered its soldiers. Then it turned and walked back into the sea, gun in hand.

As we ran, the other attackers swung at us, but we kept going toward the anotar. Midway there, Nalte shouted, and Ero Shan stopped. She had lost her pistol and was in the grip of one of the Linneaun attackers. It was quickly pulling her to the water's edge.

I drew my pistol and, aiming with extreme care so as not to hit my friend, fired several shots at the creature, trying to provoke it into releasing Nalte and turn its attention to me. Instead, the Linneaun merely pulled her along, shrugging off the impact of r-rays that would have brought any other being on Amtor to its knees.

Ero Shan bounded for the same target, shouting savagely as he swung his sword about, but his rage blinded him to the other attackers, and one was able to knock him to the ground with a mighty blow from a thick arm. Then the creature grabbed Ero Shan and dragged him toward the water. At that, all the Linneauns turned and moved back into the sea, pulling both of our companions along with them.

I ran toward Ero Shan and jumped on his attacker in the hopes of unbalancing it, but the Linneaun merely flung me off and I fell to the black sand. The enormous creature continued for the water. At a loss, I drew my gun again, took careful aim once more, and shot at the arm of the Linneaun that held my friend. After three blasts, the creature pulled its hand back in pain or surprise, releasing its quarry.

I fired again, pausing only to lift Ero Shan from the rocky beach. "Come on, there's still time to stop them." Even as I spoke, I heard the low hum of our anotar's engine.

Behind us, Duare had made it to the craft and was already taking to the air. The ship rose only slightly before she opened the throttle and swooped low over our heads. I watched with rapt attention as she lowered the pontoons, brought the anotar down on the water, and dropped anchor not far from the fleeing creatures. With the craft securely stationed, she emerged from the cockpit and stepped out onto the wing, a bow gripped in one hand, an arrow in the other.

It was somehow fitting that she'd pulled that particular weapon from storage; I had fashioned it long ago and used it when I'd first met Nalte. Realizing just now that Nalte had kept it all this time brought a lump to my throat. The primitive tool had once protected Nalte and me from all manner of threats as we made our way to safety. Now, Duare meant to use it to protect our friend once again.

Steadying herself on the front of the anotar, Duare drew the bow and loosed an arrow at the raiding party. It was impossible to see from our position whether it hit its mark, but we could hear shouting and cursing from the group of Linneauns as Duare fitted another arrow in her bow.

Ero Shan had waded out into the quiet water. He leaped onto the back of the soldier Duare now targeted. He held on and stabbed with seemingly no effect on the creature, which kept trudging into the sea without pause.

Meanwhile, Nalte shouted and struck at her attacker with her bare fists, desperate to break free and avoid being pulled under the ocean's glassy surface. But as her captor slowly submerged itself, she could no longer keep her own head above the water. Within moments, she vanished in a frenzy of splashes and foam.

"No!" Ero Shan shouted as he struck his opponent harder, stabbing and slashing with all his might until the Linneaun he rode slipped beneath the veil of the sea along with the others. My friend was forced to let go.

I resisted the urge to fire my pistol into the water where the creatures had disappeared, for fear of hitting Nalte. But it would have been all for naught anyway. The creatures were gone.

Seeing Ero Shan flailing in the water, I swam to his side and supported him while he gathered his wits. "We must save her!" he cried.

I agreed and we both swam beneath the surface, struggling to catch up to the Linneauns. They were not terribly fast, but they were certainly sure-footed, or perhaps they were just so heavy that nothing deterred them. The current that slowed us had absolutely no meaning to them or their progress. I could see them plodding along, unconcerned by the sea or by us.

When I got close enough, I grabbed the nearest Linneaun and pulled myself forward using the high crest behind its head. It must have been the one Duare had struck with the arrow. Somehow her arrow had succeeding in wounding the creature where repeated attempts with our swords and gunfire had not. Its helmet was torn on one side and dark red liquid trickled from one side of its face.

Curiously, its entire face was now encased in what looked like a giant transparent bubble. This encircled the whole head and was cinched off at the neck by what appeared to be some sort of collar. I grabbed at the bubble, only to find my hand went through it and landed on the creature's helmet. I could feel the thick dark blood that seeped from the hole in the helmet, but when I pulled my hand back beyond the bubble, the seawater washed the ichor away.

As I tried to comprehend what had just happened, the Linneaun thrust a hand at my chest to push me away, releasing what little air I had left in me. I tried to swim for the surface, but the cast on my arm impeded me and everything began to grow dim.

Suddenly, Ero Shan was at my side, pulling me upward. He towed me to the surface, where I inhaled deeply the fresh sea air. If it weren't for Ero Shan's quick actions, I would certainly have drowned.

Duare still stood on the wing of the anotar, watching us from a distance with great concern. After ascertaining that we were all right, she discarded her bow, dived from the wing, and disappeared beneath the waters I'd only just escaped.

Though Ero Shan and I were both exhausted, we did not hesitate to make as swiftly as we could manage for the point at which Duare had plunged into the sea.

When we got to the spot, we dipped our heads below the surface, looking for any trace of our loved ones. But they were nowhere to be seen.

"Let us get aloft!" Ero Shan cried in desperation. "We can fly above the sea and try to find them. We cannot let them die at the hands of those foul creatures!"

But before we could even get aboard the craft, a figure broke the surface some distance from us. It was Duare. And she was alone.

5
A LANTAR OF THE SEA

WE CLIMBED ON BOARD the anotar and pulled ourselves up into the cockpit. There we sat for several minutes, dripping and in shock at what had just transpired, before Duare was able to regain her breath and enough composure to tell her story.

"I swam down and caught up with the creatures that held Nalte in their grasp," Duare said. "They pulled her into some sort of underwater craft. The door slid shut, and though I pounded on it, my efforts were futile. The ship began moving along the seafloor at a pace I could not maintain. Only when my lungs felt like they must burst did I concede defeat and turn back to the surface." Duare placed her hand gently on Ero Shan's arm. "We must take comfort in the fact that she is alive."

But Duare's words did little to reassure Ero Shan; he was numb with shock and despair, as were the rest of us. "What will we do? We can't just wait here."

"We must find them," Duare said, "But how? When I returned to the surface I became confused as to the direction the craft took."

I was loath to admit I had no idea how to follow such a craft. It would leave no tracks upon the water as a wild beast might in the mud, and the craft made no sound that we could discern.

As I sat there in the pilot's seat, the seaborne anotar rolling gently on the water, a glimmer on the surface caught my eye.

40

The sea was bulging ahead of us. The odd phenomenon was hundreds of feet away, yet its sheer size made it unmistakable. The water rose to maybe the height of one of the huts we'd recently seen in Jovita, before suddenly exploding. I realized it was no less than a huge bubble, possibly from a pocket of air far down in the rocks, or from a massive sea creature gulping a fish.

"What is it?" Duare asked breathlessly. She was pointing to another rising bulge, this one just as large as the last.

"It can only be a bubble," I said. "But so large! I wonder if it could be a ship. Maybe an underwater vessel of some sort, venting air or moving in a certain fashion?"

A ray of hope lit up Duare's face. "It is the lantar!" she cried. "Only it is a lantar of the sea!"

At her words, I started the engine and glided the anotar on its pontoons with great celerity over the water toward the mysterious area. By the time we got there, the water had calmed, broken only by the slight waves of moonless Amtor and the occasional appearance of small sea creatures looking for food. Ero Shan leaned out the door of the anotar, scanning for another burst on the horizon. I wasn't sure if he blinked the entire time he was watching, but it was easy to see his hope fade when thirty minutes or more went by without another sighting.

"It was worth a try," Duare said, placing a consoling hand on Ero Shan's shoulder. They both continued to stare out to sea, straining to find anything out of the ordinary.

I guided the anotar slowly on a path that I felt represented a straight line between where we had originally witnessed the bubbles and where Duare indicated she believed the craft had gone. "Let's keep on this way a bit and see what turns up." In my mind, it was just as likely that we'd find something out here as we were to discover something new on the beach. Which is to say I wasn't fond of our chances either way. Tracking someone on land, you could follow footprints that might last for days or weeks, but bubbles in the sea lasted only so long, no matter how large they might be.

"Wait," Ero Shan said. He leaned so far out of the aircraft I thought he might fall into the sea. "There, in the distance. It's near the horizon." He raised his arm to show us.

I looked to see where he was pointing and found the water expanding upward like some great beast was about to breach the surface. Without a thought, I steered us toward it just as it formed into a bubble and quickly popped. A hundred smaller bubbles followed it, and then another larger bubble a few feet away, then another farther away, creating a trail of larger and smaller bursts that formed something of a trail, each coming faster than the one before it. Our craft rocked from the resulting waves.

"Whatever it is, it's on the move," I said.

"It's our only clue to this madness," Ero Shan said. "Follow it!"

Whether the hope it generated in my breast was warranted or not, I couldn't let such an opportunity pass us by. I revved the engine, and the propeller pulled us gently forward along the path of the disturbed waters.

We followed the bubbles for hours, sometimes losing sight of them and worrying we would not see them again; but always they returned. Other times we got so close to the bursts that our anotar heaved violently in the sea, waves and ocean spray pelting against the windscreen.

Duare discovered a peculiar fact early in the journey. The line we were following never seemed to turn. Using landmarks on the shore behind us, and points on the coastline to the east, we could see that the bubbles we sighted made a straight line, so straight that we wondered if it were on some sort of track, or a premade path. It helped us in our navigation and kept us from panicking if we didn't see a bubble for some time. We kept a steady speed on as direct a path as we could and eventually, we'd be back on track.

Unfortunately, we lost sight of land after a while as we

raced out across the open ocean. I felt a sense of isolation almost immediately, which was unfamiliar to me. The adventures that Duare and I went on by ourselves were terrifying and exhilarating, but I loved them. Now, a feeling of dread gripped me.

"There!" Ero Shan shouted enthusiastically. "Off to starboard, I can see a shape beneath the water."

"I was just about to say the same," Duare said. "Only farther up ahead."

I brought the anotar to a halt on the waters and we stood and peered out the windows, examining the sea in both directions. "Two objects?" I mused. "You think the Linneauns have more than one vehicle down there?" I watched as the dark mass that Ero Shan had spied suddenly turned and moved away at a right angle to us. The one at the front of our craft zipped left to right and back. "They're turning too fast to be any vehicles. It has to be some sort of fish or a…" It came to me suddenly that we might not be the hunters, but the hunted. I hoped I wasn't too late to get us out of harm's way. "Everyone back in your seats and strap in."

"What?" Duare asked.

"Rotiks," I said, referring to the monstrous, three-eyed behemoths of the Amtorian depths.

I grabbed the control stick, throttled the engine, and propelled us forward on the pontoons, trying to get us into the air as quickly as possible. We'd moved not more than fifty yards when the huge form of one of the rotiks broke the surface of the water just ahead of us. It twisted its vast serpentine body in our direction, its gigantic maw gaping open to reveal a lower jaw like the bucket of a steam shovel that spanned fifty feet from side to side.

With wild abandon, I pulled hard to the left. I felt something clip our starboard wing, as well as a strange drag from the aft, but I straightened out our course and succeeded in getting us airborne.

Though we had narrowly avoided a head-on collision with

the giant rotik, it soon became evident that something was wrong with the anotar.

"I'm having serious trouble maintaining altitude," I called to my companions as I fought against the controls. "Somebody, lean out and give me a visual inspection of the aft. And be quick about it!"

Duare did not hesitate. I felt the rush of cold air as she swung the door open. Clutching a strap from her seat, she hung so far out I feared she would fall out of the aeroplane. But a moment later she pulled herself back into the cabin.

"There's a small rotik with its jaws clamped around the aft horizontal stabilizer!" she cried.

I could have laughed at the image, had the situation not been so dire and all of our lives in jeopardy. The small fry had caught a bird many times its own size.

"Well, get it off now," I said, "or we're all going into the drink."

But Duare was ahead of me. She took my pistol and leaned back out the door, fighting against the wind as she took aim.

I saw three rapid-fire flashes from the gun. The anotar lunged up, suddenly free of its burden. Duare had scored a hit.

She climbed back in the cabin and strapped herself back in her seat beside me. "Got it," she said with a grin of triumph.

"Can you give me an assessment of the damage?" I asked. Though the plane seemed to be responding, I needed to make sure.

"Well, except for some jagged teeth marks in the metal, I think we're in the clear. The elevators appear to be undamaged."

I placed my hand upon her own. "And you?"

"Undamaged as well." She squeezed my hand. "Though I am freezing!"

Ero Shan pulled some blankets out of storage to keep us warm as I oriented our craft and got us back on our way. Ahead of us, maybe a mile distant, a huge bubble broke the surface and sent seawater flying in all directions, confirming that we hadn't just been tracking hungry fish for the last several hours.

We followed the strange trail for so long that the three of us had to trade positions: one would pilot, one would navigate, and one would rest in the back. Night fell. It was nearly impossible to see the great explosions of water in the all-encompassing darkness of the Amtorian sea at night. We had no moon or stars to illuminate our path and only the landing lights of the anotar to reflect on the waters below.

Come morning, I was navigating while Duare piloted the anotar when I lost sight of our strange seamarks. The bubbles stopped altogether for nearly an hour. Duare circled the anotar over where we had last seen them. We woke Ero Shan and apprised him of the situation.

"What was your last heading when you lost them?" Ero Shan asked as he rubbed his eyes. I gave him an indication of where we were going, and he replied, "Still straight on like last night? I say continue on that course. It's worked so far."

With a shrug, I did as Ero Shan had recommended. Duare sighed and questioned whether we might not have been following some enormous sea beast all this time. But we all agreed we had no other sensible recourse but to continue on in the direction we had been going.

Ero Shan, fresh from his round of sleep, took the controls and pushed the throttle a little harder.

Meanwhile, Duare and I went to work at removing my cast with the sharp point of a dagger. The crusty amalgam of mud and leaves had only grown more pungent with time and I was relieved to finally cast it overboard and into the sea. I tested both my arm and wrist, marveling that the unguents of the Cloud People had completely healed them.

Satisfied with the outcome of our labors, I urged Duare to get some sleep, while I fell back in my seat and watched the gray sea race beneath us.

6
SPECTRAL VISITORS

DUARE WAS THE ONE who spotted the dim outline of a landmass ahead. Several darker points on the horizon suggested mountain peaks lined whatever island or continent we were approaching. We cheered, despite not knowing whether what lay ahead would answer any of our questions or merely provide us with more.

Scanning the landforms, we tried to determine exactly where we were, so we might better decide how to proceed. We didn't want to rush headlong into a country where we were not welcome faces. Ero Shan slowed the anotar and descended until we were flying just above the water.

"Do you see that?" Ero Shan pointed toward the massive rock formations that made up the coastline.

It took me a minute to locate what he meant, but once I saw it, I was transfixed. Less than a mile from the shore was an immense structure that appeared to be either floating on the surface of the water or emerging from it. The coloring of the structure's exterior was similar to that of the tall gray cliffs that rose behind, which served to camouflage it. The architecture was foreign to us, with a central spire that rose to half the height of the cliffs. It was as beautiful a structure as I'd seen, despite its bland coloration.

"I have no idea who could have constructed this," Duare said. "I'd like to say I would recognize a striking tower such as that one, but it is like nothing I've ever seen."

As we flew closer, we noticed activity around the sides of the structure. "Are those Myposans?" Ero Shan asked.

"How could that be?" Duare looked at me questioningly. "Mypos is located thousands of miles to the north."

I would most assuredly remember the Myposans on sight. It was hard to put a race of people with humanoid bodies, fish faces, and enormous black wiry beards from my mind. Of course, the fact that they'd tried to kill my beloved Duare and me when we last encountered them certainly helped.

I was about to answer when my body suddenly seized, and pain shot through my head. My eyes were open, but I was no longer seeing Duare, Ero Shan, or the structure. In fact, I could see nothing at all of familiar Amtor. All around me for miles was dead soil. In the distance, I could see green plateaus. The heat was nearly unbearable, even compared to the sweltering, humid region of Amtor with which I was already familiar. At the thought of the heat, I brought my gaze upward and nearly blinded myself looking at the sun. It had been so long since I'd seen the sun—or a sun, as I was not sure the huge, blood-red orb above was the same that shone down on Earth— that it came to me as a surprise. The thick cloud cover of my adopted planet prevented the sun from making an appearance of any reasonable length.

I felt a presence, like someone was standing behind me, but I turned and found no one.

"Hello?" I was afraid to shout my greeting. "Is there someone there?" I heard a rumble from the direction of the mountains and turned to see clouds of green dust rise into the air. It looked like a massive line of creatures was coming toward me, though I could not tell what they were.

"Carson?" Duare said. I blinked and the foreign world was gone. Duare was looking down at me and gently nudging my arm. We were no longer on board the anotar, and I was lying on a long stretcher being carried along a narrow corridor by two Myposans. I reached up and touched the one near my head, just to assure myself that he was there and what I was now seeing was real. The fish-man swatted away my hand with a grunt.

"Duare, what is this?"

Her sudden smile showed a mix of both joy and concern. "Carson, you passed out again! One moment we were talking and then you were unconscious in your seat in the anotar."

"Glad to see you awake," Ero Shan said. "We were worried for you, so we took a chance and landed the anotar on the structure. The Myposans have been welcoming and friendly." He leaned close to me. "So far, anyway."

"This is Eront." Duare indicated another Myposan following us. "He is a member of the jong's staff and he's taking you to a room to rest. He's going to try to get us an audience with the jong as soon as he can."

"You're a long way from home, Eront," I said. "Whatever you're doing so far south seems to have worked out well for you." The fish-man simply nodded.

A lot had happened while I was unconscious, it seemed. I sat up and looked around at the palace as we continued. It seemed plain to me. The walls were smooth and bare, no artwork, no paintings, no tapestries. I swung my legs to the side of the gurney and asked my bearers to stop. The luxury of being carried around didn't outweigh my unease at being taken where my former enemies pleased. I stood with Duare's help and took a moment to gain my balance. I still felt a little off, but the sensation seemed to be fading. "Please," I said. "Let's continue." I motioned for our Myposan guide to go on.

Eront escorted us through the corridors, past several doorways that led to some shops, but more often showed storerooms piled high with crates and bins. "We have established Thayros as a major trading post for the area," Eront said. "We see artisans from a number of continents arrive daily." I noticed several humanoids wearing threadbare clothing, their faces hidden by hooded patchwork cloaks, carrying supplies along a side hall. They were followed by a pair of

Myposans armed with swords. It was hard to say whether the cloaked figures were merchants, but they moved quickly. I made a mental note to pay close attention to any other non-Myposans we might happen upon.

Our guide led us down a wide staircase to a small room with transparent, glasslike walls. To get in, we had to push through a door made of thin strips of a slimy translucent material. Once inside, the material stuck back together, and it was impossible to see where we'd entered. Eront puckered his fish lips repeatedly as we stood there, and I was unsure if this was an sign of contentment or nervousness. "Thayros is pleased to have you among us. This elevator will transport us down to the jong's chambers and an area where you can rest and ingest nourishment while we wait," Eront said. "Please enjoy the beauty of our waters." With that, the floor began to descend into the depths. I say the floor, as the walls seemed to stay in place as we drifted downward, forming a long tube that stretched down toward the ocean floor. "We would let you swim down, but I doubt you could hold your breath that long." His lips puckered repeatedly again, perhaps this time in amusement.

The see-through compartment offered us a spectacular view of the sea as we left the comfort of the floating city of Thayros and descended in the tube. As the floating structure grew smaller above us, I became aware that water surrounded us on all sides. The tube our car was in used seawater and weights to pull it down toward the bottom, leaving water on all sides of the tube, and more beyond.

Eront seemed serenely at home in these surroundings as he stared off at the sea. Schools of small fish flitted back and forth in formation at intervals in the upper regions; as we got deeper, we spotted the shadows of larger things moving ponderously through the darkness.

"What are those?" Ero Shan asked. He pointed to one of the larger shadows.

"It is a rotik," the fish-man stated matter-of-factly.

Duare groaned and rolled her eyes. "I've had enough of rotiks."

"Me, too," I said. "And you wanted me to swim down here, Eront?"

"Do not worry about the rotiks," Eront replied. "They do not venture close to the light."

"I guess I'll have to take your word for it." I watched as another huge shadow moved through the deeps.

As our descent began to slow, I looked below and saw a structure nearly twice the size of the one we'd just left. It appeared circular, shaped like a type of red onion my mother used to grow in her garden. When I thought of Earth, my knees suddenly buckled, and the familiar sensation of queasiness swept over me.

Duare noticed my condition and gripped my elbow. "Are you still unwell?"

I braced myself against the wall of the car and put on a brave face. "I'll be fine. The depth of the water must be playing havoc with me." Duare's glance lingered and she gripped my arm tighter, though she said nothing further.

The car slowed and then stopped as we reached our destination. Eront pushed outward on the thin wall and it gave way as though it were tearing apart. We followed him into a long hall that seemed to be made of materials similar to those of the elevator. For a moment we could see the ocean above us, obscured only by the transparent roof of the tunnel, before a solid ceiling appeared overhead.

I had started out at a brisk pace, but almost instantly my strange affliction caught up with me and I felt dizzy and unstable on my feet. "Could we stop for a moment? I...need to rest." I made to reach for Duare, only to discover she'd never let go of me.

Our guide motioned to the end of the hall ahead of us, and the door—the solid wooden door—that rested there. "There are sleeping quarters that we keep for visitors just beyond this portal. We have been instructed to let you rest there. Food is being prepared to sustain you."

"Are we getting a royal welcome here," Ero Shan asked, "or are we going to be fattened up and served for dinner?"

Ignoring the quip, Eront went to stand at the door for a moment, his head pressed against the wooden panel.

"What's wrong?" Duare asked. "Are we interrupting something?"

"I'm listening to make sure the hall beyond has been completely drained of water. It would cause me much dismay if I were to open it and you all drowned in the ensuing flood of the hall. The jong would be much displeased with me."

"You take as much time as you think is needed," Ero Shan said. "I respect thoroughness."

For a brief moment, a look of concern crossed Eront's face, presumably because of what he heard on the door's other side, but then his countenance immediately softened. "It's acceptable." He opened the door inward and a small amount of water flowed out, though barely enough to wet our feet. Eront sighed and puckered his lips in a manner I had come to recognize as a Myposan smile as the liquid splashed his feet. Then he smacked his lips and said, "I have been out of the water for too long this day."

He led us from the clear corridor into a beautifully carved stone hall with lightly glowing yellow globes along the walls. We could already smell something cooking nearby, giving the area a warm, inviting aroma of comfort. The smell alone made me feel slightly better.

The hall widened as we proceeded and Eront opened several sealed doors. "These rooms are available for your party to rest in. They are kept sealed and dry for our land-dwelling guests. You may choose any or all that you require. Please relax, and I will attend to the preparation of your meals." He bowed slightly.

"Thank you," Duare said. She guided me to one of the rooms and I sat down on an amazingly soft bed.

"Are you all right?" Duare asked. "I am concerned. Perhaps the Myposans have a doctor that might be of help. Or maybe we should just ask if we can leave and get you back to Korva as swiftly as possible."

"I will be fine once I rest," I said. "Please, go with the others and eat. Hopefully, there will be something everyone enjoys." I waved my companions off, putting on as cheerful a face as I could. "Once the jong is available, we'll talk to him and see if he can provide some insight into this Iralcus Iguiri."

I couldn't help but sigh in relief at finally having a moment to myself. I stood and walked around the room. One wall curved up and was completely transparent, forming something of a partial dome over one half of the room. The other half was solid stone and adjoined the outside hall. A piece of furniture resembling a tall wardrobe stood against the inner wall and a small table sat beside the bed. Walking around, I took in the long red tapestries along the doorway and inner walls before crossing to the transparent wall to look out at the ocean that surrounded us. I could vaguely make out the long tunnel that made its way up to the surface, but the floating palace of the Myposans was far too distant to discern.

Deciding that everyone was right and a little rest might actually clear my head, I forced myself to curl up on the enormous bed. Within moments, my eyes were closed, and I was asleep.

A thumping sound nearby snapped me awake. It was hard to say how long I had slept, but I suppose it was only a few minutes. I stood up, assuming someone had come to bring me something to eat. Halfway to the door, I heard the heavy thudding again, but it wasn't coming from the hall—something behind me was making the sound. I turned and nearly fell to the floor in shock at what I saw.

A stark-naked man was slamming his fists against the huge window of my room. But he was not *in* the room—he was outside it, floating in the murky depths on the other side of the transparent wall! The look on his face was one of utter terror, and it was clear from the bubbles streaming from his mouth that he would drown within moments if he found no succor.

And that face! That was the greatest surprise of all, for I recognized it instantly. It was a face I'd not seen in far too long, for it belonged to my good friend Jason Gridley. Jason Gridley of Earth! Many years before my advent on Venus, I had met him in Germany, where we had been drawn together by our mutual interest in experimental rocket cars. But how could he be here on Amtor? Had he built a ship as I had and come here to rescue me? It made no sense, but what other explanation could there be for his presence on this planet, here at the bottom of the sea and at this particular point in time?

"Jason?" I knew it was him, and yet it couldn't be him. "Jason? What do I do?" I stood stunned just a few feet away from him.

His struggle and obvious fear broke the spell my initial sight of him had cast over me, and I moved to action. I snatched up a small table that rested alongside the bed and ran to the window. With both hands, I slammed the heavy piece of furniture against the transparent barrier with all the force I could muster, but it bounced harmlessly back at me, doing absolutely no damage. I reared up and tried again. This time the table shattered into a dozen or more pieces and fell to the floor.

In a state of confusion and desperation, I pushed open the door and dashed into the hall. "Duare, Ero Shan!" I cried. "I need help!" In my panic, I found myself hitting the stone walls with a leg of the table that I hadn't even realized I still possessed.

Within seconds, my companions came charging down the hall, followed by Eront and some Myposan guards.

"What is it?" Duare asked. "What is wrong? Are you having a night terror?"

"No," I shouted. "There's someone outside in the water."
I turned and ran back to the entrance to my room. "We need
to save him. It's my friend, Jason Gridley." I entered and ran
to the window, the others following at my heels.

I stopped midway through the room. There was no one
there. There was nothing there, not even a few telltale bubbles.
Crossing to the window, I stopped and searched all around,
craning my neck as I looked up through the glasslike transpar-
ency to see if he'd tried to make it to the surface. But I saw
no trace of him.

"He was here," I said. "You have to believe me."

Duare nodded and spoke reassuringly. "Of course, we
believe you. Here, come sit down."

I pulled myself from her grasp. "We need to help Jason."

Through the window, several Myposans appeared, swimming about in the area I'd seen Jason. Three went upward,
and the others descended below our line of sight. We waited
for several agonizing minutes until they all returned. The
expressions and manner told us that they'd found nothing.

"I am sorry," Eront said. "There appears to be no one outside
in the waters. We can keep searching, but…"

"It's okay," I said. I took a deep breath and tried to review
what I had seen. The Myposans who had gathered in the room
and outside the door departed with Eront, and I was left alone
with my friends.

"The Myposans offered to have their doctor come in," Ero
Shan said, looking somewhat sheepish. "Maybe we should
accept their offer."

"I'll take another stab at resting. Maybe it was another one
of my dreams." I all but pushed Duare out the door when she
appeared ready to ask me if I needed help. "Eat your meal.
And bring me whatever you think is best in a while." I closed
the door behind me, walked to the window, and sighed.

"Maybe I am going crazy," I mused aloud to myself. "From
what dim corner of my mind did I conjure Jason Gridley?"

"What do you know of Jason Gridley?"

The curt voice came from the far corner of the room. I moved to see who it was and found a young woman, perhaps eighteen years of age, peering at me out of the shadows from behind the wardrobe. Brown, wavy hair framed her heart-shaped face and fell upon her bare, umber shoulder in the room's faint light. I wondered if she was as devoid of clothing as Jason had been. "And how do you know how to speak English?" the girl asked. "Am I back on Earth?" She seemed suspicious of me.

I shook my head. I couldn't speak for fear I was hallucinating, that the slightest sound might break the spell that had come over me. Moreover, somehow I knew, though by what means I cannot say, that I was now standing face to face with the woman who had appeared in my dream when I had blacked out while piloting the anotar. The figure garbed in the flowing, hooded gown of red and blue with whom I had engaged in the strange back-and-forth dance during my fainting spell and she who stood before me were one and the same!

"I know, I know," the girl said. "You're startled because I popped out of nowhere. Join the club, mister. I'm not exactly thrilled at the whole Cheshire Cat routine myself."

She was right. I was startled out of my wits. First an apparition of my friend Jason Gridley and now the appearance out of nowhere of this strange young woman? Perhaps I was still back in my bed in Korva, dreaming. Well, I thought, if this was all a dream, then why not play along? But the only question I could come up with was, "Who are you?"

Again the girl eyed me with suspicion, but after a moment her violet eyes brightened. "I'm Victory," she said. "Victory Harben. I'm from Earth. I guess you figured that out."

A knock at the door took my attention. "Carson? Are you awake?" Duare's voice came from the hallway. "I have some water and a little bread for you. The jong is ready for us, so you'll need to eat quickly if you're hungry."

"Yes, I'm here." I ran for the door to drag Duare inside, so she could see this girl who called herself Victory. By the time

I reached the handle, I looked back to assure myself I had really seen what I thought I had.

She was gone. I raced back without opening the door and stood in the very spot I had seen her and found I was utterly alone. First Jason, now this stranger. Maybe I truly was losing my mind. It had seemed so real.

"Carson?" I hadn't heard Duare open the door, but there she was, standing in the dim light cast from the hall. "Could you eat something?" She stopped with the tray in her hands and looked me in the eye. "What is it? Are you still concerned for your friend? You look ashen."

I took the water from the tray and drank it in one long swallow. "I'm fine. Just hungry, I'm sure. During all that's transpired I've barely taken the time to eat anything." I picked up a large piece of bread and shoved it in my mouth. It was awful, but I chewed it anyway, gaining some peace of mind that I was awake, as I knew I could not have dreamed up something that tasted so foul.

"I didn't care for it, myself," Duare said. "They make that with some combination of sea plants and water insects, all ground to a fine powder, then baked on a warm rock." She watched me closely as I chewed. "The Myposans described it in great detail to me. Too much detail." She nodded as I swallowed the piece. "But if it helps you feel better, then I suppose I could get you more."

I stopped her. "No thanks. We should see the jong now."

We left the tray on a table and joined Ero Shan in the hall as he approached with Eront and two Myposan guards with spears.

"Yron, the jong, will see you now," Eront said. He gestured to a hall just off the one where we had entered, and we walked in silence for a moment.

"You didn't tell me it was Yron," I said, the sinking feeling in the pit of my stomach only partially due to the Myposan bread I had ingested.

7
INTO THE TUNNELS

T HE JONG OF MYPOS and I had a somewhat difficult past, in that he had been my guard when I was enslaved by his people many years back. Yron had risen to jong due in no small part to an altercation between myself and the former jong, but we had parted as enemies.

"I have no love for this jong, either," Duare said. "But you are severely ill and we must throw ourselves upon his mercy. Perhaps he has had time to recall your role in his good fortunes."

A slight incline brought us to a towering double door, which the two guards swung open. Inside we found an enormous storeroom with crates and boxes stacked in neat rows. The area was dirty and smelled of sweat and smoke, a sharp contrast to the rest of the building. I could hear shouts coming from just over the boxes, but I couldn't make out the words.

We stood there, gazing at the rows of crates and waiting for the jong when I noticed something on the far wall. It was hard to discern from that distance, but it appeared there were three large dark circles. I couldn't make out what they were meant for or what they were made of, but they intrigued me. Before I could ask our guides, Yron himself stepped up to us, walking with his aides between the rows of supplies and containers.

Yron stared at me and scowled. "They told me it was you, Carson of Venus. Or whatever meaningless title you have bestowed upon yourself today. I was sure they were mistaken."

"I am happy to see you, too, Yron," I said. "How are the royal hatcheries back in Mypos? Spawning any promising little devils who might be good heirs to the—"

"You should not have come here," Yron interrupted. He looked over my friends and then opened his mouth repeatedly, as if he were straining for air. "You should turn around now and go back home in that strange flying vessel of yours." He waited, as if he truly expected us to go.

Duare broke the awkward silence. "We are here to ask for help, or at the very least, some information."

"I have none of that," Yron said.

"Help or information?" I asked.

"Neither. Both." The jong appeared flustered by the request, and by our very presence. I wondered why our appearances here had so obviously upset this usually cunning and devious leader. Had I known that it was Yron we were dealing with, I certainly would have thought twice about meeting with him so far down in his own element.

"What are you doing out here?" I asked. Yron and his people lived thousands of miles to the north in the city of Mypos, so what had prompted them to establish such a far-flung outpost? And who had built it? I had been to Mypos and seen firsthand the fish-people's poor sense of art and architecture. They certainly hadn't constructed this outpost on their own.

Before Yron could respond, Ero Shan stepped forward and demanded to hear anything that Yron knew about Nalte and the strange soldiers who had taken her. Duare interjected and described the creatures we had encountered, their craft, and how they had absconded with our companion.

Yron looked anxious, if his rapidly flapping gill slits meant anything, and said, "It sounds like you've run afoul of the Linneauns." He motioned for us to follow him deeper into the warehouse. "They are from the unexplored territories. And they come sometimes to trade."

"They attacked us and took our friend," I said. "They have

been invading cities and taking prisoners off to who-knows-where."

That set Yron's gills aflutter again and he lowered his voice. "This has come late to your people. The Linneauns have emerged to many other countries and many other races in this region of Amtor. You should count yourself fortunate."

"Fortunate? Where is my Nalte?" Ero Shan pushed forward, and I feared he'd do something to provoke Yron's guards, who followed us at a discreet distance. "If you have some insight, if you know where to find her…"

Yron seemed to find himself then, and any pretense of civility fell away. "You forget yourself. I am the jong here. I am Yron. You are nothing. You may not make demands of me." His anger made his strides suddenly faster and he moved us along through boxes and containers that were stacked on shelves and on the floor. They were marked in letters and numbers I couldn't understand, a tangle of common Amtorian mixed with strange, harsh symbols.

"Look," I said, "we appreciate the assistance with my illness and all, but if you aren't willing or able to help us find our kidnapped friend, we need to move on." The narrow aisles between the equipment suddenly widened and the room opened to an even larger storehouse. The stench of oil and smoke was more concentrated here, though it was hard to determine immediately where it originated. Between the rows I saw more and more people who weren't Myposan at work among the parts and strange objects that littered the room. The fish-people were not above using slaves to do their menial work—I had certainly found that out long ago—but the number of indentured laborers in the warehouse and up on the surface seemed beyond anything I had witnessed in Mypos. And unless there were more Myposan guards, it seemed like these prisoners would easily be able to overpower their captors if given half a chance.

"Yron, what is happening here? Who are all these humans you have captured? Where are they from?"

Yron turned suddenly and pushed me. "Did I not say I am the jong? Do not ask me these things." We stopped closer to the far side of the building. Behind Yron, three gigantic circular metal doors took up most of the wall—the dots I had seen from afar. The doors were perhaps two hundred feet tall, nearly reaching the ceiling. They resembled enormous black dishes hanging there, waiting to be brought out for a giant's meal.

Yron clapped his hands and nodded to the wall. "They are late. I want this to be over." The soldier at his side nodded curtly and bowed.

As if in response, a clang that shook the floor startled all of us. It emanated from one of the gigantic doors and was soon followed by two more of equal force. After maybe a minute of torturous silence, the enormous metal disks slowly rolled to the left, revealing dark tunnels beyond. The opening of the doors seemed to free the dense rattling sound of metal against metal. As they moved aside, the shaking in the room worsened, and I had to brace myself to keep from falling. Ero Shan and Duare locked arms to steady each other, and the Myposans did their best to stay on their feet. Yron used a nearby crate to maintain as much of his dignity as he could.

As the doors rolled to a stop, the sound from inside the tunnels increased. It reminded me of the racket caused by someone cutting metal with a dull saw, rumbling and clanging until the sound itself faded behind a hideous screech. Great billows of heat rushed out into the room and I could tell something was coming. The room shook even more.

Duare reached out and grabbed my arm, pulling the three of us together. Her face bore a questioning look and I shook my head, unable to give her an answer.

In a cloud of steam and smoke, a massive vehicle emerged with stately slowness from the center tunnel and came to rest just outside the opening. Soon, another great cloud of smoke billowed from each of the other two openings, followed again by a vehicle from each.

In the cloud that surrounded them, it was tough to make out exactly what the things were, though the sounds and what I could glimpse of them reminded me of railroad trains. It had been a long time since I'd heard one back on Earth, but the rumbling and screeching certainly could have been that of an enormous engine racing down a track and pulling on the brakes.

As the smoke finally dissipated, I found myself completely unprepared for the sight that met my eyes. While the vehicles did seem to be on a track system, the main components were nothing like an engine. They each looked much more like the torpedo I had built that had carried me to Venus. But these were not tiny models, like the ones I had seen in Jovita—each one was the same size or larger than my original craft. In fact, the vehicles appeared identical to it in every aspect save two: rather than having a nose cone at one end and the rockets at the other, these had a nose cone on both ends, with a set of modified propulsion jets on each side. I wondered if the dual nose cones made it possible to travel in either direction in the tunnels from which they had emerged. The black vessels shone in the dim light of the warehouse as though they'd just been manufactured.

I stepped forward, transfixed by the sight, curious about the changes made to the design I was so familiar with, but Duare tightened her grip on my forearm. "No," she said quietly. "Now is a good time to exercise caution."

"I'm cautious," I said.

Yron turned slightly and muttered. "Listen to her. Keep quiet."

I pointed to the rockets. "How can I remain silent in the face of these? What are they? How are they based on my creation?"

Yron's gills flapped with agitation. His lips pursed and popped air, but I couldn't help continuing my inspection of the strange abominations of my work. They reminded me somewhat of early German rocket cars I'd financed back on Earth in preparation for building my interplanetary rocket—the very same rocket cars that had drawn the interest of both Jason Gridley and myself.

The strange thought made me pause. Could there possibly be a connection between my recent vision of Jason and the torpedo-shaped craft that lay on the tracks before us? But how could there be?

With a hiss, doors opened on either side of each craft, lowering to the ground to create ramps that led down from the vehicles. A half-dozen Linneauns disembarked from each of the torpedoes, all carrying staves of some sort. The creatures from each of the flanking craft walked down the ramps to the front of the torpedoes and waited. When they were in place, a seventh Linneaun emerged from the middle torpedo. This one walked a bit more carefully and at a slower pace than the others. Once it got to the bottom of the stairs, it was evident it was dragging its foot in a slight limp. While the others wore nothing at all over their banded bodies, this one wore red cuffs around its forearms and intricate metal bands around its biceps.

We watched as the limping creature made its way toward us. The Myposans, including Yron, all clumsily took to one knee as they bowed before the Linneaun. As they did this, I took a moment to look for an escape route, only to find an additional row of Myposans had come in behind us. These were not workers; they were warriors, armed and ready for any fight we might give them. I considered shouting for my friends to make a run for it while everyone was kneeling, but I knew we wouldn't get far.

Quickly, groups of Myposans began loading crates from the room onto the vehicles.

From the craft on the right, a few people made their way down the ramp. They were of varying races, all likely prisoners captured by the Linneauns. Some of the humans who came along could have easily been from Jovita. The captives were all attached to a central chain except the very last one.

It was Nalte. One of the Linneauns grabbed her and dragged her by a separate chain that was bound at her wrists.

Ero Shan pulled away from our group and shouted, "Nalte!" He pushed past Yron and raced toward his beloved before a trio of Myposans struck him with the blunt ends of their spears and pinned him to the ground. He hadn't made it very far.

"Carson Napier. Carson of Venus." It was the red-cuffed Linneaun with the limp that spoke. Its voice resembled those of the others of its kind we had encountered on the beach, though its undertones sounded rough and haggard. "They have told me you would be hard to find. But I have done it with quite some quickness. They were wrong. When my soldiers reported they had encountered you on the shore, I had them lure you here, so that I might see you die with my own eyes. In but a short time, the Iralcus Iguiri is triumphant." The Linneaun stopped in front of us and held up his hands in victory.

So this, then, was the mighty Iralcus Iguiri of which the Linneaun soldiers had spoken with such reverence. I frowned, as for good or for ill, I have a character defect that does not allow me to be impressed by autocrats, and even less by braggarts.

And so it was that I forgot the admonition to keep quiet and replied rather brashly, "Catching me might have been easy, but holding me is the difficult part." I felt defiant in the moment. Somehow this Iralcus knew me, and his people knew my designs. I just wanted to know why.

Something like a laugh came through Iralcus' helmet. "I have heard that as well. Stories say you get captured, then you escape. You get captured, then you escape. It is a shame. I had so much to show the Carson of Venus. So much pain you have caused, so much misery. Rather than allow you time to escape, you shall just have to die here instead."

"I could just not try to escape this time," I said. "It sounds like we have lots to talk about, after all." I shrugged to show my indifference. If I was going to die here and now, I would not die a coward.

It was then that I noticed out of the corner of my eye a cloaked figure walking slowly on top of a high shelf behind us, positioned far enough from the kneeling Myposans that they were oblivious to the individual's presence. With the cloak on, it was hard to tell whether whoever was beneath it was human, Myposan, or some other race, but the stranger was certainly trying to remain unnoticed—moving from crate to crate, keeping to the shadows.

Closer to the torpedo-cars, one of the guards brought Nalte forward, until they stood just behind the leader.

"This is not a laughing matter, Carson," Yron said to Duare and me. "He is taking over all who oppose him. No one can stand against him."

"The fish-man speaks the truth." Iralcus stepped closer, until he was but a few scant feet from Ero Shan. "The Linneaun empire has slept long enough. We will soon rule all of Amtor, thanks to you." He motioned to the soldiers that had moved up next to him. "Kill him."

"Wait!" I cried. I had no idea how to forestall my fate, but I had to try. "If you're going to kill me, you have to at least tell me how I fit into all this. You have to explain why your weapons and vehicles resemble designs I created."

Iralcus Iguiri laughed again. "No. I don't, Carson of Venus. Your torpedo crashed into my village years ago and brought death to my people. You cursed us with these helmets just to breathe, to survive. I owe you nothing." He waved a hand to his soldiers and then pointed at me. "Kill him. Kill his companions. Kill Carson of Venus."

Just as the towering Linneaun guards stepped forward at their leader's command, the unmistakable hum of a ray rifle cut through the air. For a split second, I feared the soldiers had fired at me, but when I saw one of the nearby boxes disintegrate, I realized the blast wasn't meant for us. From atop the shelves and crates, the mysterious figure had pulled a gun and begun firing into the crowd of enemies, which were too many to count. Linneauns and Myposans alike shouted amid the chaos that ensued. Some ran, while a handful scanned the room, looking for the source of the attack.

As blast after blast seared through the room, I took the opportunity to lunge at Iralcus. I made it only a few steps before Yron tackled me. He threw a few half-hearted punches at me, which I easily dodged. Before I could strike back, the Myposan leader leaned close and whispered a warning. "Carson of Venus, this is not something you can win. Not here. You must flee with your companions if you wish to live."

"How swell of you to warn me." I landed a glancing blow to his head, though I admit I pulled my punch, not willing to injure him until he explained further. "Why are you trying to help us?"

"You helped me once," Yron whispered as he gripped his hands around my windpipe and began to squeeze. "Without you I would not be jong. And…"

I clapped him hard on his gill flaps and he released his grip. "And what?" I asked.

"And I regret my deal with that devil Iralcus." Yron grabbed my wrist and tried to twist it but I kicked him in the shins and he let go. "His workers built this city for me after I provided him with information about you. Now I know it was but a ploy to enslave my own people as he has done to the others."

We grappled for a moment, but it was clear Yron wasn't even trying and the fight was but a ruse.

"Take the tunnels," he said. "That is how they travel from country to country quickly and stealthily. It is your only hope." Yron punched me in the stomach, shoving a small object into my hands as he did. Before I could react, he lifted me by my belt and shoved me hard enough to send me flying past Iralcus, only to sprawl on the floor at the feet of another Linneaun. Fortunately, it was the one holding Nalte's chain, and when I opened my hand, I found that Yron had handed me a key.

I rose to free Nalte, only to be punched in the shoulder by the Linneaun holding her captive, knocking me back to the floor. My head spun as I hit the ground and my arm throbbed with pain. I looked around for a weapon but found nothing. As the guard moved in for another blow, a series of ray blasts came out of nowhere and sent him stumbling backward. One of the shots hit his helmet and he screeched in pain, bringing both hands to his head.

Not wanting to stick around to see if this had put the soldier out of commission, I grabbed Nalte's chain. Though I couldn't remove the shackles around her wrists, I managed to release her from the length of chain that kept her tethered to the guard. It pained me slightly to admit Yron was right, but we needed to get out of the storehouse, and if we went back the way we came, it would mean fighting our way out through several rows of soldiers, both Linneaun and Myposan. Not to mention we would have to make our way back up the lift and then fight our way back to the anotar. We would never make it.

"Get into the middle torpedo-car," I said to Nalte. "See if you can get it working!" She nodded, and despite the inconvenience of her shackles, she grabbed a nearby wrench and ran for the ramp.

I picked up a length of chain and leaped to Ero Shan's side. He'd managed to break free of his captors and was fighting several Myposans with his bare hands. I swung my makeshift weapon above my head like some sort of medieval mace and wrapped it around a Myposan warrior's leg. I yanked and the Myposan fell to the ground. "We're getting aboard the center craft," I told my friend. "Hopefully, we can use it to make an exit."

Ero Shan wrested a staff from one of the fish-men and dodged a blow from another. "You don't sound confident."

I forced myself to smile. "It's fine. We're golden. Not a care."

"That does not improve my estimation of our situation," Ero Shan replied, but he was grinning.

A Linneaun came crashing through a stack of boxes and landed on his back. Duare was on his chest, swinging what appeared to be a long length of metal tubing down on the creature's helmet over and over again. The warrior batted at her with huge arms, which Duare managed to deftly avoid. With one more blow to the head, Duare looked up at us. "Why are you both smiling?"

"Because everything is all right?" Ero Shan ducked as another blast from an r-ray gun sizzled nearby.

"We're leaving. Everyone get in the center torpedo," I said. "Nalte is inside already, trying to get it going." Turning, I saw our cloaked ally jump down from one crate to another and finally to the floor, only to be greeted by a circle of warriors. "I'm going to help out our new friend; we'll meet you there." I noticed a number of Linneauns on the ground, and was shocked that our mysterious savior had apparently been able to injure them when our own ray guns had been ineffective.

I ran into the fray, dodging weapons and outstretched hands as best I could. Try as I might, I couldn't find another, more effective weapon to use against the throng of enemies, so I continued to swing the metal chain at every chance. Surprisingly it made for a rather efficient, if limited weapon. It was no real substitute for a sword or a gun, but this wasn't a time or place to be choosy.

Two Linneaun guards with huge guns like the ones we'd encountered on the beach flanked Iralcus to protect him. A moment later, they added to the commotion by firing in my direction. A huge crate to my left exploded and I dived for cover, hoping to protect myself from a further barrage. While I was safe for the moment, my route to the cloaked figure was now under fire. And any other route was crowded with soldiers.

Up on the track before the great door, Ero Shan and Duare emerged from the central torpedo, lugging one of the huge guns the Linneauns were firing. It took the two of them to raise it, but after a second, they managed to fire the thing, the very force of the discharge knocking them backward. They had succeeded in destroying a long row of carts filled with metal parts, starting a minor fire and sending all the Myposans running away from the blast.

The way was suddenly and briefly clear for both myself and our unknown guardian, so I ran toward the craft, waving the hooded person to follow.

The torpedo-car my companions had entered began to rattle and steam back to life. Despite being surrounded by a host of Myposans and Linneaus, one of my friends had apparently figured out how to start the thing up again. I dodged the Myposans easily, steered clear of the Linneaus, and soon found myself being lifted into the cargo door by Ero Shan. He pulled the door as if to shut it against the bombardment of spears and weapon fire, but I stilled his hand. "We need to wait." I pointed to the cloaked figure steadily running toward us. "We can't leave without him." Without questioning me, Ero Shan continued to fire a pistol he'd found in the torpedo-car, providing cover for the figure that approached.

I held out my hand and pulled our guardian aboard. As I did his cloak fell away and I found myself face to face with Jason Gridley, the very man I'd feared drowned only hours ago. "Go!" I shouted to whomever had gained control of the vessel.

Jason breathed a sigh of relief at being pulled aboard. He turned and fired at the Myposans, but I stopped him as he drew a bead on Yron. It seemed the Myposan had found a soft spot in my heart, even if temporarily. Jason and Ero Shan helped me close and seal the doors and I shook the former's hand heartily. "I was sure you were either dead or a hallucination," I said.

"I feared I was dead as well for a time there," he replied with the characteristic grin that I recalled from our past acquaintance. "Sometimes I wonder if I'm not a ghost, jumping in and out of reality at seeming random. But I'll tell you about that later."

The ship shook as the armies outside began to paste it with more weapon fire. We were not moving, which meant our escape was not quite complete. "Who is at the controls?" I asked. Both Duare and Nalte were missing from the group. I knew both of them were quite capable of flying anotars, but I had no idea what type of controls this strange craft might use. We ran into the adjoining compartment and found both women frantically flipping switches and adjusting dials.

"Everything is marked in odd symbols," Duare said.

Nalte threw her hands up. "We'll never get this thing moving if we can't figure out what's what!"

The controls closely resembled the ones on my torpedo, despite being covered in Linneaun markings. I had to look closer to prove to myself that it wasn't in fact the same control board, but there were subtle differences that made it clear to me it wasn't. Even so, in the desperation of the moment, I flipped various switches and turned a number of dials. Nothing happened. In fact, all the controls seemed dead.

"What's wrong?" Jason looked over my shoulder. "No power?" Jason examined the console as if he thought he might figure it out.

It was good to have him with me, even if it were only for this moment. To have someone else familiar with Earth machinery might give us a fighting chance at firing the torpedo-car. And if we survived, I would like nothing better than to discuss with him why the Linneauns had so meticulously reproduced my work.

"Here's a thought," Duare said. "You say the craft resembles your torpedo, Carson? So what's different?"

It was a simple statement, but it jogged my memory. "It has two nose cones," I said.

"Maybe it has two control rooms?" Jason smiled, his own memory apparently jogged now as well, even as the torpedo shook from a heavy blast from outside.

"You two watch the doors," I said to Ero Shan and Nalte. Jason and Duare followed me past crates and supplies to the other end, where we found a door like the one we had just exited. We opened it and saw a fairly short Myposan standing at a bank of controls. He charged at us, waving a thin knife, but Duare knocked him to the floor with a single blow from the hilt of her sword. She was getting good with her new weapon.

We gave the distraught fish-man no time to recover. I scooped up his blade and together Duare and I moved in on him. "It would be in your best interest to get us moving," Duare commented.

The Myposan tilted his head.

"She said you should go," I told him. "Now." A part of the vehicle rattled outside, and small cloud of smoke wafted into the cabin.

8
ENTANGLED

ONFRONTED BY THREE armed and desperate humans, the Myposan driver needed no further convincing. He all but ran for the controls. A moment later, the torpedo-car shook, and we were rolling forward, but only very slowly. We could hear staccato rumbles on the outside of the ship, and I wondered if our attackers were beating on it with their fists, or if they'd switched to some other heretofore unseen weapons.

We rolled ahead at an excruciatingly slow pace.

"Faster," Duare said, closing on the driver with her blade.

"One moment, and you will have the speed you desire." The Myposan sat at the lone chair in front of the controls and pulled a harness around his chest. He closed his eyes tightly and held on to the harness with both hands.

Suddenly, the ship tipped forward and accelerated dramatically. The vehicle shook violently enough to knock us off our feet. I grabbed Duare by the shoulder, and as I reached for Jason, the acceleration slammed us against the wall. There we lay pinned until we finally felt the craft level off. It slowed enough that we slid onto the floor from the wall, able to breathe and relax without so much stress on our bodies.

The Myposan shifted a panel above the controls and snatched out an r-ray pistol, turning it upon us. "I will kill you all for the glory of Iralcus."

We scattered, grasping for our weapons. I came up with the small, thin blade I had confiscated from the fish-man minutes earlier and charged at him as he brought his gun to

71

bear on Duare. His first shot missed her, and before he could fire again, I buried the knife deep in his abdomen. He fell to the ground at my feet.

"Not that I'm not grateful," Duare said. "But he's the only one who knew how to guide this vehicle."

"We'll work it out," I said cheerily. "This man here is Jason Gridley, one of the top scientific minds from Earth."

Jason patted me on the arm. "You know I have no clue what you or your friends are saying when you switch languages like that, right?"

Somehow, I hadn't considered that Jason spoke only English and other Earth languages. I'd just automatically moved from one language to the other. "Well, you'll figure it out eventually, you're a smart man."

"How long did it take you?"

"I don't know, weeks, maybe a few months?"

Jason rolled his eyes. "Where are we, anyway?" he asked.

"I think we're in a system of tunnels beneath the sea," I replied.

Jason shook his head. "I mean, where exactly are we? You left Earth on your way to Mars decades ago, Carson. Mr. Burroughs said you ended up on Venus, but I never knew if he was pulling my leg when he swore the books about you were true."

I laughed in spite of myself. "Yes, this is Venus. Amtor to its residents. And it's all true. My calculations were…off, and I left out…"

"The pull of the moon. Just like in the book." Jason took a deep breath. "So I'm on Venus now."

"This is my beloved Duare." I took her hand and squeezed it, belatedly aware how dangerous things had gotten in the Myposan outpost. "She's the main reason I haven't tried terribly hard to return to Earth."

"The main reason?" Jason asked. "She'd better not speak English."

Again, I couldn't help but laugh a little. "Jason, wait until you hear the state of science here on Amtor. Radio communications are nonexistent and maps are way off, and neither are the slightest help in exploring. Some countries have an advanced power source that utilizes a sort of elemental fission and others still use rocks and sticks. There are cannibals, wizards, and despots around every corner. Oh! I built their first aircraft, and the permanent cloud cover presents all manner of problems in navigation."

"You built their first airplane?" Jason looked skeptical. "The place must be in a sorry state."

I smiled at the fact that this was the only thing he reacted to in my quick list of the horrors and wonders of Amtor. "You think that's bad? I'm officially a tanjong of the nation of Korva. That's akin to being a prince. Me, a prince of the realm."

"Do they just hand titles out to everyone that crashes on Venus? There must be a story there! And how do I get one?"

"As they say, it's a very long story. I'll elaborate when I can."

Jason's face grew serious. "I do have a question that needs addressing before we go on."

"Yes?" With so much thrown at him so quickly, I wondered what might take precedence in Jason's analytical mind.

Jason paused and took a deep breath. "What in the name of Hades are you wearing? A loincloth?"

"You don't look much better in that Myposan tunic," I said. We both laughed and I embraced him. "So good to see you again, and so good to know I'm not losing my mind. I couldn't prove you were underwater outside my room earlier today. I'd feared you drowned."

"Earlier today? How could that be? I remember being in the water and seeing you there...I don't know. Was it months ago?"

"No. Mere hours have passed, I'm sure of it," I said.

Duare stepped away from the controls and I asked her to substantiate my statement. "Yes, that is right," she replied. "You said that you'd seen him just today in the Myposan outpost."

"See, she agrees. And then the other one came…"

"What other?" Jason asked.

"The young lady. The girl. She said she knew you." It took a moment for the name to come back to me. "Victory."

Jason blanched. Then he grasped me by the shoulders and shook me roughly.

"Tell me!" he cried. "You saw Victory Harben? Where is she? I have been searching for her everywhere, across the very cosmos itself! Is she back in that huge building?"

"No," I said, and it was as if the single word took all the life and hope from his expression. He released me at once, his shoulders slumping in dejection. "She vanished, much as you did," I continued. "I turned my back and she was gone. She said something about a Cheshire Cat routine, that she hadn't meant to surprise me by popping out of nowhere. Tell me what is going on."

"It is the same with me," Jason said. "I have been popping in and out of nowhere, never knowing on what strange world I will next appear. And from your report, I suspect I may even be moving from time to time. How was she?"

"She seemed fine. None the worse for wear, I suppose. I think she may have been a bit confused by what was happening."

"She's not alone. It is an odd story, too long to explain here, but suffice it to say a mysterious force has taken hold of Victory and me, and has been hurling us from one extraordinary world to another, seemingly at random. After I vanished from the water where you saw me last, I continued to undergo a series of these strange jumps. Several months' worth, I swear." He stopped and thought about it. "Months…and then I woke up naked as a jaybird in a vast room full of furs and warm clothing. None fit me. They seemed to have been made for those people with fish-heads. I found a cloak that I could use, pulled it on and started exploring the shadows to stay hidden. It wasn't long after that when I heard your voice in conversation with someone. One of those fish-people, it turned out. I grabbed a weapon and I guess you know the rest."

"That fills in a few blanks for me," I said, "but I still don't understand. If something has been hurling you at random through time and space, why did it bring you here? What are the odds you'd run into your old wayward friend Carson Napier on far-flung Venus? And right next to a rocket car, just like the ones we were experimenting with when we first met. It's a coincidence of cosmic proportions."

"Perhaps synchronicity would be a better word for it," Jason said. "I have a theory. It's based on something I once read in a paper by a German physicist. In layman's terms, he said that connections exist on a subatomic level. He called it *verschränkung*, I believe. Entanglement. One particle can affect another particle regardless of separation by distance and time. Einstein didn't believe it and wrote a series of papers decrying the existence of this proposed ghostly action at a distance. But if the original paper was right, it may be that you and I are inextricably tangled together by the fabric of reality itself, just as Victory and I are tied to one another. That's why we all keep getting drawn together in the same place and time."

I rubbed my forehead thoughtfully.

"Do you suppose any of this 'entanglement' could be affecting my head?" I gave him a brief recounting of my recent bouts of headaches followed by blackouts, as well as the difficulty I encountered when I attempted to project my thoughts. "And I believe I saw your friend in a dream," I added. "It was during my first blackout, before I met her in person. In my dream, I never saw her face, but I somehow *know* that it was her."

"First off, I had no idea you were a master of telepathy until I read it in Mr. Burroughs' accounts," he told me. "I must admit I'm a little hurt that you've never thought to ring me up through the ether since your disappearance, but I suppose you've been somewhat busy, what with one thing and another."

"Somewhat," I said with a grin.

"Secondly, I was about to answer that I have no idea if there's a connection. I was hoping not, since it's causing you such discomfort, but when you said you saw Victory during one of your blackouts before you met her…that seems too much to attribute to chance. Couple that with the fact that my own appearances here have coincided with your new symptoms and I can reach only one conclusion—"

At that moment, Ero Shan and Nalte entered the small control room and I introduced them to my friend. The two of them, after recovering from the sudden acceleration, had gone through a few of the crates in the cargo area. They found weapons and miscellaneous parts they surmised were for the submersible lantars we'd seen and hypothesized the Linneauns were preparing to construct more of them.

In all the commotion and confusion, we hadn't had a chance to welcome Nalte back. After Duare and I embraced her, our friend related her own ordeal.

"As they dragged me beneath the water, they slipped this collar around my neck," Nalte told us, displaying the featureless ring that still encircled her throat. "As soon as my head went under, the collar released a bubble, or a balloon that enveloped my head. It let me breathe the entire time I was under. I could barely tell it was there."

Duare nodded. "We saw something similar happen to one of the Linneauns we were fighting. We damaged its helmet and something like a bubble appeared."

"I am delighted you are all right, Nalte," I said.

"As am I!" Ero Shan gathered up his love in a tight embrace, releasing her abruptly when he saw the dead Myposan and the unmanned control panel. "What is our situation here?"

"It seems to be the usual state of things," Duare said.

"It's not ideal." I agreed. "But, really, this craft appears to be copied from one that I built a long time ago—so, how hard could it be? We can figure this out."

I translated the preceding for Jason, whose expression was less than confident. "I'm on another planet, in what looks like a subway car that was built on designs from an interplanetary craft. I might not be the best assistant, but I'll certainly try."

The chair at the console was not quite my size, but I managed to lean against it. As with the other end of the craft, the console and the positioning of the levers and dials were very close to the way they were configured on my original craft. "Well. If they somehow copied the layout of my torpedo, then the controls must do the same thing as well, correct?"

"It would stand to reason." Jason stood at my side, taking in the board before us. "I mean, logically."

The red lever to my left allowed me to slow my craft in space, so I slowly pulled back on this one, assuming that it would perform the same function here. Nothing happened. "Does it feel like we've slowed down to anyone?" I asked.

"Not a bit," Duare said.

"No," Ero Shan and Nalte replied in unison.

I pulled the lever all the way back and still nothing happened. In frustration, I flipped the lever up and down quickly.

"Does that do anything at all?" Jason asked.

Sadly, it didn't seem that particular control was attached to any other part of the craft. There was no tension on it as I moved it back and forth. I shook my head. I did the same thing to another lever with the same results. I was afraid to keep messing with the foreign controls, fearing I might throw the craft into a worse position than we were in already. There was an entire array of options I could still try, but I pulled my hands away.

Jason leaned in and turned a knob positioned above the instruments I was dealing with. "Maybe they made a master control?" As he moved the piece in a clockwise direction, two large metal panels opened above the console, parting in two directions at once. As they slid back, they exposed a large clear windscreen that allowed us to see outside the torpedo-car. We were indeed in a rough, dark tunnel with little to see other than solid stone on either side of our path.

Ahead of us, we saw the occasional light affixed to the walls on either side, but we zipped past them so quickly that it was impossible to see what they were made of or how they were stuck to the surface. They managed to provide just enough light to keep us out of total darkness.

"Wonderful. Now we can see our doom coming, rather than be surprised by it," Duare said. "That is a comfort."

Jason continued to peruse the control panel. "So, they copied your look, but not your functionality?" His forehead creased as he thought it through. He stood up and looked around the room. "Okay. We know there are two control rooms: one for when we go one way, and one for when we go in the other direction."

"That's a guess as to their uses, but I think you're right."

"So, the engines must also pull double duty. One set of engines pushes the torpedo in one direction, and another set pushes it the other way, right?"

I nodded, agreeing with his logic so far.

"So maybe," Jason said, "we could brake by firing the rockets for the opposite direction?"

I offered to go into the other room and see what I could figure out. Jason followed.

"Let's both look at it," he said. "There are things I need to tell you while we work."

The aft control room was exactly like the fore, with one notable exception. There was an enormous lever to the right of the control panel, marked in some sort of Linneaun symbols. "What do you make of that?"

"Gears, like on an automobile?" Jason offered.

We leaned down and found that the long handle of the gear could be placed in any one of three positions. It was currently in the middle position. "Maybe gears. Maybe forward and reverse, with the middle being neutral or self-guided?"

Duare and Ero Shan stuck their heads into the control room to check on our progress, but we had little to tell them. "Working on it," I said. They left unimpressed.

"Let's pull the lever in the opposite direction from where we're going." Jason put his hands on the lever and looked at me for a reply.

"You're just guessing?"

"Educated guessing?" Jason replied, as he shoved the lever in the direction opposite to our craft's progress.

Instead of a jarring shake and a sudden decrease in speed, the control panel in front of us lit up and its gauges came to life.

"Carson!" Nalte shouted from the other end of the craft. "We see some light ahead. We may be coming to the end of this passageway."

I grabbed the controls and lifted the thrust to full, trying to counteract our speed. "Jodades."

"What?" Jason asked.

"Luck. It means 'luck to you.'"

The thrust kicked in, fighting our forward momentum and causing a sudden racket from the area of the forward engines. The ship thudded against the tunnel walls, bouncing from side to side. Jason and I fell and slammed into the wall as the conveyance continued its confused journey.

The entire craft shifted, and we began an upward climb at the same terrifying pace as we'd traveled all along. In the cargo hold, boxes and crates shifted, crashing against the walls. I had no idea what was coming next in our journey, but I knew I had little sway over it. I climbed forward to the opposite control room and pounded on the controls and dials in a last-ditch effort to make something work for me.

The engines thumped in a trio of terrifying explosions that ended with us slowing noticeably.

My excitement was interrupted by Duare's frantic tapping on my shoulder. "Carson," she said. "Look, up ahead."

The speck of light they'd noticed earlier shone much brighter in the window and seemed to be growing steadily. "Is that the end of the tunnel or another torpedo coming?" Nalte asked.

I didn't know, but either way, I figured our trip was about to end very soon. "Everyone buckle in and brace yourselves! Stay away from the crates, in case they shift again." I stood and offered the seat to Duare and the others. When Duare refused, we grabbed Nalte and Ero Shan and forced them into it. We figured the two of them could buckle in safely. "Jason?" I shouted. "Get harnessed in."

As we neared the light, the whole vehicle shook violently, jarring us all relentlessly. I clung to Duare as we both braced for what could be a catastrophic impact. In that tense moment, the whole torpedo was enveloped in the same high-pitched, metal-on-metal braking sound we had heard in the warehouse. We became level again and slowed quickly, as the rockets continued to push against our momentum.

My body seemed to be shaking all on its own for several minutes before I realized we'd stopped.

"We are alive?" Nalte asked, as if she questioned her senses. "No inferno of death and dismemberment?"

Ero Shan exhaled a deep breath, took Nalte in his arms, and kissed her.

Duare squeezed my hand and then embraced me. "I don't know how you and Jason did it, but we're safe. We survived."

Her arms felt warm and reassuring as always and I didn't want to let go of her. "I didn't do anything," I said finally. "Jason did it all." I needed to make sure we were all accounted for, so I stood up and, still holding Duare's hand, pulled her along into the center storage area. "Jason? We're safe."

The others followed us. "Jason Gridley!" Ero Shan shouted. "Are you all right?"

We opened the door to the far side of the craft, entering the aft cockpit quickly. Inside, we found no sign of him. We looked everywhere, but the small room was empty.

My eyes fell upon the lone gear next to the controls and I saw that it was pushed back to the middle setting. Maybe he had found a way to stop us after all.

"If he is gone, does that mean he is dead?" Nalte asked me.

"I don't think so," I replied. "From what he had time to explain to me, it seems he and his young friend are being shunted from one place and time to another by an unknown force, but so far they seem to be coping pretty well." I sounded more confident than I felt, and I knew Duare could read the concern in my eyes.

"We should examine our surroundings and see where we ended up," she said, reaching out gently to grasp my hand. The four of us moved cautiously toward the outer door.

9
CAVE OF MYSTERY

THE CARGO DOOR WAS DENTED and already slightly ajar. Ero Shan and I were able to slide it open with little effort. As we stepped out, we were startled by a cheerful cry from nearby.

"Hello there!" Jason Gridley stood a few yards away, next to a line of crates, a wide grin on his tanned face. "So glad to see you're all doing well."

It took me a few moments to gather my wits. "We thought you'd...you know...you'd disappeared into whatever void has you in its grip. When we came to the cockpit and you weren't there, I was prepared never to see you again."

My old friend feigned a mortified look and put his hand to his chest. "Oh, you thought?" He smiled. "Sorry about that. When we stopped, you all seemed to be so happy to be alive that I thought I'd give you a moment to yourselves. I slid out the door and started digging around out here." Seeing our relief, he added, "I truly didn't mean to frighten you."

It was far too soon to lose him, so I was glad to have even a few more hours to talk to him, even if he was having a little fun at our expense. I jumped off the craft and then helped the others down. Jason approached and we clasped hands and smiled.

"Don't worry about me," Jason said. "I've been around the block. And by the block, I mean the infinite cosmos." He grinned like the eternal optimist I knew him to be. "Moreover, I'm encouraged that Victory appeared here on Amtor. It means we're being drawn together, that I'm getting closer to finding her—on whatever world that may be. So, the next time I vanish, take it in stride. Just know that…I'll be fine."

Jason pointed back into the tunnel from where we'd come. "I guessed that this whole thing is automated to some degree, and I shut off the engines at the last minute. There are brakes at the end of the run that slow the craft. Had we left the rockets on, we might have destroyed those and shot off the tracks and into the hills. Thankfully, I figured that out in time."

"I told Duare you did it all. I guess I wasn't just being modest."

"Those crates have parts for some kind of vehicles, I think," Jason said. "I didn't have much time to dig through them. A few steps beyond them and you can see a couple of lifts and cranes that are probably used to assemble them."

"What do we do now?" I looked out across the rocky shore to what I guessed was the ocean again—or at least an ocean, if not the same one we had last traversed. Our location was another question. It might be an entirely different continent from Anlap. For all I knew, we could be in Strabol, the equatorial "Hot Country" that most people from this region believed to be the center of Amtor's flat disk.

"We could get back in this torpedo-car and try to return to the Myposan outpost," Duare said. "At least we'd know what we'd be facing."

"No, thank you," Ero Shan said. "Too many people with weapons in their hands and a strong desire to end our days among the living." The comment got a firm nod from Nalte.

Duare pointed to the lush land just outside the cave that housed the Linneauns' supplies and where the vehicle rested. "I hate to say it, but there are more tracks that disappear over the ridge. They appear much like the ones we followed the last time. They must assemble the lantars here and move inland with them. We could follow them and try to pursue it."

"And that turned out so well last time," Nalte said.

It was hard to argue with her; I had crashed my anotar the last time I followed them, and Nalte ended up a prisoner when we followed further.

"I have no desire to follow the tracks either," Duare said. "I believe we should explore and find out where we are before we make any rash decisions. We could have allies nearby or we could be in very dangerous territory. It's impossible to know until we identify where we have landed."

"Yron warned me," I said, "that the Linneauns were using the tunnels to transport their machines to other lands in order to conquer and take slaves. If there's another one loose here, perhaps we should follow it and find out where it's going." I didn't want to contradict Duare, but I desperately wanted to know the Linneauns' reach and strategy since such intelligence would be vital to Korva's efforts to defeat the invaders.

Jason stepped out of the tunnel and walked down to where more parts littered a sandy area and vehicle tracks crisscrossed the terrain. "It's beautiful here. Wherever here is, you know?"

"Right now, we're as lost as you are, my friend." I followed him and we stood gazing at the wall of rocky cliffs that bordered the coast.

"It reminds me of home here." Ero Shan stepped down and kicked some metal parts that were half buried in the ground.

Nalte nodded. "Me too. Do you think we could be on the coast to the south of Andoo and Havatoo?"

"You two would know better than us if we were near your homelands," Duare said. "Unfortunately, we are not welcome in either nation." Though Ero Shan was a native of Havatoo, after war broke out with Korva he had been marked as a traitor due to his association with me, the tanjong of his nation's greatest enemy. Similarly, Nalte was the daughter of Andoo's jong, but after the outbreak of hostilities between Havatoo and Korva, a coup had thrust her father from the throne and placed a tyrant with sympathies to Havatoo in power. Ero Shan had helped Nalte and her father flee Andoo and seek asylum in Korva. That ruled out any chance of help from either Havatoo or Andoo.

"Let us follow the coast toward the cliffs," I said. "For now, that seems to parallel the tracks. If we discover we are in enemy territory, we'll stop and reformulate our course of action."

"That is a sound plan," Duare said, and the others readily agreed.

We each took a weapon from the vehicle, a more time-consuming process than expected, as the majority of those we found were built for Linneauns. These were too big, too heavy, too bulky for us to carry and use effectively in the event we encountered trouble. Ero Shan managed to find a Myposan pole arm that he was comfortable with, while Nalte took two long blades that seemed to be of Linneaun design. They were light and thin, and hence easy to wield—perfect for Nalte. Jason was happy to hold on to the gun he'd commandeered at the warehouse, while Duare and I found a serviceable sword and pistol, respectively.

We set off, walking parallel to the coastline as the clouds darkened above us. When we came to a wide river, we decided to follow along its banks rather than attempt to ford the rapid current. The river ran the same general direction as the tracks we'd found, leading us to believe those aboard the vehicle had reached the same decision. The path began to turn rocky as we approached a long stretch of cliffs close to the coastline. Great water birds found shelter high in the crags as the wind picked up.

After an hour making our way along the rocky terrain, we decided to stop on a low cliff near the shore. I volunteered to climb to the tip of the nearest peak and scout the area ahead. My ascent wasn't terribly difficult as the slope was slight and the peak not all that high. Still, when I got to the top, it allowed me an open view of the way forward. For better or worse, our path seemed to consist of an unending field of rocks and a rough go for the foreseeable future.

"Any good news on the horizon?" Duare climbed up behind me. I grabbed her hand and pulled her up to where I sat.

"I'm afraid not. More boulders, more crags. Nothing much to see for miles."

Duare laughed. "Nothing much to see? Just look at this," she said. "Look at the way the clouds fall behind the mountains and the colors dance on the river. We may be the first people to ever stand in this very spot. You are most certainly the first Earthman to stand here. We should not take a moment of our lives for granted, my love."

The sights of Amtor were always a thrill to behold, and I welcomed the reminder. I returned Duare's smile and drew her close. No longer was she the cold, spoiled daughter of Mintep, the jong of Vepaja. During all of our adventures together, she had bravely faced whatever challenges confronted us. Her experiences had matured her outlook on life, and at that moment I loved her more than ever. "You're right. I need to take a moment whenever I can to enjoy our life here together."

"I understand you have been having a rough time of it lately," she continued. "I know it is a bad time to tell you to be thankful for your life and the beauty around you." She put her arm around me, and we were silent for a time while we both stared off at the beauty around us. "Carson? With everything going on, the sudden appearance of your friend Jason, the threat from the Linneauns that reminds you of your old rocket, do you find yourself missing Earth? I mean honestly missing it."

"I do, sometimes," I admitted.

"If Jason or Victory gave you the opportunity to go back with them, would you?"

"Duare…"

"No, I understand. I would not take offense if you wanted to go home. It is just something you need to think about if the situation presented itself."

Home? Earth seemed so far away and so long ago. I smiled. "I am very happy here."

"That's not the question I asked." Duare stood. "Think about it. You do not have to answer now, but you should think on it." She rose to rejoin the others.

Ah! There she was, the Duare I remembered of old. Proud and able to make my heart ache on the turn of a dime.

The clouds, ever present on Venus, darkened with the threat of rain as I watched Duare make her way back down to our companions.

I stood for a moment, staring at the river as it flowed on toward the great ocean. For just a few seconds I pushed the Linneauns and our mission to the back of my mind. I thought about the creatures that swam in the water there, the birds that soared over them. It felt good, standing on that rock, letting the breeze blow the crisp air across my face. I took a last breath and followed Duare's path down to our friends.

"Duare tells us there's more of the same ahead," Ero Shan said. "That will be rough."

"I agree," Nalte said. "I wish I could say all this climbing has not taken a toll, but…"

"I have no notion of how long we were in that Linneaun craft," Ero Shan said, "or even what time of day it is. But I am weary from our trials and I fear the weather will turn at any time. We should rest soon and get some sleep."

"Let's find a cave or some other shelter," I said. "I'm pretty sure I saw a couple of places in the valley ahead that would work well."

As if on cue, the sky broke and large drops of rain began pelting us. The unexpected ferocity of the sudden storm drove us toward the hope of sanctuary among the rocks ahead. We climbed across the treacherously slippery rocks but couldn't seem to escape the winds that had arisen with the sudden weather. Ero Shan was in the lead, doing his best to guide us to a safe refuge.

Meanwhile, I concentrated on trying to conceal the fact that I was not feeling well again. It didn't seem as serious as the other times I'd felt poorly, though the symptoms were similar. My head ached and my stomach was upset. I wanted to chalk it up to the recent battle and to the fact that I'd eaten some of that awful Myposan bread, but the pain increased steadily.

"A cave!" Ero Shan cried, his voice nearly lost to the storm.

Nalte helped Duare along. "Did you hear that? Ero Shan has found shelter." I nodded and did my best to smile in light of the news. We jumped from the rocks into the gravelly mud below.

Ero Shan was waiting and all but pulled us toward the mouth of a cavern nearby. "I looked in and did not see anything at the mouth of this cave," he said, "so I think we should chance it, even if it isn't deep. The entrance is fairly wide and will give us at least some protection."

We crowded inside as far as the light would allow. "Thank you, friend," I told Ero Shan. "That rain felt as though it were trying to fight its way through us."

Jason had apparently arrived at the same conclusion. "Feels like everything on this planet is trying to kill us!" he said, shaking his whole body in the manner of a drenched German Shepherd.

"You get used to it," I said. "Well, unless it kills you first."

Duare made a fire with dry sticks and weeds from the ground inside the cave, using a lighter from her pack to get it going. We all peered into the depths of the cavern revealed by the campfire's glow. The yawning cave continued on, gray and rocky, sloping somewhat upward until it disappeared in the darkness.

"This should do." Nalte removed her covering and shook it out by the entrance. "I would say it is better than being out there. We'll need to keep watch, to make sure nothing else has made its home here. All manner of creatures could be trying to get out of the weather. There could be targos, tharbans, serpents."

"You aren't exactly making me feel safe here." I rubbed my temple, hoping to massage the headache away.

"I am sorry," Nalte said. "It is always best to be prepared. Have you ever heard of the amsts that infest the coasts to the south of Andoo? Tiny mites that crawl along in dark, wet places, waiting for prey? They burrow into your skin, usually around the neck, eventually causing you to bleed to death."

I had not heard of amsts, but I could have lived without knowing about them.

"No," Ero Shan said. He was gathering branches, twigs, and leaves to throw on the fire. Some animal must have dragged them into the cave thinking to build a den. "You're thinking of the tunnel worms. The amsts are the flying insects that nest in their victims' ears when they sleep and then feast upon…"

I raised my hand and interrupted the zoology lesson. "Thank you. I will cover my head with a blanket to keep out unwanted intruders, but I don't need to know about everything that can kill me right now."

Nalte shrugged and proceeded to pull a dry blanket out of her pack.

"What are they saying?" Jason asked.

"You don't want to know."

I busied myself for a while fashioning two torches out of some of the material Ero Shan brought back, wrapping some fabric from my pack, along with dry grass and weeds to serve as kindling, around bundles of thicker limbs I had tied together. I lit one torch, grabbed a sword and r-ray, and walked deeper into our temporary home. "I'm going to explore a little and try to clear my head."

"Oh, watch out for…"

Duare interrupted Nalte with a curt shake of her head, stopping her from her predilection to plant terrible images in my mind.

The passage sloped gently upward, twisting to the left and narrowing as it went. I felt reassured that any large creatures that might want to pursue us would have had a hard time squeezing through the confining space. The torch gave me a good view for about twenty feet in front and behind me, but there was little to see beyond jagged rock.

I was vaguely aware of Duare calling my name from back down the tunnel. Head swimming, I continued on without reply and turned from the main passage at the first fork that presented itself. I had the overwhelming feeling of being drawn along the path before me, reinforced by the fact that the pain in my head had begun to subside with each step I made in that direction. By the time I saw a blue glow in the passage ahead, I realized that I was all but running in my need to discover what it was up ahead that so forcefully demanded my presence.

The passage opened up into a wide cavern with the azure light seeming to emanate from a well in the middle. It was nothing more than crudely placed stones stacked in a circle, but even from the distance of the opening of the chamber where I stood, I could hear water dripping quickly from above. I looked up and found the light was coming from the same crack in the rocky ceiling that delivered the water. I knelt and pulled water up with my cupped hands and drank it. I was about to take a second mouthful when I noticed something sprawled on the ground by the far wall. From the entrance, I'd mistaken it for a group of rocks. Now that I was closer, I could see it had the general shape of a man.

I stood and raised my torch in one hand, my sword in the other. Seeing no movement, I stepped over cautiously. It may have had a form like a man, but it was like no variety of human being I had encountered before, nor did it resemble in the slightest the armadillo-like Linneauns. What lay before me were the mortal remains of a tall, thin humanoid with four arms and long legs. Tusks of some sort protruded from its mouth. In all, it had to have been fourteen or fifteen feet tall. The skin color, if the torchlight was to be believed, was olive green. It was naked save for a harness and belt that seemed made to hold the broken sword at the creature's side.

Standing there alongside the thing, I felt my headache suddenly vanish completely, as if a switch had been flipped.

"Carson?" Duare entered the chamber behind me. "I have been calling you. Are you ill again?"

"I'm sorry if I worried you," I said. "I got distracted by another headache, but I'm feeling better again." I motioned to the remains on the cave floor. "Look at this. Do you know what manner of creature this is?"

She approached and lowered her light closer. "I have seen nothing like it in our travels."

"Neither have I," I said, though the creature somehow seemed strangely familiar.

I considered taking at least the hilt of the broken weapon so that we could examine it further, but for some unfathomable reason I could not bring myself to touch the creature or anything in contact with its body. It was obvious from looking at it that the thing was quite dead, so I couldn't imagine what I was afraid of. Did I think the ghost of a six-limbed green man was going to haunt me for not treating it with more respect?

"We should return to the others," said Duare. "We all need sleep."

"No doubt..." Yet I lingered there, staring down at the corpse.

"Carson, are you sure you are feeling all right?" Duare reached out and lightly stroked the back of my head. "These strange attacks worry me. Suppose you had blacked out again in here and we found you floating face down in that well?"

I smiled and took her hand in my own.

"You paint a charming picture," I told her. "But I'm actually feeling better than all right." I gave my head an experimental shake. "No pain, no cobwebs—nothing! I know this may sound strange, but I think whatever it was has gone now— hopefully for good. It had gotten pretty bad again a little while ago, but as soon as I started into the tunnel I sensed something drawing me in this direction, and I could feel the pain leaving me the closer I got to this cavern. Then—" I snapped my fingers. "Gone!"

She gazed down in perplexity at the grotesque body.

"You believe that it—he—wished you to find him here?"

"I don't know what I believe at this point. Jason thinks that he and I are cosmically tangled together in some way, as he is with the girl, and that's why he keeps appearing near me. We were starting to wonder if that was somehow causing my whatever-it-was. Maybe this gentleman also came from someplace other than Amtor, and that had the same effect. Do you think that for some reason my head can detect disruptions in the fabric of space and time?"

"That would not be a skill I would want to perfect," said Duare. "But you do have an unusual head. I wonder if it has something to do with your thought projections, which have also seemed to be affected?"

"I wondered the same thing." I shrugged. "If old Chand Kabi were still around, I'd consult with him on the matter. As it is, I think Jason and I need to have another go at unraveling the whole thing before he disappears on us again."

We returned to the mouth of the cave where Ero Shan had already dozed off. There we found Nalte keeping watch with a pistol in her lap. "Did you find anything?" She yawned and, looking like she might be about to fade into her own slumber, stood up.

"Just a dead-end tunnel and some remains," I said. "Nothing we need worry about now, I suppose."

"Where is your friend, Jason Gridley?"

"What?"

"I saw him head down into the tunnel just before you did, while you were busy making your torch. I thought you knew. He went first, then you, then Duare." Nalte suddenly looked worried. "You did not find him between here and where you say the tunnel ends?"

"Are you sure that's where he went?" I asked. "And without a light to guide him? If he had gone that way, we would have run into him." I took my leave and ran back down the passage, calling Jason's name, but I found nothing. There had been no time to say good-bye this time, but I remembered his words and tried my best to believe he was well.

I returned to the group empty-handed.

"Perhaps he went down another side tunnel," Nalte offered.

"No," I said. "I just checked the main tunnel, and it ends a dozen feet after the fork, with no other branches."

Duare agreed and we all stood there mystified.

"You two sleep," Duare said to Nalte and myself. "I will stand the watch."

Nalte nodded and put her weapon on a nearby rock. "Wake Ero Shan to replace you. He has slept since you left."

I put my own weapons down and pulled out my blanket. My pack served as a lumpy but useful pillow as I covered myself. The rain came down as fiercely as it had when the sky first opened up, but it had a fine rhythm that set my mind free of the jumble of mysteries that had plagued us for the past several days.

Someone was shouting in my dreams. When I awoke, I was vaguely aware that something was amiss. My body felt colder than I would have expected and when I sat up, it was with some difficulty. I raised my arm to find that I was mostly covered in mud and I was stuck in it.

"What has happened?" I cried.

"The rains caused a mudslide farther up the cave!" Ero Shan shouted. "It is all drifting our way!" He was half covered in black muck as he slid about gathering his things and trying to give Nalte a hand. "I was on watch for creatures and beasts, but the mud came with no warning."

With Duare's help, I stood. The mud was up to our ankles and rising fast.

My gear was a mess, but I hoisted it over my shoulder anyway, and slid my dripping sword into place. Outside, the rain had abated, with only a few drops spattering the ground as we stepped out into the open world.

We followed the river for an hour until the mud began drying and hardening on our skin. Eventually, we could take it no more and we stopped to wade into the water and bathe ourselves.

"Finally," Ero Shan murmured. "The more it dries, the more it itches."

"And its odor is foul," Duare said. She moved deeper until the water was up to her neck, scrubbing her arms and wiping the mud from her face. "Why cannot we hide out in a lovely palace once in a while? Someplace beautiful and smelling of soap?"

We all laughed and continued our ablutions. Before long, however, we were interrupted by a splash near the bank, farther up the river. The sound was followed by words spoken softly between what sounded like two people, though it could have been more. Nalte peeked out from the river grass that had hidden us from that direction as we washed. "I see three females," she whispered. "They appear to be fishing with spears and longbows."

"Are you sure they are women?" Ero Shan asked, peering through the grass beside her. "They are large, muscular."

Duare and I edged forward and took a look for ourselves.

"From their stature and crude weapons," Duare said, "I would guess they are a Samary hunting party."

She and I exchanged glances. "Great," I said. "The Samary."

Years ago, when we had been traveling in what we now assumed to be this same region, a Samary tribe had taken Duare as a slave, and it was only through guile and determination that I had been able to free her. The Samary were a race of warrior women known for their strength and courage. Though their culture was primitive, they were not to be trifled with.

"It is not the Samary I am worried about," Duare said. "If we are close to Samary lands, it means that Havatoo is not far away." She was right. In Havatoo, we were all considered enemies of the state due to our siding with Korva in the intermittent, though persistent war. And though Ero Shan had once dreamed of returning to his home city, he had given up such plans years ago after our further tangles with the technocratic state convinced him of the immorality of its leadership. Even though the ruling body known as the Sanjong had eventually lifted the termination order it had placed on Duare and me, they had reversed that decision following the outbreak of the war. If we were captured by the Havatooans, all four of us would be put to death.

"Should we turn back and take our chances in the tunnel?" Nalte asked.

We were startled by a grunt from behind us. Turning, we beheld a dozen Samary warriors with raised bows and spears, all fairly shaking in their eagerness to loose their weapons upon us.

10
THE SAMARY

THE SAMARY WARRIORS pushed us along with their spears and pikes. They were all tall muscular women, wearing animal skins and armed to the teeth with primitive weapons. They said little, except when ordering us to move faster or to change direction.

While all of them were larger than the average human, one stood out. That warrior had skin the shade of the desert sands of Noobol, meaning slightly darker than the bronze tones of the others. She was scarred on her arms, chest, and thighs, with a thick cut that began at one temple, crossed her high-bridged nose, and ended on the opposite cheek. Her face was further marked by a series of dots that appeared to be tiny burns administered in a straight line from her lower lip, down her chin, and ending at her neck. She was easily a foot taller than the others and her muscular arms were like thick logs. Of all our captors, she carried the most supplies, brandished the broadest sword, and was still somehow the most sure-footed. While the rest of us were slipping in the mud created by the recent rain, she stomped along with nary a concern. Around her neck hung a thick pendant with a rough, clear blue stone.

"Are you the leader here?" I asked.

"Silence," she said with a curl of her lip.

"I just assumed you'd be the leader since you are obviously the superior warrior." I hoped flattery would get some sort of response, but no luck.

Ahead of us, several bluffs had come into view and we saw

more of the Samary milling about near one side of a rope bridge. This ran high above a tributary of the nearby river, but we managed to cross it with ease, as the fiber that composed it was thick and well maintained, unlike the next one we came to. That one was frayed and we wobbled with each step as we crossed. Thankfully, it wasn't nearly as long as the one before it.

We passed from one craggy stretch to another, moving over sharp blue rocks. Windows and doorways were carved in a pattern along the cliff face. In the middle, a rounded area formed what seemed to be a communal gathering space. A few elderly males sat weaving river grass into baskets. The men were nowhere as impressive as the women we'd encountered, being smaller in stature, their arms thin and pale. They eyed us briefly before returning to their weaving.

We came to a choice of three tunnels leading into the rock face. Our captors shoved us through the central tunnel, which snaked around and sloped downward until it opened into a courtyard surrounded by rock. Here, many more Samary walked among cooking stations and food preparation areas. Several of the men were skinning a basto in one corner, expertly brandishing their knives as they removed the inedible portions and placed them aside. On the opposite side of the open-air kitchen, children ran about screaming and singing, oblivious to the group of prisoners being pushed along just a few feet away. A few Samary males who weren't cooking or tending to the offspring began to follow us, giggling and pointing.

"What have you brought us?" one of them asked.

Another held a hand over his mouth in mock terror. "Look at them. They must be fierce hunters." He broke out in laughter and pushed his nearest companion.

The group of men grew larger as we proceeded into another passage that wound around, lit by dancing flames of orange in sconces carved out of the rock. They wore long scarves about their wrists and waists. The dye from the cloth had worn off, staining the men's skin the color of their garments. They came to look at us in colorful waves: a group of blue-smeared, a group of red. Some tried to touch us but were quickly rebuked by the warriors escorting us.

Our guards brought us back out into the open air, though this time we came out on a terrace overlooking the river. Perhaps terrace was too fancy a word for it—it was simply a large, flat area carved into the rock, ending in a cliff over the rushing water. A group of women, sitting comfortably on large piles of reeds arranged around the edge, chatted while gazing out over the water below. Nearby, two doorways carved out of the stone led to passages that disappeared into the rock.

An older woman with braided silver hair sat a few feet back from the main cluster. Her own seating arrangements were larger, higher, and probably considerably more comfortable than those of the others, the pile of reeds framed by branches bound by lengths of dark rope and cushioned with layers of grass and animal skins. Her face featured the same pattern of dots as that of the large guard, but her marks covered the entire area below her mouth and continued around her neck. Her powerful body was adorned with other prominent scars, including a series of cut marks that began on her upper arms and led down to her knuckles. Her right hand seemed gnarled, the fingers gathered together and unmoving. The picture of casual authority, the woman reclined with her eyes closed as we were brought before her.

"My most honored chieftain," the large one said. "we have captured these strangers trespassing on our land. They were observing some of our warriors near the fishing well."

We waited, but the chief said nothing.

"Your excellency?" I looked at the warriors guarding us and noticed they remained perfectly still as they waited. "Should we come back?"

"Quiet," said the large warrior.

"Perhaps we could come back later." I didn't look forward to facing an irate ruler if we disturbed her slumber. I'd learned from experience that it was wise to let sleeping chiefs lie whenever possible.

Eyes still closed, the chief made a series of sharp clacking noises, sounding like nothing so much as a newborn cave lizard calling for its mother.

"I'm sorry..." I said.

Again, she made the sound.

The large guard rapped me solidly on the back with her pole arm. "You. Quiet. The chief will not be spoken to by a yellow-haired ar-edyl."

"Ar-edyl?" Another sharp clack-clack came from the chief.

"Ar-edyl. It is an outsider that is a man," the guard said. "All men are edyl and should mind their words to the chief. Men who are outsiders would do well to just keep their words to themselves."

Another of the warriors who had escorted us stepped before the leader. "My most honored chief, these outsiders spied upon our fishing party as we returned from the river. We surrounded them as they concealed themselves behind tall weeds. They were painted in mud to further hide themselves from our patrols."

"We were not concealed,"Duare said. "We just had some bad luck in the rain. We meant no..."

A guard jabbed her with the dull end of a spear. "Silence."

The chief finally turned her head to examine us with a scowl. "Who are they? They are not Samary."

"No, my chief."

"My name is—" The guard whacked me again before I could finish.

Once more, the chief made her clacking noise.

Duare stepped forward. "I am Duare, janjong of Vepaja and royal emissary of Korva, and these are my companions..."

"You know the unruly one?" The chief pointed lazily at me with her good arm.

Duare nodded. "Yes. I do know him...he's..." I could see Duare assessing the Samary as she spoke. "He's my servant.

He carries my equipment and cleans my clothing when I have need."

The chief stared at me in anticipation, almost daring me to speak. Her mouth appeared poised at the ready to clack at me again, but I refrained and merely nodded. I could not, however, keep the smile from my face upon hearing Duare essentially call me her valet.

"I am Chief Syto. Why are you here? Why were you stalking our warriors?" She still appeared unconcerned by us, and her questions sounded perfunctory.

"My companions and I have recently run afoul of a Linneaun by the name of Iralcus Iguiri," Duare said.

"I don't know that name," the chief said. "I cannot help you." Syto poked at a pile of fruit sitting next to her throne of reeds, to all appearances amused by a berry that fell off its stem and proceeded to roll to the ground.

"We escaped from him, but now we're trying to track down one of his enormous weapons—a giant war vehicle that resembles a lantar. The Linneauns used one like it to destroy a village near our home and we would like to stop this one from creating more death and destruction."

The large warrior stepped forward again. "I do not know what a lantar is, but what the outsider speaks of sounds like the machine we encountered in the forest a few days past."

"Haln, know your place," the chief said. "You live to protect me, yes?"

Haln nodded.

"Guard the door, then."

Nalte joined the conversation. "You have seen the machine? Did it attack your people as well?"

Syto sighed and waved around her head as though an insect was vexing her. "There are too many foreign voices in the air."

"We only want to help," I said.

Chief Syto jabbed her finger sharply in my direction, clacking angrily. The males that had followed us from the courtyard snickered and pushed each other, their eyes glinting as if they took obvious pleasure in seeing me chastised.

"Our mighty warriors encountered a thing such as you describe. They dispatched it." Syto yawned and squeezed a piece of fruit between her fingers.

I was astonished, and as I opened my mouth to question her, Duare patted my arm and spoke before I could. "Dispatched it?"

"Yes, killed it in the forest, I believe."

Still tactful, Duare asked, "Killed it? Killed the machine? May I ask how?"

"With rocks, I believe." Syto threw a berry at me and seemed delighted when it bounced off my forehead. "Yes. Rocks."

The four of us exchanged glances, certain the chief was making up a story. We weren't the only skeptics. A couple of her warriors, notably the largest one, seemed slightly uneasy with their leader's assertion.

Duare kept her tone reverent and even. "If their machine has spared you," she said, "I assure you another will come for you in future days and wreak much havoc. We just want to prevent that from happening."

"Let them come. Our warriors are the mightiest in the land." The chief held her good hand high and waved it dramatically in the air, which elicited roars of approval from the warriors on the terrace. The guards around us raised their weapons and shook them, hooting as the cheers crescendoed.

"These Linneauns are enslaving anyone who opposes them," Duare said. "Those who survive their attacks are dragged off to work as slaves in their factories. We could use all of the strongest warriors we can find to oppose them. Release us and send your people to help us. Together we can end this threat long before it comes back to bring destruction upon your village."

"No." The chief picked a berry from the plate next to her and popped it into her mouth.

From behind Syto, Haln said, "Mighty chief, my apologies,

but I saw that rolling weapon with my own eyes. We are strong, but it is enormous. At the very least, we should observe it, so we can prepare in case it threatens our village."

The chief sat back again in her opulent throne, and then clapped her hands twice. One of the other women seated near the cliff quickly stood, came over to the chief, and leaned close to her. After Syto had whispered a few words, the woman ran off through one of the carved doorways next to Haln. The chief selected another berry and shoved it in her mouth. Red juice dribbled down her face and dripped off her chin. She chewed slowly before she finally swallowed the juicy morsel.

"I have heard your words," Syto said. "I have carefully considered them." As I waited for her decision, I couldn't take my eyes off the line of dark juice that remained under her lips. "You may go and find this machine. I task you with destroying it, if you can." The men in the back guffawed. "I am not indifferent to the threats of the outside world, but I cannot send an army to assist you, so I will provide you with a single valiant warrior to guide you through this territory on your quest. Our fiercest fighter will offer you a deft hand in combat and a single-minded ferocity the likes of which you've not encountered." Her words gave me hope, even though she spoke them with the same indifference she'd used with everything else she'd said.

"We thank you," Nalte said.

"I have handpicked this warrior." Syto pointed toward the doors with a handful of berries and a mock flourish. "Jodades on your journey."

Standing in front of one of the main doors was the statuesque warrior called Haln. She all but blocked the opening, and I marveled again at her muscular form and sheer size.

The assembled Samary tribespeople gasped audibly when the chief indicated Haln. When the sound died down, they began murmuring among themselves.

Forgetting myself, I thanked the chief. "We are grateful

for your generosity." My gratitude earned me the requisite sharp clacks.

"Thank you," Duare said. "With your warrior, I feel we can defeat our enemies with ease. I am sure Haln is a fierce and capable fighter."

Seemingly invested in our discussion for the first time, Chief Syto tossed aside her handful of berries and rose from her chair. She waved at Haln. "Stand aside." As Haln obeyed, Syto pointed with her good hand to the doorway in the rock. A small male stood at the threshold. Completely hidden until now behind Haln's imposing bulk, he stood perhaps half her height at a hair over four feet tall. There was a satchel at his side, but he carried no visible weapons.

"There," said the chief. "That is your warrior."

Behind us, the males began tittering again.

"He...will be acceptable, O Chief," Duare said, her face carefully expressionless.

The rest of the tribe was laughing now, some flat-out guffawing—all except for Haln. "I protest," said the giant warrior stiffly. "Duh-nee is not one to be sent off with outsiders to face the unknown dangers."

"Are you saying your mate cannot take care of himself?" the chief asked.

"Duh-nee is a fierce fighter when the need arises."

"Then he will fight alongside the outsiders," Syto said. "I have spoken and there is no more to the matter."

In a second, Haln's face went red and she clenched her fists. "Then I will go, too."

"You are the chief's high guard," one of the other women said. "You cannot just leave."

Haln removed her necklace with the clear blue stone and tossed it so that it landed near Syto's feet. "If my beloved must go, then I will go too."

Syto's face grew red as well. "You will not leave me. It would mean banishment from the tribe. You would never be welcome here again."

"You have left me no choice." Haln turned to Duare and nodded. "You have our aid for as long as it pleases you."

"Are you sure you want to do this?" Duare asked.

Haln nodded. "I am certain."

"Thank you," Duare said. "You and your mate are a welcome addition."

Duh-nee pushed past our little group and whispered, "We should leave while we can." He dragged not only his satchel, but a larger cloth bag that seemed to be bursting with sharp objects and bulky pieces. We did as the little man directed, walking off in a line following Duh-nee toward the tunnels from which we'd entered. Haln was last in the line, walking confidently in the face of every one of her fellow warriors and tribe members. The faces of the fighters withered beneath her proud, icy glare. The men in the back were no longer laughing.

We left the Samary village unchallenged, crossing the rope bridges and passing into new territory, guided by Duh-nee and Haln. After walking in near silence for an hour, Duh-nee announced we were officially beyond the borders of the territory claimed by Syto's tribe. Ahead, we would enter territories occupied by other tribes, and wild, unclaimed forests. Haln climbed a ragged trail to the top of a hill, instructing us to wait at the bottom. She stared back in the direction we'd come, silently taking in the home she had left behind.

"You are Duh-nee?" I asked the little man. "I am…"

"Ar-edyl," he interjected with a bleak nod. "A man from the outside. So am I now."

We rested until Haln came back and led us off into the unknown. It was still rough going, with more rocky terrain. The constant climbing wore us down quickly, though neither of the Samary seemed too affected. Nalte lamented the fact that we no longer had our anotars to make the journey easier.

"It's just as well," Duh-nee said. "We could not have flown, anyway. Haln is afraid of great heights."

"They do not frighten me." Haln's face was hard like stone. "Nothing frightens Haln."

"Oh, and targos," Duh-nee said, referring to the giant spiders of Amtor. "They really terrify her."

"Duh-nee," I said, beginning to suspect that the little man was simply listing off his own fears, "I understand Haln was a guard for the chief and led patrols around your territory. But what was it that you did, exactly?"

"I was in charge of our supply storage. It was my duty to ensure we kept enough food on hand for each season, and to properly care it for so that it didn't spoil." He seemed to have pride in his work and straightened visibly as he explained it to us. "I also counted the arrows in the weapons room to make sure everyone had enough. They let me count a lot of things, really."

After a moment, Haln cleared her throat. "He is also a valiant warrior," she said. "In addition to counting sacks of grain."

"Grain." Duh-nee nodded. "I'd forgotten about grain. They had me count grain as well."

I frowned and considered it fortunate that we had at least one mighty Samary warrior among us.

11
SWORDS FROM THE SKY

WITH TWO ADDITIONAL COMPANIONS in our party, we headed off from the Samary territory. Our main objective remained the same as when we had departed the Linneaun tunnel: to follow the tracks of the war machine.

"Can you not just go to the army of Havatoo?" Haln asked. "We could use one of my people's boats to make our way upriver. Surely that nation would help destroy this metal beast."

Duare and I looked at each other.

"Our nation is at war with Havatoo," Duare said. "We are not welcome."

"She's right," I said. "We'd all be marked for immediate termination if we returned there."

Ero Shan pressed on with the matter at hand. "So, we follow the tracks of the machine until we catch it?"

"Best to keep to the forest as we pursue it." Haln pointed off to the trees that rose up a small distance from the destructive path that the great machine had created as it went. Crushed wild grass, smaller trees, and shrubbery withered in the impressions left by the treads. "The trees will give us cover, and there's a hill ahead that might allow us a better view of where our quarry goes."

We moved along the border of the great plants that grew among the massive trees, the foliage becoming so thick and high at times that we had to use our swords like machetes to cut it back. Though the air remained cool,

106

soon we were all perspiring with the exertion of making a trail.

Well into the afternoon, Haln pointed through the trees to an area beyond the forest, where I could see clouds of gray smoke rising over the hills. "Perhaps your machine has struck again," the Samary said.

We moved as fast as we could, keeping an eye out for the attack vehicle as we went. The terrain was difficult, covered in briars and waist-high grass, but we managed as best we could.

At last we crested a hill and a small village came into sight. Several fires were burning throughout the settlement. From our position, we could see a dozen huts, a few larger buildings in the center, and a fence that encircled it all. Haln and Duh-nee ran faster at the sight of the destruction. At least five of the huts were either on fire or had burned to nothing but ashes and embers. A massive hole marred one side of the largest building, surely the result of a blast from a Linneaun weapon.

We sprinted toward the dingy fence as we got closer to the village, trying to keep up with the Samary. The gray smoke billowed from all around, filling the air with the smell of burning grass and wood. It became harder to see Duh-nee as he ran directly into the thick of the destruction. Haln stopped short and surveyed the area, looking as though she'd smelled something rotting. We quickly understood her expression as the smoke began to swirl, twisting in the air despite the lack of any wind or breeze anywhere about us. As we drew closer, three dark, winged humanoid forms flew out from behind the cloud, voices raised in shrill cries.

"Klangan!" Nalte cried and drew her sword.

The cries of the winged men increased as they swooped toward us. The klangan—the singular form of the word being angan—are a beautiful people when they aren't trying to kill you, and these were no exception. Their faces resembled a bird's in many respects: feathers grew in the place of hair, while their long noses looked very much like eagles' beaks.

However, though feathers covered their heads and the lower extremities of their torsos, and they had feathered pompons much like the tails of birds, the great wings jutting from their shoulder blades were more akin to those of bats, consisting of a thin layer of skin on a frame of narrow bones. The majority of the klangan I had previously encountered had dark brown or black skin, but many of these appeared to have a reddish-purple hue to their bodies beneath the colorful collage of feathers.

Their high-pitched battle cries grew louder, and the trio swung their maces and swords above them. The lead angan shouted out an order to attack. With that, a dozen more of the flying warriors emerged from the cover of smoke above the village. All of them dived for us at high speed, dark wings beating in the air. Most held deadly spears, while a few dangled ropes with which to snare us. Thankfully none of them had guns or we would have been dead before we could have lifted a hand in resistance.

I fired my pistol into the flock of bird people, scoring a hit. My target cried out and plummeted to the ground.

"Everyone stay close and watch out for each other!" Ero Shan cried. "Klangan can drop from out of nowhere." He moved into the lead of our group and drew his sword. Haln picked up a large rock in each hand and stood waiting, her mate behind her. As the first group of klangan got closer, she threw one of the rocks and another angan went down.

They closed on us so swiftly I scarcely had time to fire again before they were upon us. I counted more than two dozen descending, forming into groups and splitting off to combat each of us. We turned our backs to each other as best we could, forming a defensive circle. With Duare at my side, I attacked the first two klangan that came at me.

Though we were all experienced fighters, to be attacked from the air put us at a significant disadvantage. It would be only a matter of time before our adversaries overwhelmed us.

A pair of klangan managed to grab hold of Duh-nee using

a rope, and lifted him nearly over my head before Haln realized what was happening. With a cry of rage, she grabbed one of the klangan by his wing and pulled the bird-man out of the air. Drawing him close, Haln pummeled the angan until he let go of her beloved. Wisely, the other attacker released Duh-nee and rose higher into the air, avoiding Haln's wrath.

"What I wouldn't give for an anotar right now," Duare panted between sword thrusts. "We could at least fight them in their element."

"Or better yet, flee," I added, for the angan spears were coming at us from all angles and becoming more difficult to block.

Haln suddenly let out a fearsome warrior cry. Duh-nee dropped to the ground, flattening himself in the grass. I assumed he knew something I didn't, so I shouted for everyone else to duck. My warning was just in time, for Haln began spinning her halberd over her head with a speed that resembled the rotating propeller of an anotar. As she spun it, she drew closer to the klangan, moving around the perimeter of the circle we had formed for protection. One of the klangan swooped down and grabbed Nalte's arm, but Haln's blade cut into its shoulder, leaving a trail of crimson across its upper arm.

My pistol raised, I followed the path of destruction and mayhem Haln left behind her as she confronted the cloud of wings and spears. Three klangan fell to the ground by my weapon and more by Haln's. Our efforts rallied the spirits of our companions, and soon more of our enemy plummeted out of the sky and lay dead or injured.

Working together, Ero Shan and Nalte rushed one of the attackers from behind as it flew down at Haln, managing to grab it by the leg while deftly avoiding the creature's long talons. The flying warrior was so startled, he let go his spear in his attempt to remain airborne. But it was too late for the bird-man to recover. My friends pulled down hard with all their weight and simply yanked the angan out of the sky.

Now that the bird-man was on the ground, he no longer had the advantage. The angan, unsteady on his short, stocky legs, drew his short sword and jabbed at the two humans vexing him. While Ero Shan advanced upon the angan with his sword, Nalte circled around to the side and rushed their opponent, kicking viciously at one of his legs, knocking him down, and sending his blade flying across the field.

The angan who had originally signaled the attack had hovered far above the fight but never entered it, so I took him for their leader. He angrily shouted orders to his remaining flock, pointing with his spear as the battle raged. I shot at him twice with my pistol, missing both times, but it was enough to frighten the flying commander into retreating and calling for his warriors to do the same.

Haln took a few last swings at the klangan as they withdrew, wounding one as it tried to fly to safety. I could have fired at them while their backs were turned and taken several down, but I lowered my gun and watched as they grew smaller against the gray sky. I'm not sure they would have done the same for me, given the same opportunity.

The only prisoner we'd captured squirmed and flapped from Ero Shan's and Nalte's grasps and tried to take flight. "Let him go," I said. "We can't really take a prisoner with us, and we can't turn back now to imprison him."

Exhausted, I sat on the ground and watched the klangan fly off into the distance, high above the treetops. They moved erratically, not in the precise formations they had employed during their approach. We heard them chattering among themselves in agitation until they flew out of our sight.

"Is everyone safe?" Duare asked. "Anyone injured?"

Ero Shan and Nalte shook their heads and produced a waterskin, which they proceeded to pass around.

"How about you two?" I asked Haln and Duh-nee. Haln crossed her thick arms and grunted in reply.

"We are both fine," Duh-nee said. "Thank you for your concern." The little Samary began ticking off his fingers as if he were counting in his head. Finally, he nodded curtly and grinned, as if pleased with his tallying. "I estimate that the six of us were able to defeat more than sixty of those flying men. That's ten or more each."

I cleared my throat at the highly exaggerated estimate but didn't have the heart to tell him he was giving us more credit than we deserved. Had we faced that many klangan, we would all be dead.

Duh-nee turned toward his mate, who looked as if she had been insulted. "Of course, some of us may have had a hand in more of the combat than some of the others, but still…it's a great victory." He pulled a slight stack of yellow books from his bag and wrote something in one of them with a thin ashen twig.

The water came to me and I took a long drink. When I was finished, I stood and motioned for the others to do the same. "Come, we need to explore the village. Maybe we can find a survivor or some trace of where everyone went."

As we set out to begin the grim search for victims of the latest attack, we heard a loud groan from the nearby trees. We raced to the edge of the forest, searching for the source of the noise. Suddenly, we heard crackling and crunching from the branches above us as two klangan fell from the thin prickly trees to land at our feet. One of them let out another pitiful lamentation as he landed.

We lifted our weapons, ready to fight.

The two klangan stood with some difficulty, picked up their spears, and held them defiantly. "Come no closer," the largest one said. "We can still give you a good fight, whether we can fly or not." He had a streak of white that covered one ear and ran down to his neck. Otherwise, he was stark black as the starless night. His companion was red as a fox from head to toe. The darker one stepped forward. "Stand aside or be destroyed."

"Listen," Duare said. "You're both clearly injured." She nodded to a blackened wound on one of the smaller angan's wings. "If you surrender your weapons now, you may travel with us safely until you can rejoin your fellows."

We all stood out of the range of their weapons, but Duare was the only one to put her sword away. "We will not fight you. You stand no chance against us."

"We can fight. That is enough." The larger angan had spoken again, while the smaller seemed less anxious to get back into combat. His injured wing looked worse off than his companion's and he appeared ready to retreat at the first chance.

"We are willing to let you leave, if that is your wish," Duare said. "That is your choice. But you are both unable to fly and I understand the forests and mountains are thick with all manner of creatures eager for a meal. You can travel with us, and we will protect you. Once we reach the pass, you can leave. It is safer there."

Guarding one of the klangan that had just tried to kill us was not something Duare had discussed with me. I would not have been as enthusiastic or as forgiving as she. Nor were the klangan ready to join our party. "I would sooner sleep in a tharban den with blood smeared on my feathers," the larger one said.

"Why would we do that, Messapossamee?" asked the other angan, apparently so unimaginative that he missed his companion's metaphor.

Messapossamee raised his wings in a menacing stance, looking like a predatory hawk. "We are under orders to kill these humans," he said. "Do not treat with them, Breemak."

"Listen," Duare said, her voice weary. "You are both clearly proud warriors, but there is no shame in getting assistance to survive and fight another day." She nodded to the dark wound on Breemak's wing. "You both need rest, so I say again, if you surrender your weapons now, you may travel with us safely until you feel well enough to fly, or you can rejoin your fellows."

I caught Duare's eye and drew her some distance away

from the others. "These klangan just tried to kill us," I whispered. "Are you sure we want to do this?"

Duare motioned to the winged men. "They're obviously hurt, and no real threat to us. Besides, perhaps they can be of some use."

The klangan's ears must have been better than I would have expected, for at that moment Breemak stepped toward us and asked, "Why would we not survive?"

"Shut your mouth," Messapossamee said. "Let us go."

I thought that would be the end of it and the two klangan would leave us, but the one named Breemak surprised me by turning and hobbling after Duare."

"Wait, please," he said. "Talk some more as to what you think will kill us in the forest."

"We are not going to travel with our enemy," Messapossamee said. "We have sworn an oath to kill them."

"No." Breemak held up a hand to his companion. "I swore to fight them. There's a difference. I have fought them. My promise is fulfilled." Breemak turned to us and advanced slowly. "Please. Continue describing the deadly things."

"There are spiders," Ero Shan offered.

"Spiders? I am not afraid of spiders." Breemak turned and started back to Messapossamee, and then stopped suddenly. "Unless they are large. Are they very large spiders?"

"Oh, yes." Nalte joined in. "There are huge spiders. And they have…" She appeared to think for a moment, as if conjuring the most fearful thing in her mind's eye. "They have a thousand eyes and two heads."

"What?" Breemak asked. "Two heads? Ghastly!" He moved closer to me and wrung his hands. "Wait. A thousand eyes altogether, or a thousand eyes on each of their heads?"

"Each of their heads," Ero Shan said.

The angan shuddered, his feathers rustling.

"And they have long tails with more spiders growing out of them," Haln added. The warrior woman spoke with great conviction, though she was perhaps not as skilled in the art of lying as she was in fighting.

Breemak seemed suspicious of Haln's addition of the tails, but he scurried forward on his short legs. "I will allow you protect me until the pass." He handed his large spear to Duh-nee and stood behind the two Samary. "Please do not lose this spear, it belongs to my sister." Both Haln and Duh-nee seemed taken aback but they made no objection as the wiry creature crawled around them. "Good-bye, Messapossamee the Mighty. I will see you back home if the thousand-eyed spiders do not eat you."

"Two-thousand-eyed," Nalte said.

We watched as Messapossamee stalked off into the distance, following the same general direction as his companions who had fled by air. The angan stopped no less than four times to glare back at us with his beady eyes. Breemak winced each time, but made no move to rejoin his erstwhile companion.

Once Messapossamee had disappeared over the hills, we turned back to the burning buildings. "Let's see what we can find among the destruction. Maybe we can still help someone," I said. "Ero Shan, find a good vantage point and watch for those klangan. I'd hate to be surprised by them again."

Before Ero Shan could even respond, Breemak waved his hands. "Don't bother. They aren't coming back."

"How do you know?" Nalte asked.

"You vanquished them," Breemak said. "They have no support from a larger group of soldiers, so they won't attack again. Since you managed to defeat them when their numbers were so great, they won't dare return without help. That's the way they think." Breemak looked to the skies. "The way we think, I suppose."

Seeing the wisdom in that and giving the angan the benefit of the doubt, at least provisionally, we turned to the village to look for any remaining injured or dead.

"Don't bother with that, either." Breemak sat down on a nearby rock and swirled his hand in a patch of mud at its base until his long, heavily nailed fingers were caked with the dark soil. He gingerly slathered the mixture on his wound, wincing as he patted it gently and spread it in circles.

"Why not?" Duare asked.

"There wasn't anyone here when Iralcus Iguiri ordered these dwellings to be destroyed. His soldiers had cleared all the little pink groundlings out days ago. They are likely already in the mines or the pits or wherever they get their resources. Anyone who won't join him willingly, joins him unwillingly." Breemak flicked the mud from his fingers onto the ground, wiping the rest on his legs and chest. "There is not a third choice. Well…death. I suppose that is the third choice. Join willingly, join unwillingly, death. Three choices."

"You have met this Iralcus before?" Nalte asked. "Is he the one who ordered you to burn the village and attack us?"

"I have not met him." Breemak stood and wiggled his injured and now mud-caked wing around a bit. "I do not wish to. His soldiers raided the settlement to enslave the villagers. They did it as a warning to others. And yes, he ordered my commander to have our flock burn the village and look for the one with the yellow hair." He lifted a hand in my direction.

"Why?" I asked.

The angan shook his head. "That I do not know, but I have heard things. I've been told he hates you, Carson of Venus. He hates you with a heart that burns like the flames that lie beyond the clouds."

I looked at Duare and we shared a puzzled glance. I thought again of the words Iralcus had spoken back at the Myposan outpost about how I had caused a calamity among his people. I felt the weight of his accusations that my carelessness had condemned them to death.

We made a quick survey of the village to gather anything

useful that had survived the flames and carried on by foot toward the pass, following the tracks left by the Linneaun vehicle. The long path wound through the trees and down along the mountainside.

I was far from certain about the wisdom of bringing the angan along with us, but thought it might be worth the risk. The klangan I had encountered were soldiers of fortune. They were splendid fighters but knew little else besides obeying their superiors. Since Breemak was now separated from those superiors, perhaps we could find a way to use him to our advantage as Duare had suggested.

We'd walked only a few miles when the angan spoke. "How do you do this?"

"What?" I asked.

"This." Breemak pointed at his feet. "This…walking. It is exhausting and tedious."

"You get used to it," Duare said.

Breemak shook his head. "Never. It is awful." Then, slowly, he fell to the back of the group. A few minutes later he spoke again.

"You there, big one. You are large and muscular." He was looking up at Haln. "Surely you could carry me."

Haln didn't answer him, other than to scowl.

It was quiet for a moment until Breemak took another angle. "You know, to my people it is a great honor to assist the members of one's flock when they are injured. It is one of the greatest gestures one can make for another."

Haln leaned close to her mate, her broad face creased in doubt. "He says it would be an honor. I should do that. I am honorable."

"No," said Duh-nee.

"But…I can't say no to his greatest gesture."

"He's lying."

I watched as Breemak leaned a little closer to hear the conversation.

"I don't think he's lying," Haln said.

"I do not lie." Breemak leaned in even closer until he was right in their midst. "I am Breemak the Truthful."

Duh-nee sighed. "He just wants you to carry him. Tell him no."

"But…"

"If we are attacked or in peril, he will run off at the first chance. There is no honor in the lives of the klangan. They ally themselves with whomever offers them the greatest chance of profit."

Haln turned and looked at Breemak tentatively. "No."

With a bristle of his wings, Breemak sighed. As he walked, he noticed me watching him.

"You there," he said. "You are not entirely without merit. I am sure your companions consider you handsome, and your yellow hair not at all grotesque."

"Thank you," I said, waiting for whatever was about to come.

"Did you know it is a great honor in my culture to help a fellow warrior when he is injured?"

"I'm not an angan," I said.

"I am willing to bet if you asked one or two of your companions for help, you could muster the strength to carry me the rest of the way."

Duare laughed. "Carson is certainly a man of honor."

I shook my head. "No."

The angan flapped his wings in frustration. "Perhaps walking is even worse than giant spiders."

It was not easy to continue to follow the tracks with Breemak's constant grumbling about walking and his growing desire for food. His observations about the rest of us—our clothes, our hair, and our mannerisms—wore thin quickly. The klangan I have known have all been great talkers, but Breemak was the worst I had yet encountered. His prattling only added to the exhaustion we all felt from the battle and the rest of our tribulations.

"What do you say we find a place to sleep?" I asked the others.

They readily agreed. Haln walked around the area, searching for any signs of predators or enemy soldiers on the ground. Ero Shan and Nalte climbed a nearby tree to look for an area that could provide us shelter. I gathered what food I could from the woods and shrubs. As Duare had invited the angan along, by mutual assent the job of guarding him fell to her.

Nalte waved from a high branch for us to climb up to join them. She and Ero Shan presented us with a cluster of branches and leaves that came together to form a sort of natural room that was large enough for all of us to fit rather comfortably inside. The leaves could be parted on the floor of the shelter in order to get a clear view of the ground below, giving us warning should any unwelcome visitors come searching for us. It was perfect for the group.

"A fine resting place," I told Ero Shan and Nalte. "We can eat the berries I managed to pick and restore our strength."

Haln looked around at the structure. "Something feels wrong. We should find shelter elsewhere."

"It's perfectly fine," I said. "There is plenty of room for all of us, and we can't be too choosy right now. Let's get some rest and we'll move on early in the morning."

The leaves rustled as Duh-nee made a spot for his mate. "Come. This will serve us well. Sleep. You will feel better. You have been on edge since we left the village." Reluctantly, Haln knelt beside him and pushed a few leaves around. She put her weapon next to her, curled her broad arms around Duh-nee, and was snoring within a minute's time.

I chuckled and moved close to Duare for warmth. Soon I began to fade into my own slumber.

Sleep did not come as easily for Duare. "What do you think will happen?" she asked. "What if this Iralcus Iguiri can bring others under his control? What of the Thorists? Will they oppose him, or will they declare some sort of treaty and rule together? The Thorists still have a vast amount of might and influence and are likely the only people with the power and the willingness to join him as equals."

I had been groggy when she started her barrage of questions, but I was soon wide awake and considering the immediate consequences of the Linneaun leader's appearance in our little part of the world, and the damage he could inflict upon it. "I don't see this Iralcus sharing power. He seems like he wants to be in charge, or nothing."

"But what if he makes an alliance with our enemies—the Thorists, the Sanjong of Havatoo…"

"In truth, we've only seen a handful of these Linneauns. They seem to have some interesting weapons and means of transportation, but once the jongs of larger cities and nations get organized, they'll stop Iralcus," I said, and I believed it. Until we got some sort of count of his troops and his other capabilities, we had no reason to think he hadn't just been lucky so far.

Our angan guest had been listening from his own little nest of leaves a few feet away. "Our leaders would not have just given up to a few of those Linneauns," he said. "I know not how many soldiers his army contains, but those we saw were so powerful, so seemingly indestructible that we surrendered on the spot without a fight. He turned and shuffled some leaves again, grunting in disgust. "No. We saw enough."

"Is it possible the Linneauns are already working with the nation of Havatoo?" I wondered aloud. "We are following but one machine. It would stand to reason that if they planned on attacking the major cities, they would have certainly brought more of their weapons." Unless, I told myself, they weren't planning to attack. Havatoo has defenses and would fight back. Someone like Iralcus would know that. If they were already allies, there would be no need for a brigade of land-sea craft, or lanjotars, to use the word Duare had coined for them, a contraction of the word "lap" (land), "joram" (sea), and "notar," (ship).

"I know not of their alliances beyond my people and the Myposans," Breemak said. "But I think anything is possible. I think you are fools for following this machine. You should have turned back by now."

I thanked Breemak for his help and his opinion, and agreed to organize a discussion in the morning on the subject. There was no use worrying and I feared we were keeping the others awake. I put my arm around Duare and again felt the world drifting away as I neared sleep.

"I am pleased you are all comfortable," Breemak said. "How wonderful for you." He sighed and rustled around, but everyone slept despite the noise.

I did not know how much time had passed when we were startled awake by a scream from Duh-nee. He was shouting that Breemak was going to kill him. I was alarmed to see that Breemak was indeed standing over him with a knife that I recognized immediately as belonging to Ero Shan. However, the angan thrust the knife upward, and into the canopy of branches above us, rather than at Duh-nee. Breemak swung again, with his whole hand disappearing into the leaves. "Can you aid me?" he cried, suddenly desperate.

I admit I was at a loss as to what was going on until I saw what appeared to be a white stringy substance dripping from Breemak's hand when he withdrew it from the canopy. The pale material looked much like webbing, and it dawned on me.

"Tarel," I said, referring to the strong, silky fiber produced by the targo, the giant spider of Amtor. I reached for my sword and Haln for her halberd. She sliced upward, close to Breemak, but with such precision as to not even bump him. Part of the branch above us collapsed and the targo shoved its head through the hole, its giant, crablike pincers clacking. I thrust my sword at its face, and Haln sliced near where the body still crawled on the limbs above us. I slashed at the beast's powerful jaws, in an effort to keep it from biting our angan companion and injecting its paralyzing poison into him.

From beside me, Duare unsheathed her sword, which she had taken a liking to since our initial encounter with the Linneauns. She swung upward, striking at the base of its head and nearly cutting clean through it. The targo went limp, its head lolling to the side. Blood dripped down onto the floor of our hidden room from the dead beast.

"You're getting good with that thing," I said, indicating her sword, and she smiled back at me, clearly proud of herself.

Breemak pushed himself away from the carcass of the beast, trying to tear off the tough, stringy webbing as he went. "You said there were creatures on this journey. You said I shouldn't go out alone. I thought you were just trying to scare me. But here it is." He clawed for the entrance to our little room and made his way out. "I should have stayed with Messapossamee. My chances were better with him."

We all thought following Breemak out of our hideaway might be a good idea, considering the circumstances. The corpse of the targo might attract other predators and more trouble. Gathering our weapons, we climbed down in the low evening light, our senses suddenly attuned to every little noise and crackle. We moved away from our previous hiding spot and found a clearing in the forest in which to camp out. We had entered a rocky area, and the ground was lumpy and uncomfortable to lie on, though a thick layer of weeds helped somewhat. Breemak agreed to take the first watch, as he was sure he would be unable to sleep. As the rest of us stretched out on the ground, Ero Shan told me privately that he would keep one eye open to watch the watcher, as he did not trust Breemak any more than I.

The rest of the night passed uneventfully. After what seemed like hours of drifting in and out of sleep, we convened to discuss our best course of action. I already knew Breemak supported fleeing. Duh-nee and Haln were all for a fight and wanted to pursue the machine. Ero Shan and Nalte were willing to do whatever I decided. They just wanted to help in whatever way they could.

Duare stood up and walked around, yawning as she stretched and tried to wake up.

"Duare?" I asked. "What is your vote in the matter?"

As I waited for her answer, the morning air was suddenly

alive with a whistling sound that I couldn't place. It was not a bird or forest creature, but the noise got louder and higher pitched. It sounded almost like my space-faring torpedo as it had hurtled into the air from the mile-long track I had constructed on Guadalupe Island on Earth all those years ago. I looked up and saw a yellow streak descending on us.

"Run!" I shouted at everyone.

The group scattered and headed back into the forest just as an explosion tore apart a row of small trees across the meadow from us. Coming over a rise, the Linneaun lanjotar advanced on us, smoke rising from one of its forward cannons.

It appeared that the question of whether to flee or fight had been answered for us.

12

FOREST FIGHT

W E SCATTERED AGAIN in the wake of another blast from the machine. Some ran for the cover of rocks and others for the safety of the trees. While I recognized the latter as members of the same enormous species common to most Amtorian forests, these must have been mere saplings, as they rose only a thousand feet into the air and were not quite a hundred feet in diameter. On closer inspection, I decided that they were probably members of a variant species, for unlike the mature colossi with which I was familiar, their branches ran up the trunk almost from the base.

As I settled behind a boulder, I heard shouts. Duh-nee and the others were pleading with Haln to stop. I peeked from cover to see the giant warrior running alone toward the massive, towering machine, swinging her huge sword over her head as she charged. The lanjotar was still some distance away, leaving plenty of time for the Linneaun gunners to get their sights on her.

I could spy several warriors on top of the machine, much as they were when I first encountered one of their tanks. I lifted my r-ray rifle and fired off a few shots. I didn't have a good angle and my targets were still quite far away, so my shots went wide. I needed a better vantage point, so I examined a tree nearby. The branches were low enough and sufficiently close together that I felt confident I could climb up until I was nearly level with the machine's upper deck.

As another explosion sent dirt and debris into the air nearby,

I shouted to Duare and Ero Shan, who had found shelter a few yards away. "Stay there while I get a better shot!" I ran to the tree and gripped a limb.

"Be careful!" Duare cried, but I was already making my way up the tree.

The tree's branches were spaced exceptionally well for climbing. As I neared my target area, I found a long, thick branch that allowed me to swing to the next tree, which would serve as an even better roost to get a shot at the Linneauns.

I lost sight of Haln and the tank as they dipped into a small valley and out of my sight. Below me, Ero Shan, Duare, and Nalte took the opportunity to move closer to the machine's path and find better cover. I saw our new companion, Breemak, preening his injured wing and chewing on some weeds, looking for all the world like a spectator in a sporting match, as he craned his neck to watch the action from behind a large rock.

The enormous tree I had chosen for safety and a good line of sight shook at the approach of the lanjotar. It swayed enough that I feared I might be dislodged, but I clung to the thick, sturdy limb and managed to hold on.

Within moments, the members of my little group were treated to their first look at a mighty Linneaun lanjotar. The craft was just as huge as I'd remembered, boxy with enormous treads on either side. Its armored hull was dark gray like the barrel of a Colt pistol back home. If the tree I'd taken refuge in was nearly a thousand feet tall, then the Linneaun war machine had to have been two hundred, top to bottom. It was even more daunting than I remembered.

From my perch, I had a good shot at the lanjotar, though I had to wait a few moments for it get clear of some trees that blocked my line of sight. I steadied my aim and fired multiple times. The blasts struck the side of the terrible machine but caused no visible damage. The r-rays, which affected only living matter, had no effect upon the metal hull, of course, but I was aiming at the Linneauns themselves. I knew our pistols had inflicted little damage upon the first group of Linneauns we had encountered, but I hoped the more powerful rifle I'd taken from the Linneaun's own stock inside the torpedo might change the equation.

My first shots at the soldiers on the roof of the craft went wide, missing them all completely, but I took my time with my next salvo. Success! One of the Linneaun soldiers stumbled backward and disappeared from sight as it fell from the back of the ship. The others turned and pointed in my direction. Though I was concealed, they must have traced the r-ray blasts back to their source.

The machine's main gun, which jutted from the front of the craft, suddenly moved and fired, launching another projectile in my general direction. It exploded somewhere below me and the massive tree shook.

I fired again and saw another Linneaun soldier fall on the deck. Another roar of the great cannon followed. This time, my tree not only shook; it tilted slightly in the direction of the tank. Peering below me, I found the machine's big gun had blown away a huge section of the trunk and weakened the tree as a whole. I gathered up my rifle and quickly climbed back the way I had come, hoping to find the branches that led to the other tree. The trunk creaked and crackled, snapping the whole time as I scurried like a squirrel to get to another safe limb.

But it was no use. A tremendous crack and a sudden jolt warned me that the last part of the trunk had disintegrated. The massive tree began to fall over. At that point, I grabbed the thickest branch within reach and hung on for dear life. I took a deep breath as I prepared myself for the possibility that I might not survive a fall from such a height. Below, I heard shouts from my companions, but the roar of the cannons muffled the meaning of their words.

My fall was brought to a sudden halt when the tree to which I clung crashed into the thick branches of another tree that was nearly its equal in size. I could see where the two had become entwined some fifty feet above where I clung. Considering I was more than two hundred feet from the ground, I decided it would be prudent to climb higher and reach the adjoining tree, but I had no time. Then I heard a deafening crack and the trunk of my own tree resumed its fall, crashing through the other trees below, snapping branches as it went. Whether these slowed my fall, I cannot say, for it was truly a horrendous ride. Before I knew it, the whole thing crashed to the forest floor, the impact slamming me against the thick bark and hurling me off the trunk. Immediately, I could hear shouting, the crack of branches snapping, and the sound of metal on metal.

I found a foothold and steadied myself before climbing up to the top of the felled tree. Smoke rose from an area ahead. The crown of the tree had landed on the tank, tearing one side of the boxy vehicle clean off. From where I stood, I could see inside the top level of the machine. Black smoke issued from somewhere deep in the lanjotar's interior.

On top of the vehicle, on the part of the roof that hadn't been destroyed, a single Linneaun guard with a rifle slung over its shoulder stood turning from side to side. I wagered it was looking for any of its companions who had been standing there just moments ago. Unfortunately, its search for its fellows brought its eyes on me. Its disorientation and fear quickly turned to anger, and it began raining gunfire in my direction. Before I could react, Haln pulled herself on top of the vehicle, and grabbed the soldier by the shoulder, swung it around, and tossed it off the back of the machine. She waved happily to me and I slowly raised my arm to return the greeting.

For a moment I was puzzled how the Samary warrior had managed to mount the two-hundred-foot-tall vehicle. Then I espied a series of rungs running up the lanjotar's side, which began just above the tank's massive treads. A thin cord dangled from the lowest rung to the ground. Haln must have attached a rock to the cord and thrown it with such force that she was able to loop it around the rung more than fifty feet above! I later learned that the cord itself had come from Duh-nee's seemingly bottomless bag of tricks.

From the smoke billowing out of the machine's lower level, two Linneauns emerged and stepped out onto the fallen tree. Seeing them, Haln jumped down to land between the two. She swung her pike at one and then the other, causing them both to instinctively step away from her. She pursued one, slashing and pressing her attack. While the Linneauns seemed to move as slowly as when we'd fought them earlier, they were also as powerful and impervious as before and could hold their own in combat. They used their thick arms to block blows and swing at Haln, stomped forward with thick feet, and did their best to catch the Samary warrior off guard. But Haln was far too agile.

When the opportunity presented itself, she landed her pike square on top of one fighter's helmet, which cracked open, releasing a hiss of green-tinted vapor. The Linneaun reached up and grabbed for the helmet, desperately trying to keep the two pieces of its headgear together. Haln moved on to fight the other aggressor, pressing it backward now that she could focus on just one.

I couldn't help but stare at the injured fighter as it struggled to keep itself alive.

"Help me," it wheezed as it fell. There on the broad trunk the soldier lay sprawled, part of its helmet broken off and releasing another greenish cloud. I moved closer.

Then and there, I saw a Linneaun face for the first time. It had a surprisingly small head, with almost pointed, mouselike features—tiny black eyes, a black bristled nose, and a mouth hidden far beneath the snout. The gaping hole in the side of the damaged helmet exposed tubes and gears, spongy squares, and other components I could not identify.

Though the soldier was an enemy, I couldn't stand by and watch it die. "How?" I asked.

It replied with nothing but a series of gurgles and sighs.

I picked up the helmet and tried to fit it back on its head, struggling to put the two pieces back together, hoping that it would help somehow. Unfortunately, it didn't. With a rough gasp, the warrior stopped breathing. I stared at the pieces of its headgear in my hand, trying to make sense of them. That the helmet had kept it alive I was certain, but what did it mean? All the Linneauns I had so far encountered had worn helmets. I wondered if their species breathed something other than air. And what had Iralcus meant by saying I had cursed the Linneauns with the helmets?

I had no further time to contemplate the biology of Linneauns. The shouts of combat drew my attention back to my companion, and I ran down the slanted trunk to assist her. Three more Linneauns emerged from the torn side of the machine, advancing quickly enough to get the better of Haln. Two of them pressed her, swinging their arms and wide-faced axes. She fell onto the tree trunk, quickly pinned by the force of the dual attacks. I was blocked by the third of their number, unable to assist her.

From the shadow of a thick side branch, Duh-nee emerged, brandishing a pair of thin, pick-like daggers. Based on our previous experience with these formidable creatures, I greatly feared for the smaller Samary's life. My expectation was that if his mate couldn't hack her way through the strong Linneaun skin bands, the diminutive man had little hope of doing anything substantial. I was quickly proven wrong. Duh-nee jabbed at the enemy rather than slashing as most of us had. He came around the side of Haln's attackers, stabbing one of them three times in rapid succession before landing a blow that sank deep into the Linneaun's side. The creature howled in pain and swung at Duh-nee.

"Get between the layers!" Duh-nee cried. "Strike where the bands meet!" He avoided the aimless swings of his adversaries and struck another blow, this one just below the creature's shoulder.

With the odds evened, Haln managed to shove her

remaining attacker off balance and far enough away to pick up her pike. Following her mate's suggestions, she began thrusting the weapon at the fighter's chest and abdomen. In desperation, her opponent stopped attacking and did its best to defend itself, blocking and parrying her efforts. It was eventually distracted by the fall of its fellow Linneaun, stabbed and bloodied by Duh-nee, and Haln was able to jab quickly through its defenses. The pike's thick blade slipped easily into the Linneaun's chest and it fell, sliding over the edge of the massive tree trunk and disappearing into the leaves and branches below.

At the sight of its defeated comrades, my own attacker retreated, ducking back into the craft. Before I could give chase, I was hailed by the rest of my friends as they climbed up to the same area where Duh-nee appeared. "Our Samary friend made a discovery," I said. "These soldiers are vulnerable if you can land a strike in the gaps between the long strips around their bodies."

The information brightened Ero Shan's weary face. "They aren't invincible, then? That's heartening news."

Armed with that knowledge, we cautiously made our way into the broken machine. Three warriors engaged us almost immediately, but we made quick work of them, owing to our superior numbers, our newfound knowledge of how to defeat them, and the fact that each of them seemed afraid, or certainly less confident in their skills than those we had fought before. Understandably so, now that they were outnumbered and had seen us slay their comrades. Even so, fear seemed an incongruous emotion to find in these huge beings that had all but ignored us upon the occasion of our previous meeting.

We searched the craft, looking for any information that could tell us more about the Linneauns, their past, their location, and how to defeat them.

"A shame that the tree destroyed this craft," Ero Shan said. He admired the vehicle as we continued. "It would be a daunting addition to the Korvan battle fleet, to say the least."

Everything inside was set slightly higher than we were used to, owing to the Linneauns' great statures. Haln, the largest of our number and the one who should have been least fazed, still marveled at the enormity of the whole environment. The Samary weren't known for their amazing feats of technology, and they didn't mix much with the more advanced peoples of Amtor. The battle vehicle, which intrigued the rest of us, must have seemed like a moving mountain to her.

"This place smells bad," Haln said. "I do not like it at all." She sniffed the walls and poked at the furniture. "A rolling cavern is what it is."

"My fierce tharban, you are not wrong," said Duh-nee. "This seems to be where they slept, fought, and ate." He covered his nose as he moved along behind his mate.

I made my way to the area where they had loaded and fired their great gun. It was littered with more of the shells that resembled my old torpedo. Some were attached to racks in the wall, while others rolled free about the floor. All were identical.

"Surely there is an explanation for this." Duare had followed me into the room. "I do not see how they could have created so much from your ideas without your help."

Something outside caught my eye. Through the targeting portal in the artillery bay, I saw a group of objects darting through the air in the distance. "What's that?" I leaned forward to get a better view, drawing Duare closer to the glass as well. She focused on the objects I indicated, outlined in the dark sky.

"Havatooan anotars," she said. "And look. Ground troops as well."

I saw them, too. "This doesn't look like a fight we can win right now."

"Agreed," Duare said. She stepped back out into the main hall of the upper deck. "Everyone, gather your things. We need to get out of here immediately."

I followed her out and secured my weapons.

"What is wrong?" Duh-nee asked. He and Haln were waiting at the giant hole in the side of the vehicle.

"Havatooans are on the way," I said. "We don't want to be here when they arrive."

"Or we can stay and talk with them," Duh-nee said. "They may have answers or offer help in defeating a common enemy. Our people are...if not friends with the Havatooans, at least neutral. We could use an ally now."

"No," I said. "It's too risky."

"Would you like me to add up our number of fighters here? Any addition to that count would only be an improvement."

"Or we could fight them." Haln shrugged.

Nalte helped Ero Shan up onto the tree. "Havatooans? They arrived quickly. Do you think they were already nearby?"

That thought hadn't occurred to me. "Why, do you think they could be in league with the Linneauns?"

"It's a possibility," Nalte said. "They certainly would not side with us in any matter at present." Ero Shan nodded in agreement.

A loud yawn interrupted the silence and Breemak stood up from a nest of leaves on a nearby branch. "I have to agree with our Samary friends," he said. "What would be the harm in getting the fine people of Havatoo to assist you? All this walking can finally be over." He groaned as he stretched his wings experimentally. "And they are very smart. Maybe they can help heal me and I can go home."

"As I have explained before," Duare told him, "due to the ongoing conflict with Korva, we four are enemies of the state in the eyes of every citizen of Havatoo. They have orders to put us all to death. We would not survive the day." She picked up her gear and walked down the slant of the tree trunk, Nalte following behind as they crawled their way through the limbs.

"I can't ask you to continue with us," I told the two Samary and the angan. "It actually might be wiser for you go to them in some respects. The Havatooans got here awfully quickly. So either they are out actively hunting the Linneauns, or they

are in league with them and were here to meet one of Iralcus'
emissaries. Whatever the situation, my friends and I can't
stick around to find out."

"So," Duh-nee said, "if those Havatooans are joined with
the Linneauns, and they see we have destroyed one of their
giant fighting caves and killed all their warriors, they will
most likely be angry with the lot of us." The two Samary
looked at each other meaningfully before moving to catch
up with Duare and Nalte.

Breemak and I stared at each other before he made a noise
somewhere between a dissatisfied grunt and a squawk. "Stay
here with Breemak the Agile."

"We're going," I replied. "Jodades." I could see three anotars
sweeping between the trees and approaching swiftly, so I
turned and ran for the rest of my party.

"Well, this limits our options severely," I said when I caught
up. "We can't continue south for too long before we get to
the sea." We had other directions we could go, but one would
take us back to the great river, which could be traversed only
at certain spots. The other direction would also take us to
the ocean quickly. We could go back to the Samary village,
but to drag them into a fight with the technically sophisticated
Havatooans would mean certain death for many of Haln and
Duh-nee's people.

"They are not likely to help us at this time." Haln was
matter-of-fact.

"I say we take our chances in the tunnel again," Ero Shan
said. "If we return to the Myposan outpost, perhaps we'll
have the element of surprise on our side. And maybe Yron
would be sympathetic, as you have indicated, Carson."

"We don't even know if that same tunnel would take us
back where we started," I said. "Maybe there are more paths
to take." We climbed down the trunk using branches and
foliage that could support us and took a moment to quietly
assess whether we had been sighted and would have to deal

with pursuers. Seeing none, we moved on hastily, lest that situation change.

"Walking is terrible, but somehow running is even worse," Breemak shouted from on top of the tree trunk, where he had been surreptitiously following us. "Can we be done for this day?"

13
END OF THE LINE

I T WASN'T JUST BREEMAK; we all had cause to complain on the journey back to the tunnel. The rains turned every path we took into a soggy, muddy mess. We stayed close to the boles of the giant trees whenever we could, trying to keep ourselves concealed from any other trouble that might be looking for us. It was a damp, chilly, and altogether miserable journey.

As we approached the tunnel we sighted the torpedo-car, still visible through the yawning mouth of the cavern. We decided to rest a bit on a nearby hill before entering the tunnel.

Breemak took the opportunity to remind us of how much his feet hurt and of how tired he had become of walking. Finding no outpouring of sympathy from the group, he eventually quieted down and roosted like a sulky bird in a clump of weeds halfway up the little rise.

Duare sat down in the tall grass at the base of the hill and drank from the waterskin. "Taking this murderous vehicle back is not my favorite idea."

I wasn't particularly fond of the plan myself. We had discussed it over and over as we walked, with no real consensus on how to proceed. All I knew was that most of us were not welcome in Havatoo, and that was enough to convince me to turn around. "There's no sense continuing deeper into Havatooan territory," I said. "We'd risk running into our old friends and the Linneauns."

"Not to mention any beasts that decide we look like a fine meal," Nalte said, accepting Duare's offer of water.

134

The foliage rustled at our back and Breemak sat up, blades of grass stuck to his feathers. He pointed a bony finger toward the torpedo-car. "That is the vehicle you have talked so much about? It looks much worse than walking. Much worse."

"We will be fine," Duh-nee told him. "Surely a fierce angan warrior like you is not frightened by a metal egg?"

The bird-man shook his head. "We do not like..." Breemak struggled for the right word, "closed up things like that. We prefer space to open our wings and feel the winds."

"Were you not listening to the others tell their story? At the other end of this tunnel, there is a wide open space for you to do just that," Duh-nee said. "Just get on into the vehicle, sleep in comfort, and we shall wake you ever so gently when we arrive."

"There is plenty of wide open space right here."

Duh-nee nodded. "Then you are afraid of the strange craft."

"Of course," Breemak said. "Just look at it. It screams death."

"No one died when we got in it," Duare said, doing her best to help Duh-nee encourage our angan companion.

"Well, the Myposan driver died," I said. When Duare frowned at me, I added, "But that wasn't the vehicle's fault."

Duh-nee moved close to Breemak, as close as he could without getting knocked over by an errant wing. "I must be honest, my friend. My mate, Haln, has never been in a vehicle of this sort, and I may need your help in keeping her calm."

"Calm?"

"Yes," Duh-nee said. "I am giving you...something to do."

"Are you ordering me to help you?" The angan's eyes narrowed.

Duh-nee thought on that for a moment. A look of clarity came over the small man's face. "Yes. This is an order."

Without an instant's thought, Breemak stood up. "I will help you."

In the time it took Duh-nee to convince Breemak to continue, Ero Shan, Nalte, and Haln had already made it to the vehicle. It was hissing to life when the rest of us caught up to them in the cockpit. With a final nod, I set the machine in motion. Knowing that just about everything about our transportation was automatic took most of the pressure off me this time. All I had to do was hit the mechanism to get us moving and, if Jason's and my theory was correct, the ship and the tunnel would handle the rest.

As soon as we began accelerating, Ero Shan went into the storage area and tore open some crates. "Surely they have food here. It cannot be all parts for their machines." He threw some thick metal rods out onto the deck with a clank. "I am on the verge of eating this metal."

"Over here," Nalte said. "I've found something." She hefted a pair of large tubs she had come across in the back of the storeroom.

The group converged on Nalte, myself included. I hadn't been aware of how hungry I was until the possibility of food was mentioned. We pried open the lids from the large tubs and found some sort of pasty, dark substance that smelled ranker than spoiled milk. Everyone backed away except Breemak, who leaned closer and extended his hand. He pulled it back completely covered with the dark stuff. He lapped at it with his thin tongue and smiled.

"Tastes like mashed sea worms. Delightful." He shoved his whole hand in his mouth and slurped.

I recoiled at the stench of the food, not to mention the sounds that Breemak was making. "I don't think I can eat that. There must be other food here somewhere."

Nearby, Duh-nee pushed a few things aside in another large crate. "I'm afraid there is not much else left. Certainly no food. Mostly big shiny armor plates, and these other heavy shells. Sorry."

Breemak took one of the tubs for his own and sat down next to Haln. "Would you like some? Suddenly this vehicle is not so bad, is it? I am not at all concerned." He scooped out more of the foul substance with his hand and licked it off his fingers. Haln, unflinching, dipped her fingers in as well and brought them to her lips. She didn't look happy with the taste, but she swallowed the stuff and took some more.

After exchanging a round of pained expressions, the rest of us followed suit with the second tub. It tasted as bad as it smelled, but we ate it because we had no idea how long we would be stuck in the torpedo-car. I dabbed my finger into the tub and tried to hold my breath as I ate in a vain effort to reduce the effects of the foul smell. It burned my throat as I swallowed and felt like caked mud going down. "How can you stand to eat so much of this?" I turned to ask Breemak, but he was already asleep on the floor next to Haln. His beaklike nose was still covered in the pasty food, and his tub was nearly empty.

At the end of our repast, I informed Duare that I was going to try to reach out once more with a mental projection and contact Taman. I took leave of my companions. If I could somehow manage to establish a sympathetic connection with the jong, he could send help from Korva and I could provide him with the valuable intelligence we had gathered about the Linneaun threat.

Settling in a secluded spot behind a row of shelves in the storage room, I took a moment to get comfortable on the swaying floor and drew in a deep breath. I formed a picture of Sanara in my head and focused on the jong. I did not know if he and I were in psychological harmony, which would be required for me to project my mental image to him, but we were good friends, so it was worth a try. My mind reached out for him. I envisioned the palace, the airfield, the gardens, but to no avail. The harder I tried, the more distractions broke through. Memories of what had led me here intruded. Lisant Or, Jovita, Vot, the Samary, the Havatooans—they all clouded my efforts. Again, I focused on Taman and tried to send my image along with a message, reminding myself of the difficulty the last time I had reached out. At least there was no head pain this time, for which I was very grateful. I imparted what I could about Yron, the

Myposan base, and our suspicions about Havatoo and the Linneauns.

I opened my eyes, still sitting alone on the floor. I had failed. The jong had neither seen nor heard me. With a sigh, I returned to the others.

The rocking and swaying of the torpedo-car had a hypnotic effect on all of us. I sat on a box next to Duare while Ero Shan and Nalte rested on a makeshift platform they had created out of some boards balanced on a pair of boxes. It was clear that either the Linneauns didn't sit down or the torpedoes weren't meant to carry large numbers of them. There was absolutely no comfort to be found in the car.

The only one who didn't rest was Duh-nee. He seemed quite content to wander the storeroom as he rearranged the contents of the crates, totalling them as he went and making marks on the wall with a sharp piece of metal to indicate how many items he'd found. It was the first time I'd seen him smile since I'd laid eyes on him.

"What do we do if this thing doesn't take us back to Yron's palace?" Duare asked.

I put on my own best smile. "Perhaps that would be fortunate, my beloved. Maybe it will drop us off in Korva, though I sincerely hope the Linneauns don't have a back door into our homeland."

A clattering at the back of the craft brought our attention to Duh-nee. "Sorry to interrupt," he said. "I'm taking stock of what weapons are available to us." We examined the array of dangerous-looking objects he had assembled in an orderly line on a countertop. "We have three handheld pistols, five extraordinarily long swords, six very thin daggers, two knives, and four of those rifles that we can't possibly carry on our own. I would take the thin blades, but..." he patted the bulging satchel strapped around his neck. "I have all the weapons I need."

I was impressed with his initiative and resourcefulness. "Thank you, Duh-nee. That will be a big help to us. Why don't you rest? It's hard to say what we'll encounter once this thing stops."

"I can keep watch first," Nalte said. "I'll alert you if anything happens."

I smiled. Nalte was as brave as the day I had met her so many years before outside of Kormor, the city of the dead. I felt reassured by her presence on this strange journey we had undertaken, as I did by the company of Duare and Ero Shan. And I had to admit the resourceful Duh-nee and the fearless Haln were growing on me, as well. Eternal optimist that I am, I hoped Breemak would also prove to be an asset, though I doubted it.

Duare and I found a spot to get comfortable, stacking tarps and other softer materials in a corner and curling up together. I was asleep from the sway of the cars and the noise of the engine in moments.

Duh-nee had just awakened me for my turn at watch, when we noticed light coming from the direction of the control room. Through the cockpit windows we saw that the dark rock of the tunnel walls had given away to a transparent substance. We were underwater, but likely not far. I could see what appeared to be waves moving some distance above us, and we were surrounded by colorful fish and abundant plant life. I stood transfixed by the sight, while Duh-nee went to rouse the others.

Haln shrank back from the scene. "Are we sinking? Are we trapped under the sea?" She stayed by the doorway.

"No," I said. I'd already forgotten how foreign some things must have seemed to the unsophisticated Samary warrior. "The walls are still there; we just can't see them well."

"It resembles the material we saw back at the Myposan outpost," Duare said, "in the tunnel when we went below the surface."

Nalte pointed off in the distance. "There are more tunnels over by that outcropping."

"Look—over there!" Duare pointed out half a dozen Linneauns laboring on a rocky ledge not far from us. They seemed oblivious to our approach, moving with measured slowness as they piled and shifted rocks in what appeared to be the construction of a new part of the tunnel. "They don't seem to have any problem operating underwater."

"It's beautiful down here." Duh-nee said from behind us. He'd moved to stand next to Haln. "The water is so clear."

Our ship had begun to rise at a sharp angle toward the surface. In a moment, we had left the water and entered another series of transparent tunnels that led toward an enormous building that sat on the edge of the ocean. Much like the Linneaun lanjotars we'd encountered, the entire edifice was stark and undecorated. It was essentially an enormous cube a mile and three-quarters to a side, the rear of which disappeared into a mountain behind it.

Ero Shan seemed stunned by the sight, his nose pressing against the portal. "Is this perhaps the Linneaun home city? Or merely a fortification of some sort?"

"Well, we will soon find out," Nalte said. Our torpedo-car turned and entered the structure alongside several other tunnels.

Breemak had been silent for some time. I had assumed he had dropped off to sleep again, since this seemed to be his default in crisis or times of stress. "I think we need to stop," he said now. "You should really reverse our course."

"We can't," I said. "It's on autopilot."

"That is unacceptable. There must be a way. We cannot be here." His feathers began to shiver as if he were suddenly cold. "I betrayed my fellow klangan, and in turn betrayed Iralcus and the Linneauns. They will kill me." His wings folded close to his body and he shrank back against the wall. "They'll kill you, as well. They hate you even more, Carson of Venus."

"There is nothing we can do," Nalte said. She reached out toward the bird-man as if to reassure him, but Breemak moved away from her touch.

"It'll be over soon," I said. It looked as though the track we were following stopped just ahead of us, and the vehicle was already slowing.

"That is what I am afraid of," Breemak replied in a low voice.

The doors slid open automatically as we came to a stop and the ramps emerged, extending silently to the ground. We peered out into what amounted to a rail yard. Several torpedo-cars stood with doors open to admit cargo from huge carts pushed by Linneauns, while others sat idle. None of the workers came close to our car or even took notice as they went about their duties. We watched as a Myposan departed one of the cars.

"Well? Duare asked. "What do we do now?"

"We wanted to find the Linneauns to make them stop their advance," Haln said. "Here we are. It looks like a fine place to begin." She thumped her pike on the deck.

While I agreed with Haln in principle, I suspected that our preferred methods for achieving our common goal differed wildly. "If we start fighting here," I said, "there's no telling how many soldiers will come running to attack. We'll never get out of this staging area. Let's scout out the place a little and see what we're up against."

"He has a point," Duh-nee said. "Let us count the number of enemies first."

"Do as you will," said Haln. "I will be ready to fight when it is time."

Behind Duh-nee, I saw Breemak trying to look inconspicuous among the crates deep inside the adjoining compartment. "Are you going to stay?" I called back to him.

The angan sat up with a sigh. "Someone must remain here to guard the vehicle in case we need a quick escape. I bravely volunteer to be that guard."

"There is more safety in numbers," Duare said. "Come along with us."

"No, thank you. I will stay here in order to save the rest of you."

"It would be foolhardy to face down the Linneaun warriors alone," Nalte piped in, trying to cajole the angan as well.

"I betrayed my flock," Breemak said. "That is bad enough. But these Linneauns? Iralcus Iguiri? That is a mark on me I cannot hide. They will kill me for my treachery as soon as I step foot outside the vehicle. Go." He nestled deeper in the crates and boxes until he was lost from sight.

"You know," I said, "they'll likely get around to unloading the crates from this thing eventually."

"Then hurry back before such a thing occurs!" came Breemak's muffled voice from amid the stacks of boxes.

Haln had ducked into the storeroom while we talked. When she returned, she rummaged among the boxes until she had uncovered the huddled form of the bird-man. "I do not use such things," she said, handing him a small pistol, "but you might find it helpful."

"Thank you." Breemak took the weapon and examined it gravely. "Perhaps this is the very weapon that was used to shoot me, thus setting in motion the entire terrible ordeal. Who knows? Maybe it will bring me better luck in this situation."

"Close these doors when we leave and lock them. We'll make three rapid knocks on the door followed by two slow knocks if we come back, so you can know to let us in." I held my hand out to clasp his, but he only huddled deeper in the nest of boxes. "I'm wishing you good luck."

"You did not want me to join you on your journey, but you allowed it anyway. Why?"

"I didn't want you to join us because I had no idea what lay ahead," I told him truthfully. "I knew it would be dangerous, and that you were injured. I figured that if you came along in that condition you would either slow us down or get yourself killed."

"So why?"

I pointed to Duare in the other room. "It was my mate's idea that we bring you along so that we could protect you until you got better."

Breemak brushed aside my extended hand. Then, much to my surprise, he opened his arms and enveloped me with his wings. He released me after a few seconds and burrowed back into his hiding place.

Duare smiled at me as I entered the control room, but she said nothing.

The remainder of the party exited the car and made our way as casually as we could down the ramp. Haln's accoutrements and weapons clanged together as she walked; fortunately, the noise was barely audible above the din of torpedo-cars braking and workers shouting to one another as they loaded and unloaded crates.

Running on metal tracks resembling the rails of an earthly train, the cars were confined to predetermined paths that kept them from colliding into one another. We made our way alongside a succession of empty cars, using them for cover to lessen our odds of being spotted. Moving from one vehicle to another, we passed from the loading yard to a stack of boxes near an entryway. There we waited for the flow of cargo to subside, and the number of Linneauns along with it.

Ducking inside a nearby doorway, we found a warehouse stacked with boxes and crates on one side and partially assembled vehicles on the other. Until now, we'd faced only one of the enormous lanjotars at a time, but here we could see the parts for dozens of the battle machines.

"If one of these things can destroy a village," Ero Shan said, "what might a group like this be able to do?"

Nalte frowned. "And these are just the parts for them. How many have they already built? How many are out in the world, spreading out across Amtor?"

Duare and I exchanged a bleak look. The Linneauns' capabilities seemed to be well beyond what a tiny group such as ours might be able to take on.

"Carson?" Duh-nee motioned me over to a nearby crate and showed me more of the shells the machines fired. "I was counting the number of boxes and needed to see what was in them."

"How many?"

"I have to estimate, but it seems like there are six rows of thirty-six of these shells in each box."

The two of us turned to stare at the boxes stacked up to the high ceiling. "Over there are the much smaller ammunition shells for their long guns. I have not even begun to calculate their number."

I was starting to feel that I didn't want to know anything more about the storage area. It was dispiriting and, honestly, would not help us learn more about the Linneauns themselves.

"Maybe we should we return to the torpedo-car," Nalte said. "This is an immense arsenal. We should see if we can make our way home and warn Taman, so our people can at least begin to prepare for the invasion that must surely be coming."

Duare agreed. "I know there is more here at stake for you, Carson, but we are talking about a threat to the entire region, and perhaps all of Amtor itself. We should find a way to turn back if we can."

"If we are to return home," I said, "it must be with a comprehensive report on the strength and capabilities of this new enemy. And if we can, we must learn of their plans."

"More complete information is useless if we are dead," Duh-nee said. He climbed up on a crate and disappeared into the shadows. I could hear him counting softly to himself in the darkness.

"Then go," I said. "Return to Breemak and take the torpedo-car wherever it will bring you. Warn our people and any others that will listen. I will stay to gain the intelligence for Korva and report later." I looked at Duare and the others. "I would feel better if you were all safe."

Ero Shan broke the silence that followed. "Do not speak that way. We would never leave you behind."

Haln raised her huge pike. "I am bored here. Perhaps there is a fight somewhere waiting to be started?"

Duare's eyes flashed with excitement and courage. "Well said. Where do we go next?"

I laughed and shrugged. "Let's see where these parts are going."

We made our way around the outer edge of the stacks of supplies and parts, trying to locate an assembly area for the weapons. Other than in terms of sheer scale, the operation appeared to me to be no different from that of our plants back in Korva, where we manufactured anotars for the royal army. There, we built one anotar at a time and needed only about six skilled craftsmen for assembly. Here, dozens of Linneauns, and even more slaves, welded and joined parts together.

"What do you think they're using to fuel their vehicles?" I asked. "I've noticed the exhaust does not resemble the propellant I used in my torpedo. In fact, such propellant would be highly inefficient, as it would be exhausted after only a brief time and have to be replaced after each use."

"It is a mystery," said Ero Shan.

The heat was almost unbearable even here in the observation area from which we looked down to the factory floor; it was hard to imagine what the people inside the work area were enduring. The Linneauns were like no other creatures any of us had ever encountered, however, and there was no way of knowing how the heat impacted their alien physiology.

"We should help the enslaved ones," Haln said. "If we free these people, they will come to our aid here and fight their captors." The Samary's deep resonating voice was hard to argue with. "Arm them and we will be invincible."

"I want to agree with you," I said, "but even in this room these people are outnumbered by members of Iralcus' army. And that's just one factory. We have no idea how many more are in this structure. Let us explore further. Now is not the time to free them."

"It is never the time," the giant Samary said. "Haln is growing annoyed. When is the time?"

"My glorious warrior, that time will arrive," Duh-nee said, coming to my rescue. "Now is the time to allow the others to use their talents. I am sure they value your skills and realize how very, very desperately you want to put them to use." The little man gave me a discreet jab with his elbow. "Don't you, Carson?"

I assured him that we did, and then spurred our party on into the next area. The walls there were blackened with smoke and looked roughly chiseled from the rock of the mountain we had seen rising behind the structure. We pushed deeper into the complex, trying to make our way as quietly and inconspicuously as possible.

In most of my past exploits, I had had only Duare's well-being and my own to be concerned with. Now, there were six of us to be accounted for. Among that complement was a very large Samary fighter itching for a fight, which only made our odds at being discovered even worse. Our one advantage was that no one was looking for us. We encountered very few Linneauns in our path that weren't intensely focused on doing a job. No doors were guarded, no passages locked.

"How is it that this facility is unguarded?" Nalte asked. "Surely they have reason to be on the lookout for their enemies. Our forces would definitely be on the alert at a time like this. I mean, they have all but declared war on the entire region."

It was a good question, but whatever the answer, I was glad for the lax security. "Maybe they've never been attacked before, and they feel safe in the seclusion of their rocky fastness?"

"It could well be that all they know is attacking," Duare said. "Defending may not be something they have ever had to do."

"Fascinating," Duh-nee said. "Are you suggesting that before they began their onslaught of our territories, they had never had to fend off any enemies, and therefore they may not know how?"

"I will teach them. Just point the way." Haln's demeanor had grown sour as we talked in the shadows. Her mate patted her on the arm in an attempt to calm her.

We climbed a metal staircase to a walkway that took us high over another factory area. In an enormous room below us, Linneauns used pulleys and chains to lift gigantic curved metal segments high enough for others to secure them onto waiting structures. Smoke had blackened the walls and drifted in clouds throughout the room. Even as we moved high above the numerous workstations, the heat from the equipment was severe. When we got closer to the center of the room, it hit me like a physical blow.

I stopped to rest and get a good look at the separate pieces, trying to extrapolate what they would be once they were assembled, but it was too soon in the process to tell. Each part was huge. Whatever the final product, it was going to rival the size of their boxlike war machines.

Duare tapped me on the shoulder, sweat streaking her beautiful face. "Ero Shan has scouted ahead and found a door back into the main structure," she told me. "Let us leave here before we all burn to a cinder." The walkway led to a small room, and we ducked in gratefully, closing the door behind us and enjoying the instant relief from the oppressive heat.

Ero Shan stood next to another door on the other side of the room. "I checked and there is not a soul out in the hall. This does not seem to be an industrial area. It's just a long white corridor with no exits other than a very large set of doors at one end. The other end is very far away, and I was unable to determine where it goes, or if there are any other passages that way."

"I wonder where those large doors lead," I said.

Ero Shan shrugged. "Your guess is as good as mine."

We opened our door just far enough to get a look at the area described. He was correct on all counts. "Okay," I said.

"I propose half of us go down the hall to find out what lies beyond those doors. The rest can cover us from here. If something goes wrong and you need to retreat, head back the way we came. Make your way to the torpedo-car with Breemak and get out of here."

Haln raised her pike, her broad face stern. Before she could speak, I said, "Of course, you're coming to check out the doors with me, Haln. I'll need a powerful warrior at my side in case there is a fight." In truth, the last thing I needed was someone of her size drawing unwanted attention to us, but I was hoping that our luck would hold and we wouldn't encounter any Linneauns. The Samary nodded with a smile of satisfaction and handed her pike to her mate, then took a moment to decide which weapon to take instead. She toyed with a short sword, returned it to Duh-nee, and then tested the heft of an axe. It seemed to satisfy her, and I waved to her and Duare to follow me.

Keeping close to the wall, we crept slowly down the long hallway to the great doors. The walls themselves were of white stone, carved into large blocks that had been piled one on top of the other. I tried to identify what type of mineral or rock composed them, but it was nothing I'd previously encountered.

Haln's patience had evidently run its course. Suddenly she pushed out from the wall and began to sprint the remaining distance toward the end of the corridor. I watched in dismay, not daring to cry out and alert a potential guard on the other side of the door to her presence. With Duare and me still thirty yards behind her, she gripped the metal handles and slid the doors aside.

I recognized the square room beyond as an elevator car of some size. Inside stood three startled Linneaun warriors.

My heart dropped into the pit of my stomach, but Haln practically beamed upon seeing the creatures and promptly swung her axe at the closest enemy. The blow didn't pierce the thing's hide, but it was knocked off balance and stumbled back farther into the car.

Fearing that even the powerful Haln would be overwhelmed by a trio of opponents at such close quarters, I ran to join the brawl, Duare close at my heels. As I leaped over the threshold the car gave a jolt, the doors clanged shut behind me, and we began to rise.

Duare had not made it into the car. I landed heavily on the floor, closer to the feet of my enemy than to those of my friend. One Linneaun swung his thick arm down, barely missing me as I rolled toward Haln. I leaned against the wall for support as I got up, drawing my pistol and firing two shots in quick succession. The first merely sizzled harmlessly on one of their chests, while the other missed entirely, hitting the far wall of the elevator.

The Linneauns and Haln stared at me. I put my gun away and drew my sword.

"I will fight the two large ones." Haln lunged at the pair of foes nearest to her. I was left facing the third Linneaun who, while marginally smaller than its comrades, was still a huge brute in its own right.

The creatures bore no weapons, but that was not necessarily an advantage to me. Each of their powerful arms, huge and jagged as rock, was just as deadly as any sword or axe. My own attacker swung its mitts like concrete, missing me but denting the metal wall at my back. I remembered our lesson from the woods, that stabbing along the lines of their bands was the best way to injure them, but we were so close that I had no room to do so. My foe had no such restrictions against me. It swung its fists repeatedly, putting me on the defensive as I dodged and blocked the blows.

The elevator rumbled as it ascended. At times, our shifting weight caused the whole car to slam against the outside wall, but it kept moving nonetheless. Near the door I spied a simple switch, which I assumed controlled the car's motion. Flipped up, as it was while we fought, and the car went up. Flipped down and the car should reverse course. We desperately wanted to go back down. That way our fellows could help in the fight, and we could keep the Linneaun warriors from sounding any alarm.

Meanwhile, I could hear Haln's laughter erupting from the other side of the car. She finally had her chance to throw off her restraint and do what she'd wanted to do all along: cause injury to something, anything. Though she was tall, the Linneauns were taller still, which should have given them an advantage, but Haln didn't appear to be fazed. She pushed one fighter away with her axe, then thrust the sharp edge into the other's chest, managing to bury it between the bands. The Linneaun screeched and fell, writhing on the ground. The other fighters stopped to see what had happened, and Haln took full advantage of the sudden lull. She swung the axe again and connected with her other opponent right below the helmet, slicing into its neck. That foe fell to the floor of the elevator as well.

The third Linneaun was dumbstruck, shuffling from side to side while it eyed Haln and me. I charged, sword tip forward, and stabbed the creature, but my jab missed the weak spot between its bands and glanced harmlessly off its natural armor. My efforts were rewarded with a punch to the side of my head that sent me reeling against the wall.

Haln took over before I suffered further injury. She was shouting again—some sort of warrior cries that echoed in the car. Tiny sparks of light burst in my vision as I tried to stand and help her, but I couldn't get to my feet. My head throbbed and I fell back down on my side. Through blurry eyes, I watched the Linneaun land a couple of solid swipes on Haln, but in the end, she prevailed, using the hilt of her axe to pummel the other fighter's head.

She picked me up and propped me against the wall. "You fought well for a male. Are you all right?"

I nodded, but with each movement of my head, the car seemed to spin a little. I pointed toward the doorway. "There's a switch. Pull it before we get to the top."

Haln eyed the switch and touched it gingerly with a finger. "This?"

I nodded. "Yes, flip it down. Not too hard." Likely no one in Haln's tribe had ever even seen an elevator before. She'd done well enough in the torpedo-car getting to the Linneaun fortress, but that only involved sitting and bearing her experience on the strange craft. "The handle. Just gently pull it down."

She grabbed the handle a little more firmly and tried to pull it completely out before moving it correctly, putting it in a neutral position that was neither up nor down. "Like that?" The car came to a complete stop and a look of pride came over her.

"Great, but now move it just a little more to get us going back down to Duh-nee and the others."

But before she could complete the task, the elevator doors opened on two startled Linneauns. The last thing I saw before the pain in my head became unbearable was Haln pulling the two creatures into the elevator.

14

A VILLAGE IN AMBER

AWOKE TO DUARE standing over me, speaking in urgent tones to the others. "Now is the time for us to take what we have learned and return to the jong. We cannot fight these Linneauns like this. We need help!"

"I agree," Nalte said.

"He's awake." Ero Shan leaned down and clasped my shoulder. "How do you feel?" He gripped my hand and pulled me up to my feet before my head was ready. The room spun just enough that I reached out to the wall for support.

"Like a basto just steamrolled over me and then came back for another pass," I said. "But I'll be fine. Just give me a moment."

It was then that I realized that we were still in the elevator. "Where are the Linneauns Haln and I fought?"

"We deposited them in one of the nearby rooms," Ero Shan said, examining the side of my head where I'd been struck. I reached up to my temple, and when I looked back down at my hand, I saw a mudlike substance on my fingers. "We put some of the salve on it that you got from the Cloud People," he explained. "Your arm seemed to respond well to it, so we hope it will have the same effect on a head injury."

It was certainly still tender to the touch, and I wasn't sure about their supposition regarding the medicine, but it probably wouldn't make things worse. "I caught the end of your discussion. You're thinking of turning back?"

"We weren't sure if you were going to make it," Duh-nee said. "Your whole face was an odd color."

"Sorry to have worried everyone. At least this time I had a reason for blacking out. Why are we still in the elevator?"

Duare squeezed my hand, her dark eyes reflecting a mix of concern and relief for my well-being. "After we hid the Linneauns' bodies, we saw some activity down at the other end of the hall. You were still here in the car, with Duh-nee guarding you. We were afraid to move you and also worried the enemy might see us, so we sneaked back in."

Haln pried open the door a sliver and peered out. "Still a lot of them down there. Maybe we should charge them and frighten them away."

"I don't think that's wise," Duare said.

Further discussion was interrupted by the elevator car suddenly shaking and rumbling back to life. Before we could act, we had begun to move upward again. "Did someone hit that lever?" I asked.

"It was not me." Haln held her hands up in the air.

The switch we'd used to move the car up and down during the fight was still set in the neutral position. I lurched away from the wall, fighting the effects of the blow that had knocked me out and that were now compounded by the mounting speed of the car's acceleration. I flipped the lever downward, hoping to halt or at least slow our ascent, but to no effect. Moving it in the opposite direction brought no reaction either.

"Looks like we're going up," I said.

After we had cleared the initial few floors, the elevator walls suddenly became transparent, revealing a beautiful view of the bay below the structure and the mountains and the sea stretching out beyond. A great mountain range loomed in the distance that hadn't been visible from our torpedo-car.

Nalte pointed to one of the peaks. "Do I see lights over there? It looks like a group of them, where those two ridges meet." We gathered closer to inspect the area she had identified, but it was difficult to decide whether we were looking at a compound of lighted buildings or being tricked by the late afternoon sun.

While the view from the portal was breathtaking, it was maddening that we couldn't see in the other direction and determine what was inside the massive structure itself. The facility's cyclopean size could allow for dozens of floors. I feared that additional factories and assembly areas lay inside, producing more war machines for the assault on the region.

"Imagine how many lanjotars they could make inside this one building," Duare said, her thoughts paralleling my own.

"Too many," I replied.

We rode the elevator up in silence for several minutes until the car began to slow. "Everyone stay out of sight when the doors open," I said.

We flattened ourselves against the front wall on either side of the doors, but a peek around the corner when we arrived confirmed no one was in the immediate vicinity.

Cautiously exiting the car, we found ourselves in an enormous open space that must have composed most of the huge building. Curiously uninhabited, it stretched before us for what could have been a quarter mile, both the flooring and the towering walls on three sides made of the same transparent material we had seen in the elevator. An enormous double door centered the back wall, flanked by several other portals that might have been sized for Linneauns. In the very center of the space stood a large block of some sort. Throughout the area, thousands of candles burned on posts, their flickering light reflecting from the glasslike walls, giving the appearance that the room itself was on fire.

"I've never seen so many candles in one place," Ero Shan said.

Duare stood with mouth agape, taking in the awesome sight. "Such a huge chamber," she said. "What do you suppose its purpose is?"

Nalte's wide eyes roved about the massive space. "The glow is eerie. I am not sure I want to know."

I drew my gun and proceeded forward, my steps echoing in the vast room. "Well, let's see what we find."

We made our way slowly across the transparent floor.

Ero Shan stopped after a few yards and knelt, pointing down below. "Look at this." We gathered around and gazed down upon a small village far beneath the strange glass. The houses and huts were built on a flat area of the rocky coastline, nearly level with where we'd entered the structure aboard the Linneaun torpedo-car. I guessed we were close to a thousand feet above the village, the details of which were impossible to make out at that distance.

"Over here," Duare said. She'd walked to the center of the room to examine the boxy object we had noted. She looked up at me with a wry smile. "It's some sort of telescope."

I shook my head tiredly. "Great," I said, recalling our last misadventure, in which a passing whim of the jong of Loton had sent us on a perilous quest to retrieve the components of a telescope. It was an undertaking during which Duare and I had nearly met our demise on multiple occasions.

The base of the object seemed to have been coated with some kind of frictionless substance; Duare was able to push it easily forward and back over the transparent floor, peering down through it the whole time. The block itself acted as a colossal magnifying glass, bringing everything below us into sharp relief. We could make out not only large objects such as buildings and wagons, but also—when Duare tinkered with a small control bar she had discovered on the instrument's side—the minute details of small objects, such as shovels and hammers, cups and plates. Moving the block as far as we could to one side, we found a wide swath of destruction just outside the town—a deep scar that cut through the earth and didn't end until nearly the other side of the settlement.

"Why would anyone build a structure this enormous over their village, as if encasing it in glass?" Nalte asked. "Why not replace it if they have the means? Why leave it around when you have technology far superior?"

I didn't have an answer that made sense yet, but Duh-nee offered a theory. "Maybe it is a sacred place to them," he said. "We have areas for burial and for ceremonies. Perhaps that is why they leave this intact, as a gift to their ancestors."

"Could be," I said. While the others pushed the large magnifier around, I walked to the window that overlooked the bay and the ocean beyond. It was an incredible sight from that height, with an unimpeded view of the water and mountains, some of which were topped with snowy peaks. In the bay below, the tunnels of the torpedo-cars stood out as dark lines that shot out to sea and disappeared into its depths.

"No one is walking around in this village," Haln said. She was kneeling on the glass, her face nearly pressed on the floor.

"It appears to be deserted," Ero Shan told the Samary warrior.

Haln seemed unconvinced and continued to stare down through the glass, as if waiting for the slightest movement.

Perhaps it was simply the power of suggestion, but I thought I spied a speck of blackness moving up high in the sky far out across the water. Before I could call it to the attention of my companions, however, I lost sight of it.

Just then a great commotion arose from behind us. I spun around to see hundreds of Linneaun soldiers pouring into the chamber like agitated ants from the great towering doors in the building's rear wall. There was nowhere for us to flee, and before we had done more than draw together into a defensive circle, the soldiers had stormed all about us.

As we stood there, clutching our drawn weapons but knowing we were vastly outnumbered, the mass of soldiers parted and Iralcus Iguiri came shambling toward us down the open way. I stepped forward to meet him. He paused dramatically, then raised his red-cuffed forearms like a vicar addressing his flock of sinners.

"You are determined to deliver yourself to me, Carson of Venus," he intoned, his hollow, otherworldly voice hoarse with emotion. "You escape from me at the outpost of our

Myposan vassals, you escape from one of my lanjotars and a squad of my troops, and yet now you come directly to Iralcus Iguiri of your own volition."

"You posed an intriguing mystery to me," I replied. "I guess I couldn't walk away without finding the answers."

"You have appeared most fittingly here in our holy temple above the shattered village of H'Kriani, just as we are about to begin our daily ceremony to honor the innocent Linneauns who died there at your hand. A coincidence perhaps, but I will take it as a sign." He motioned to his soldiers. "Lower your weapons, all of you."

"What sort of trick is this?" Ero Shan asked.

"No trick. You are safe here. We would not dream of killing you in the temple of our ancestors."

I wasn't reassured by his statement. Though my companions and I retained our weapons for now, we were surrounded by hundreds of armed enemy soldiers, and the fact that they weren't pointing their guns directly at us meant little. Plus, he hadn't said they didn't intend to kill us eventually—only that it wasn't going to happen here and now.

"At this moment," Iralcus continued, "thousands of my people are walking the halls around the base of the structure for the daily memorial observance. Should you wish to leave, you will have to make your way first through my soldiers gathered here, and then through the populace below. Each and every one of them would be proud to carry you from our sacred land and kill you elsewhere." The Linneauns around him murmured their agreement.

I squared my shoulders and gazed up at the creature who held all of our lives in the palm of his hand. "You claim that I am responsible for all of this," I said. "I want to know what you mean."

"I told you." Before Iralcus' voice had trembled with emotion. Now he spoke almost casually, as if lecturing a child. "Many years ago, your rocket fell from the clouds and crashed into my village. Naturally, we rushed to investigate this strange phenomenon. Something emanating from the crash site sickened us. Thousands of my people perished in the days and weeks that followed, and had I not raced to develop the apparatus that allows us to breathe, the rest would have died as well. Your name, Carson of Venus, will forever be celebrated as that of the man who brought my people out of isolation and ruin, the man who gave us the tools for greatness." He paused. "Just as it will forever be condemned as that of the demon who brought murder and despair among us. This is true now and it will be true until the end of the Great Voyage. Now drop your weapons and come with me, if you wish to look upon the depths of the injury you visited upon the Linneaun people before you meet your fate.

I turned to regard my little band of companions and the circle of giant warriors surrounding them. Duare and I looked into each other's eyes for a long moment. Then, with a shrug, I lowered my weapons to the floor.

15

EXHIBIT OF DEATH

RALCUS MOTIONED ME toward the towering doors and the two of us left the enormous room. We walked unaccompanied down a stark hallway that smelled of fresh soap and something akin to bleach. There were no doors on either side of us, though a large one loomed ahead. I watched Iralcus as he walked, gauging his limp and wondering how quick he was. Perhaps I could outrun him if I needed to. His steps were short, and he seemed almost elderly with his hobbling gait.

"What are you thinking, Carson of Venus?" Iralcus asked. Do you hope that once we are alone you can overpower me and free your friends?"

"Just wondering why you don't just get it over with," I lied. "You already said you want me dead."

We had almost reached the door at the end of the corridor before he spoke again. "I know you have been considering the outcome of a fight between the two of us since you laid eyes on me. You are confident you can win." Iralcus laughed. "You are wrong. I have survived this long without falling to my challengers. You certainly are no threat." He turned the handle and pulled open the door. "Why have I not killed you? Because I need you to see and to understand the magnitude of your crimes against the Linneaun people before you die."

We entered a large room bustling with activity. Dozens of Linneauns moved around tables, huddled near workstations. In front of them lay a long line of half-assembled helmets.

159

The workers reached into nearby bins, pulled out filters, and snapped them into the helmets before stacking them on carts nearby. It took a moment or two for them to notice our presence. Then the production halted as they each dropped to one knee and looked away from their leader. Iralcus continued without a word to his people, leading me up a set of four wide steps that brought us to another door. "Here we are." He pushed the door open and waited for me to enter.

In typical Linneaun fashion, the chamber was beyond spacious and contained nothing but a large display in the center. Even from half the room away, I recognized the object on display: it was my old torpedo, the craft that had originally brought me to this planet. Most of it had been skillfully reassembled, but I also noted a collection of miscellaneous parts that lay strewn about the area. I saw bolts and jagged sections of metal on the floor, bits that likely didn't fit anywhere precisely. The front of the torpedo was the most severely damaged, with a good half of the cockpit exposed, and the main control board only partially intact.

"You recognize it, yes?"

"Of course I do. I built it." I couldn't help but quicken my step as I approached my faithful craft, displayed here like a museum piece with its guts hanging out for all to see. Some sort of translucent protective coating encased it.

Iralcus nodded and walked around the display. "You built it. You flew it. You jumped out of it. You let it fall without a thought. You killed my people." His voice faltered and he made another sound then, as if he were on the verge of choking. When the moment passed, he pointed to the craft. "Killed them with this. But we are Linneauns and so we did not merely curse our fate and bury our dead. No, we tore this monstrosity apart and learned from it. We learned your..." He was flustered, searching for a word. "...means to make it move, we figured out your methods for guidance, your air tanks...all of the science of it. And then we figured out how to make this alien abomination work on Amtor. Everything you see, right down to this building, has been made with your science."

"You speak of science," I said, "so let me do the same. You told me earlier that something leaking from my ship poisoned your people and made them fall ill. That makes no sense. My rocket's propellant should not have had that effect. Besides, it was almost completely exhausted, burned up upon takeoff. There would have been only trace amounts—"

"Silence!" Iralcus screamed. "Your race knows nothing of Linneaun biology and how it was affected by the noxious emissions. Only the providential discovery of the long-hidden archives of the Ancients just prior to your rocket's crash permitted me to develop the breathing apparatus that saved my people."

I wondered if Iralcus could be right after all. The Linneauns seemed to be entirely unrelated to any other form of life I had heretofore run across on Amtor. Could the trace elements of my torpedo's propellant have been so noxious to their kind that it had reacted to their strange biology in the manner of a highly infectious disease? Had I truly been to blame for unleashing a plague that had wiped out so many?

A cold chill ran down my spine as I stood there, considering Iralcus' words and my possible guilt in the tragedy that had struck the Linneauns. Looming over us as if in silent testimony to my captor's accusations was the great torpedo that had carried me to Amtor. The rocket and its sudden reappearance in my life transfixed me. Staring up at the old crate, as my friend Jimmy Welsh had affectionately called my torpedo, I could almost feel the cushions of the seat beneath me during that fateful flight. Vividly, I relived the feelings of dread that had coursed through me as I watched helplessly while the pull of the moon drew me inexorably out into the vastness of space, there to die, as I fully expected, a slow and solitary death.

"You made this death for my people," Iralcus said, "and then provided the means for those of us who survived it to prevail as a species! From your ship we created missiles and bombs and guns. We had none of that before. Your onboard library and the illustrated primer proved most useful, as well."

"You found the primer," I said, suddenly understanding how deeply the discovery of my ship must have affected the Linneauns. When I had left Earth for Mars, I had taken with me a hundred or more highly specialized textbooks that encapsulated the most crucial innovations my world had achieved since the birth of civilization. Included among them were works on the science of rocketry and twentieth-century warfare. Though I had not believed I would ever return from the Red Planet, I had brought with me the information required to construct another torpedo, should it ever prove necessary. And should I not return, I believed it might serve me in good stead on a world named after the god of war to be able to recreate the most powerful weaponry of my own planet.

Included in my library was an exhaustive pictorial primer that a linguist friend of mine, a fair genius of a man, had developed for the self-teaching of written English to an inhabitant of another world—Mars, in this case—who knew not a word of the language. This primer was meant to serve as a sort of skeleton key to my library—and Iralcus had found and used it to his own ends.

"My people are a highly imitative race." Iralcus pointed to the torpedo. "Before this thing crashed down from the clouds, we were craven pacifists, cowering from our enemies in our hidden settlement. In only two decades, we went from fearing the world outside to conquering it with war machines the likes of which Amtor has never before seen."

"Science is what you make of it," I said evenly. "As is life itself. You could have found a way to use the advanced knowledge in that ship for something positive. You could have made your nation a world leader in science and technology, rather than twisting the information into a means to conquer those weaker than yourselves."

He gave an unpleasant laugh. "Oh, Carson of Venus. How surprisingly naive you are! You've been on this planet a good long time; you know how it works. No one here helps anyone else. Alliances are short, but fear is something that takes root and grows."

"You could have changed all that. You still can."

"I would think you would have learned better by now." He motioned me away from my torpedo. "Come. Let me show you something else." I trailed behind as he strode toward the doorway, taking one last glance over my shoulder at my creation.

"Do you ever wish you still had that craft? I mean, the functioning version—all shiny and waiting? Would you have used it to go home by now? Do you miss your planet? These are things I wondered about you." We walked down the stairs, back to the outer assembly room. "It must be difficult being so far from home."

"I have my moments," I said. "Sometimes I miss the short ribs and lima beans at Johnson's on Central in Hollywood so much I can't stand it. Back in my movie days I spent many a lunch break there. In all honesty, after all my years on Amtor, I would settle for the cold ham sandwich from Woolworths. But most of the time I'm just fine."

"Every word you just spoke is utter gibberish to me." He turned and moved for a different set of doors from the ones through which we had entered. As he spread them wide, I found myself shielding my eyes from the blaze of light beyond. We passed outside onto an open-air balcony, which I estimated was on the opposite side of the building from where my companions and I had entered the immense structure.

Iralcus walked to the edge of the balcony and leaned out over the railing. I joined him there and looked down on what he had been so eager to show me: a huge tower that rose out of the foot of the mountains, alongside which loomed a single massive torpedo, secured at the top by a metallic arm and walkway. Aside from the fact that it stood upright rather than resting on its belly on a mile-long track, the thing was a dead ringer for the torpedo I had constructed back on Earth. The body, the placement of the engines, everything about it mirrored the torpedo on display just a few rooms away. Near the gleaming rocket, a second tower seemed to be in the early stages of construction. Dozens of Linneauns swarmed around the structure like ants acting as one entity.

I thought back to Duare's question: Would I go back to Earth if the opportunity presented itself? The means to do just that now stood in front of me. In that moment, I knew for certain that it was an opportunity I would never willingly choose to take. Venus was my home now. Here I had lived a life like no other inhabitant of Earth could imagine and here I would die.

"Planning a trip into the fires surrounding Amtor, Iralcus?" I asked.

The Linneaun turned and gazed at me through the two black half orbs of his helmet. "Because I have read your books, I know that the flames beyond Amtor are just a myth. Do not rule out that after I conquer this world, I shall cross the void of space and subjugate yours. No, Carson, this torpedo is not a rocket ship, and you will never go back to the world that is your home. What stands before you is exactly what I have called it: a torpedo. That is, a missile. But a missile armed with a warhead unlike any you have ever dreamed of, thanks to the knowledge I have recovered from the archives of the Ancients."

I suddenly felt cold all over. "Explain."

A hollow, haunting laugh came from beneath Iralcus' helmet. "You think your anotar is a marvel of modern in-novation, what with its engine powered by the annihilation of the substance lor by applying the element vik-ro upon the element yor-san. The annihilation of lor in such a manner releases a tremendous amount of energy. I think you are intelligent enough to realize there are other uses for such a release of energy besides powering an engine."

I shook my head, not quite sure what to say. "You're telling me this torpedo is armed and ready?"

"Most assuredly."

"You're mad, Iralcus," I said. "You'll never succeed! Amtor is a far bigger place than you can imagine. Once they get wind of your plans, its people will band together and wipe your soldiers from the face of the planet."

Iralcus nodded thoughtfully, his expression hidden behind the helmet. "Korva will be the first to go," he said, "not because of its military strength, though it has become mighty indeed under your advisement, but because it is dearest to you. Then we will strike Havatoo, and one by one the nations will fall before the Iralcus Iguiri." He gave a short laugh and turned, pushing me ahead of him back toward the door.

Before we made it to the entryway, I caught a flicker of motion from the corner of my eye. Once more I thought I saw something moving on the horizon—a black dot, maybe two? Iralcus shoved me through the door and back inside.

We made our way in silence back to the enormous room in which we had left my companions. I was alarmed to find them on their knees in front of a group of Linneauns whose banded bodies were painted white. These warriors held immense axes at their sides.

Iralcus pushed me forward to join the others. "By your association with Carson of Venus," he proclaimed, "you are all judged compliant in his crimes. You may not have been in the evil device that devastated my people, but you are all guilty and will face the same fate." Iralcus pointed to the white-stained creatures behind the group. "These are the Sarn, the Keepers of the Law. Now, go with them away from this sacred place and meet death at their hands."

Axes raised, the members of the Sarn advanced toward us. At that moment, an uncanny whine like that of a great swarm of angry hornets began to resonate through the chamber. I turned my head to see an anotar, brightly painted in the colors of Havatoo, racing straight for the building. Behind it a squadron of similar ships streaked into view.

"Everyone get down!" I cried to my companions. I dropped to the ground just as a brilliant flash of light filled the enormous window before me. The floor shook beneath our feet as a tremendous explosion rocked the building.

16
TRUTH AND LIES

THE LINNEAUNS WERE COMPLETELY unprepared for the attack, and a good many of them were hurled to the floor as the building shook violently, among them all but one of the members of the axe-wielding Keepers of the Law. The Linneauns' bulky armor made it difficult for them to regain their feet, leaving most to lie flailing on their backs like inverted turtles.

I pulled Duare to her feet. "Let's go!" Wasting no time, we snatched up what weapons we could before our enemies regained their composure.

I immediately lunged at the single Sarn who had remained standing. My long dagger missed its target and glanced off the creature's armorlike bands. It was quick to respond, hefting its axe high and slicing downward with it, narrowly missing me. Its move gave me the opening I needed, and before the Linneaun could raise its heavy axe and make a second swing, my dagger had sunk deep into the skin between its bands. I shoved away the corpse as Haln appropriated the mighty battle-axe that dropped from the creature's lifeless hands.

Before we could decide on an escape route, the elevator opened again and several dozen Linneaun warriors pounded into the room. I was distracted from the chaos within the chamber as motion outside once again caught my eye and a pair of anotars painted in the colors of Havatoo streaked past the great window. As they dived out of sight, several more explosions rocked the building.

"What is this?" Iralcus shouted. "Get me an update!" One of his soldiers raced to the elevator, no doubt off to assess the situation, as Iralcus himself stomped to the window and pounded the glass with an immense fist. "The Myposans? Yron dares treachery against me?"

I pressed my nose against the same glass several yards away to get my own update on what was going on outside. Iralcus was right. Below us and just offshore, a small fleet of hundred-foot-long Myposan biremes cut through the waters. In the air above them, most of the anotars bore the colors of Havatoo, though I also caught sight of a handful that were unmistakably part of the fleet I maintained for Korva. Smaller boats rode the waves, darting back and forth among the larger vessels.

I looked over from the window to find Iralcus staring in my direction. "Get Carson Napier, now!" He pointed a long, crooked finger in my direction. Two of his white-painted guards moved toward me, their axes gleaming under the room's bright lights.

Iralcus followed, stooping to grab an axe from the warrior I'd slain. He swung and missed me, slamming a fist against the window in rage. "You have brought these armies here to defeat me, but I will slay them all. Iralcus Iguiri will be triumphant." He swung the weapon again.

I thrust my short sword for the seams of his hard shell. Before I could even tell if I had connected, Iralcus' enormous arm slammed into my chest, knocking the air from my lungs and sending me reeling to the ground.

A new series of explosions rattled the titanic building and the sky outside lit up with flashes of fire. Iralcus continued toward me, axe at the ready. "Our cannons are even now answering the overtures of the traitorous gnats outside, and you, Carson, are finished here."

"This is not over, Iralcus." I brought my sword across the front of his head, leaving a deep scratch in the glass of one of his eye coverings. "We are not done fighting."

The Linneaun leader stepped back, swiping my weapon away. "You are deluded, Carson of Venus. This treachery is an unexpected turn, but in the end it will serve only to hasten our spread across Amtor."

Briefly, I wondered what Iralcus meant when he spoke of treachery. Of course, I knew the Myposans had struck a deal with the devil, one that Yron later lamented. Had the Havatooans also initially joined the Linneauns' cause, only later to change their minds and broker an alliance with Korva and Mypos?

Just then, an explosion of incredible proportions filled the window as one of the Linneaun cannons below discharged and an anotar took a direct hit. Iralcus gave a great roar of triumph as the doomed craft split in two and erupted in a ball of flames. Continuing on their trajectory, the fiery pieces crashed through the long window before us. As shattered glass flew through the huge room, the two flaming sections of the aeroplane spun across the floor on either side of us, plowing through the mass of confused Linneaun soldiers. A crack formed in the transparent floor under one section of the wreckage and began to creep toward where I stood. I watched in horror as more fissures shot out from the larger one and snaked toward other areas of the room.

Utter chaos filled the chamber. I searched desperately for my scattered companions through the sudden veil of smoke and fire. A group of ten enemy warriors had surrounded Haln and Duh-nee; now they stood frozen in their tracks in the face of this massive change of fortune. Duare and the Sarn soldier had continued their duel during the explosion, but the Linneauns near Ero Shan and Nalte turned tail and ran for the exits when flaming debris from the crash tumbled near them. Unfortunately, the elevators were still in service: for every Linneaun that fled or stood immobilized by shock, five more poured into the room.

I was racing to assist Duare in her battle with the giant warrior when Iralcus Iguiri emerged from the swirling haze of smoke that was rapidly filling the chamber. Fire and ash blackened his armored bands, but he advanced without the appearance of concern. The black smoke rippled off him as he stepped from the fiery mess. Each step of his large feet seemed to hasten the floor cracks that still moved in our direction.

"Stop!" I shouted. "This is a grand fight we have going on here, but if you advance any farther, you'll shatter this floor and hurl us both to our deaths." He continued forward as if he hadn't heard me, one heavy step after another. I looked to the broad strip of white rock that encircled the room, hoping it would be sturdier than the glasslike material that composed the floor.

At that moment, the whole building seemed to shake. There came a tremendous cracking sound, and the section of the flooring upon which I stood lurched down several feet with a sickening screech. I flung myself to one side and grabbed a thick section of the clear floor, holding on with one hand as I watched the great chunk of glass upon which I had just been standing twist and turn on the way to the ground far below.

Fingers bleeding, I clutched the sharp edges in order to keep myself from following the broken section down. The sounds of combat around me fell away until I heard nothing but my own breathing, ragged and desperate, fearing the slightest breeze would cause my fragile handhold to break free.

Iralcus Iguiri loomed suddenly above me. His thick talon-like toes hung just over the edge of the broken glass on either side of my clinging hands, and I could see the great battle-axe poised to swing down and end my life.

"Death is almost too good for you after the sacrilege you have brought to this holy place," Iralcus intoned. "I should have your skin flayed from your body and slowly roasted over the Flame of the Ancients."

"You don't have to go out of your way," I said with more bravado than I really felt. "Perhaps some other time?"

Iralcus drew his arms back, axe raised to crash down on my head, when suddenly he recoiled as a chunk of debris came out of nowhere to crash against the faceplate of his helmet.

I managed to crane my neck to look behind me and saw Duare and Ero Shan across the great chasm at the edge of the broken floor, furiously hurling hunks of glass and anotar parts at the Linneaun leader. I could have cheered at the sight!

Iralcus quickly regained his footing. Batting away the fragments of debris with one hand as if they were flies, he returned his attention to the matter at hand—that is to say, ending my life.

"Wasted effort, human," he snarled. "You will never—"

I heard a great cracking noise. Then the floor beneath Iralcus suddenly gave way, plunging the two of us into the open air and toward the village hundreds of feet below. For the briefest of moments, I saw Iralcus hurtling through the air some distance from me, looking like nothing so much as an armadillo curled up into an almost perfectly spherical ball. Then I closed my eyes and pictured Duare in my mind, knowing it would be the last mortal thought I ever had.

Half a second later, I felt something warm wrap itself around me, and instantly my whole body seemed lighter and my descent slowed. I opened my eyes and looked up into the face of an angan.

"I am Breemak the Swift," said my unexpected savior. "And I have arrived just in time to—*whoa.*" We dropped faster for a few seconds and I could feel Breemak's muscles shake as he strained to maintain his grip on me while preventing the two of us from slamming into the rapidly approaching ground. "Ready yourself," he said. "I'm going to let go."

The angan released me and I fell free for a moment before I crashed into one of the thatched huts. The roof slowed my fall as I passed through it, but the impact still knocked the wind from me. I landed on my stomach after breaking through some hammock-type bedding. The floor was mostly dirt and rock, and felt cold against my face.

I made a half-hearted effort to rise to my feet. I wanted to lie there and recover from the vast assortment of cuts, contusions, scrapes, and bruises I had acquired over the past few days. Finally, I forced myself to roll over. I surveyed the room in which I had landed. Aside from the hammock I had crashed through, I could see a few basic items: a pitcher, a couple of containers, a chest with tools on top, and some rags.

I was about to call out for Breemak when Iralcus' voice sounded from somewhere outside the hut.

"Your little angan friend saved your life, Carson Napier." His voice sounded weaker than before. "Carson of Venus. Murderer. Pariah of Amtor." He broke off into a fit of coughing. "Where are you, Carson?"

I marveled that he had survived the fall of several hundred feet without the aid of an angan, especially since he had already sustained several wounds. I remembered the sight of him curled into a ball as we both fell. Maybe when a Linneaun assumed such a defensive form, its banded armor plating rendered it nearly indestructible?

"You're alone now, Iralcus," I said, my own voice sounding weary. "Your painted soldiers aren't here to help you. Call this off before I have to destroy you." I had no idea how to back up that kind of talk, here in a broken-down grass hut in the middle of my enemy's territory, with an entire army of indestructible armadillos waiting in the wings and a huge building about to collapse on top of my head. But I would find a way. I pushed some rusty tools off the top of the nearby chest and pried it open.

"Call it off?" Iralcus sounded nearer now. I could hear his halting footsteps not far from the hut. "This is not a petty quarrel between two kazars over scraps of food. We cannot just walk away and have done with it."

"I'd be okay with that at this point," I said reasonably, hoping to stall him long enough to find something useful. "If you just want to open the doors, my friends and I will walk away." The tools in the chest were bigger than I was used to, owing to the Linneaun's larger stature, but I pulled out two thick stone hammers and felt their heft in my hands. "I mean you did say you would rather not kill me on your sacred land."

The wall behind me exploded as Iralcus ran through it, the momentum of his charge carrying us both straight through the far wall. For a moment we both lay on the ground in the center of the village. Iralcus recovered first and heaved back onto his feet. His helmet was gone, probably shattered in the fall.

For the first time, I looked on the face of Iralcus Iguiri.

It was an unremarkable face. He looked much like the other Linneaun I'd seen without his helmet in the forest, though Iralcus was obviously considerably older. His long, pointed face was lined with a scrub of white hair on each side along his jawline. A similar stripe ran from just above his eyes all the way back to the collar that pointed up from behind his head.

It took me a moment to realize that, unlike the fallen Linneaun in the forest, Iralcus had gone on breathing—though admittedly with some effort—after the destruction of his own helmet. Squinting, I made out what looked to be tiny filaments leading into his nostrils from larger tubes rooted in a small pack affixed to the back of his short neck.

"You still have a chance to make good on that impulse not to kill me on sacred ground," I said, from where I lay nursing my new bruises on the rocky ground. "We can walk out of here like sensible folks and talk about how my people and yours can get along."

"You want to know about my people?" Iralcus asked. "My father lived in a hut just like this one. He worked in the mountains, clearing rock and debris so our village could push farther inland and keep our people safe from the ocean storms." The Linneaun leader bent down and picked up a long-handled piece of equipment similar to the small hammers I still clutched. I couldn't tell if it was made to be a weapon or a tool, but the rock at the end was nearly half as big as I was. "My father broke great boulders with a grirwar just like this day after day. Used it to kill wild tharbans that attacked him as he worked. Many an enemy felt its wrath, as well. He didn't need rockets and rays to make his way, and he certainly never needed a helmet on his head just to survive." It took some effort, but Iralcus hefted the large weapon up and held it with both hands. "But you took that away. Your arrogance killed him and so many of our people…"

"I didn't know where the rocket would land, and I didn't know anyone lived on this planet. If I truly wronged you and your people, let me make amends and help you."

"Ignorance, then? Your ignorance killed many of my people. And if I hadn't stepped in to lead them, your ignorance would have killed my entire race."

"Lies! You lie to Carson of Venus just as you lie to your people!" The source of the exclamation was hard to pinpoint, for above the eternal gray skies of Venus, the sun had passed beyond the towering cliffs against which the dead village nestled, casting the whole scene about us in an eerie gloom.

"Who dares speak to me that way?" Iralcus peered into the murk, his thin mouth stretched back in a sneer. "I will kill you for that."

I heard the rustling of dry grass behind me and turned to see another Linneaun. It was shorter than the other soldiers I had seen by about two feet. On its arm it wore a band identical to the one Iralcus bore, only this one was yellow and caked in dust. "I know full well what you did, Iralcus. I was there."

"Salde? You are not worthy to speak to me in that tone. I should kill you where you stand."

"I am the leader of all builders," Salde said, "your equal in all things."

"You lead the women, good only for creating. You are not the equal of any warrior." Iralcus turned his gaze back to me.

"Yes, I am a woman, but there is no difference between

the builders and the soldiers," Salde said. "Soldier is an artificial caste you invented to consolidate your power. Power that you unlawfully seized by fabricating the lie that this human's craft poisoned our people, and that only you had the cure to save them. You know as well as I that Linneaun means Builder in the old tongue! We are all builders, the perfect workers: tireless and nearly indestructible. We were grown in the vats of the Ancients to serve them. So it says in the sacred archives of the Ancients—those who created us to excavate their massive tunnels, which you have appropriated for your own malevolent ends."

"You are the one who lies," Iralcus said, but something in his rough, hollow voice sounded uncertain. "No one is permitted into the sacred archives but me. You could not know what the records say."

"Not all Linneauns are loyal to you," Salde said. "Even among the soldiers, there are those who question the dangerous direction in which you have been leading our people. I have indeed been to the sacred archives, while you were busy with your war, and it was there that I discovered the truth."

"What are you saying?" I exclaimed. "That my torpedo was not responsible for the disaster that befell Linnea?"

"The poison did not come from your rocket, Carson of Venus." Salde stepped forward, raised her strange, double-jointed arm, and pointed a long, crooked finger at Iralcus. "No, it came from your resurrection of the forbidden knowledge of the Ancients, Iralcus Iguiri—the very knowledge that nearly destroyed them. You caused this calamity, with your experiments to weaponize the action of vik-ro upon the substance yor-san, resulting in the utter annihilation of the substance lor in which the yor-san is found. Instead of simply releasing the energy from the destruction of lor, as these humans have done to power the engines of their flying machines, sea vessels, and lantars, you used the knowledge of the Ancients to bond the active elements with a gas. You, Iralcus, poisoned our people, creating the disease that spread among us when the gas leaked from your laboratory. But the timely crash of this human's rocket on the edge of our settlement only days before the accident provided a convenient scapegoat. You blamed it on the one you call 'the Carson' and said the gas leaked from his ship. And then, only days later, you provided the 'cure'—the masks in which we are all now imprisoned—and set yourself up as the savior of Linnea."

"Lies," said Iralcus calmly, but I saw the long fingers of his hands curl up into fists that shook with rage.

"I watched from the next room," Salde continued. "I saw the reaction when you bonded the elements, and witnessed the smoke and green haze that hissed out of the great tanks in your lab immediately afterward. You ran from the room, enveloped in the poisonous cloud. While you fled for safety, more of that gas poured from the room, and out through the roof. It spread so quickly that no one could avoid it."

Iralcus brought the massive grirwar up to point it at her. "Silence. You know nothing. Return to the factories and await my punishment."

"You hastened the death of so many, including your own father," Salde said. "In your haste to get away from what you'd done, you carried traces of it with you. You brought your father's death to him as you begged him for help."

I had risen to my feet when Salde appeared. Now I backed away from both of the Linneauns, suddenly wondering if I had already exposed myself to the infectious gas.

"Do not worry," Salde said to me, seeing my action. "It does not affect your species—only Linneauns."

"I said, silence!" Iralcus swung his grirwar then, missing Salde by mere inches and stumbling under the weight of the weapon.

I ran to Salde's side. The instinct to protect is a natural one, but I had a moment's surprise when I realized that it was a Linneaun that had aroused it in me. I had experienced the same brief struggle between sympathy and animosity in the forest when the soldier's helmet had broken off.

Grunting under the strain, Iralcus lifted his mighty weapon again. The hammers I held suddenly seemed inadequate.

I stepped in front of Salde. "Iralcus!" I called out. "Why do your men die without their headgear, while you survive?" I hoped to draw Iralcus back into the conversation and thus avoid getting my head split open.

"He gets all the newest developments," Salde answered for him. "The soldiers are lucky if they get fresh filters for their helmets."

The grirwar swung through the air, so close I could feel its wind on my face. "Stop talking!" Iralcus screeched. Dropping his cudgel, he darted past me in a sudden fury and swung out with a massive fist, knocking Salde heavily to the ground as I stumbled back.

Though the hammers were awkward to wield, I struck back with one and then another. Both scored hits but bounced harmlessly off his unyielding frame.

I swung again with all my might, this time targeting his head. My blow landed with a thud and Iralcus cried out in pain. I swung again, hitting him in nearly the same spot. Emboldened, I pressed my advantage and struck him a third time.

Iralcus dropped to his knees. I heard the dry grass rustling behind us and turned to see three of the white-painted Linneauns running toward me. I helped Salde to her feet. "Is there any way you can stop them?" I asked her.

"They won't listen to me," Salde said. "They are Iralcus' guard. But I will certainly try to fend them off while you kill him."

"Kill him?" I asked.

"It is the only way. So long as he lives, his warriors will do what he wants them to. Only a new leader can hope to change things."

I looked down at Iralcus. He was bleeding from several

spots on his head, but still struggled to rise. The hammers in my hands suddenly felt even heavier than they had earlier. "I can't do that. He's helpless."

The pale guards reached Salde and she blocked two, while the other managed to get around her and race for me. While I engaged my attacker, Iralcus lurched to his feet and half ran, half stumbled off in the direction from which his guards had appeared. I wanted to shout, to make him stop somehow. As much as I couldn't bring myself to kill him when he was down, I was certain that once he made it back to his people, he would be virtually impossible to catch again.

As Iralcus reached the tall grass, a shrill cry brought my attention to a lone figure perched atop one of the nearby huts. Breemak spread his leathery wings and launched himself like an arrow up into the air, swerved abruptly, and shot down toward the Linneaun leader. The bird-man's brief flight ended as his taloned feet thudded into Iralcus' back, knocking him over onto the grass. Breemak clawed at the Linneaun's un-protected face as the latter's screams filled the air.

Iralcus swiped at Breemak with a thick arm, knocking him aside. He stood and the two faced off, both obviously injured and struggling to keep standing.

The white-painted guards abandoned Salde and me, rushing to defend their leader.

"Breemak!" I shouted. "There are more coming your way."

Realizing that he would be gravely outnumbered, the angan leaped into the air and glided out of reach just as the guards arrived at Iralcus' side.

With a shoulder under each of the struggling Linneaun's arms, the white guards dragged him off and out of sight into the ruins of the dead town.

I caught up with Breemak as he landed with a thump on the ground and crumpled into a heap. "Are you all right, my friend?"

The angan looked up at me. "I am in some good amount of pain. How much pain are you in? I am likely in more."

His wing looked worse than it had before, and he had sustained several other injuries from the fall and his valiant fight. "You did well," I said. "You saved my life." I lifted him onto his quaking legs and supported him at my side as we waited for Salde to join us.

"You should have killed Iralcus," she panted, sounding puzzled. "He would not have hesitated to do the same to you."

"You could have killed him?" Breemak looked at me in surprise. "That would have made things a lot easier."

I supposed neither of them were wrong, but I could not kill Iralcus in cold blood. I was not a monster like he was. I would either bring him to trial for what he'd done, or I would wait for another chance to decide things in a fair fight.

"Where is he going?" I asked Salde.

"I do not know," she replied. "The doors lead to the inner hallways, and he can go wherever he wants from there."

As we made our way out of the dead village, I looked up at the ceiling so high above us and wondered how my friends were faring. It had been utter chaos when I fell through the floor. I only hoped they could hold their own until help came.

"You are concerned for your companions?" Salde asked. "My people are there to help them."

"I thought Iralcus said your people were builders, not warriors?"

Salde gave a snort of laughter. "And who do you think builds the weapons that the soldiers utilize in their conquests? The builders, no?"

We made it through the doors and found the hall beyond was nearly empty, making it easy to spot Iralcus and his men just before they disappeared through another door on the far wall.

"That tunnel leads outside to the rocket launcher," Salde replied to my inquiring glance.

"The rocket equipped with the yor-san warhead?"

"Yes," she said, her voice thick with concern. "If they reach it, it may be the end of everything."

17

TORPEDO OR BUST

WE STOOD IN THE DOORWAY and stared down the tunnel where Iralcus and his soldiers had disappeared into the darkness moments before. "Is there anything else out there?" I asked.

Salde shook her head. "No. It is an enclosed area, surrounded by mountains. Iralcus could not get out of there without climbing out, and no Linneaun has ever tried that."

"So, either he's trapped," I said, "or he's desperate enough to try to fly the rocket out of there." There was a third possibility. Maddened by the realization that his long-awaited victory might now be out of reach forever—not to mention his failure to accomplish the death of the one person he hated most on Amtor—would the Linneaun dictator use the rocket's deadly warhead to wreak as much havoc on the planet as he could before going out in a blaze of destruction? I pushed through the doors, cautious to make sure no one was lying in wait for us. As we moved farther down the passage, we came upon a dead Linneaun guard, with a thin, pick-like dagger in his chest.

"Did Iralcus kill one of his own men? And if so, why?" Salde asked. "It makes no sense."

"No," Breemak said. "I think I recognize that weapon." He looked at me for a moment. "It is of Samary craftsmanship."

"You think Duh-nee and Haln have been here?" I asked.

"I've seen the little one use these," he replied, "and I hope the woman is with him, because it could be a rough time for him alone against Iralcus' guards."

"Duh-nee is clever," I said. "He wouldn't take on more than he could handle." I hoped it was true.

We pushed on until we reached an iron door. "This heavy portal," Salde said, "was created to keep any debris or flames out of the tunnel after the rocket's engines ignite. Beyond it is the launch area."

"I've been meaning to ask what kind of propellant Iralcus' rockets use," I said, recalling the mystery Ero Shan and I had discussed earlier. "The torpedo-cars don't seem to use the fuel that I employed in my interplanetary rocket."

"The smaller missiles used a liquid propellant just as your old rocket," Salde replied, "as it is simply more practical. But the larger torpedoes, such as those in the tunnel and the one outside for which we are headed, are propelled by the annihilation of yor-san. They are a hybrid of your ship's design and the lost science of the Ancients."

That made sense. Iralcus had found a way to power a rocket much more economically and efficiently than my terrestrial torpedo. It also made his innovation much more powerful, to such a degree as to threaten the current balance of power on Amtor. The horrifying thought strengthened my resolve. We could not let Iralcus escape.

Breemak looked pitiful, bleeding from several wounds and limping on his short, stocky legs. "You should stay behind," I said. "You look terrible."

"If only you could see yourself," the angan said. It was clear he was determined to remain at my side.

"Salde," I said, "you at least should consider staying. If you are the leader of the workers, we need you alive at the end of this."

Before she could refute my logic, angry voices and the stomp of Linneaun feet filled the hall. At least a dozen soldiers flooded through the door at the far end, blocking off our only means of retreat. "That settles that argument," Salde said.

"I guess so." I grabbed the handle of the large metal door and turned it. My companions helped pull it open and we ran outside to the launch area. Here the great torpedo and the giant tower at its side stood surrounded by rock walls and charred ground. At the tower's base, as we had guessed, Duh-nee fought with a group of Iralcus' white guards. But to my surprise, he stood back to back with Duare rather than his powerful mate.

I ran headlong toward the embattled pair, hoping to aid Duare and the diminutive Samary before they were over-powered. Shouts came from behind us as the Linneauns pursuing us reached the iron door. At Salde's urging, we had barricaded the door behind us with some pieces of discarded metal we encountered on the other side. We knew it wouldn't hold for long, but at least it might buy us some time to help our friends.

I surprised one of the white guards, slamming into him with all my momentum and knocking him into the base of the stairs that led into the launch tower. "Duare," I panted. "I am so glad to see you safe!"

"Carson!" She seemed equally relieved at the sight of me. "Safe is perhaps an exaggeration, but at least we are alive. I would give you a proper embrace, but..." Duare continued to swing her sword against the warriors that had all but surrounded her and Duh-nee. "My hands are quite full."

The ground around the rocket and tower was littered with scraps of metal that had spilled from crushed and broken crates. As they reached us, Salde and Breemak each chose something roughly dagger-shaped with a sharp point; they combined forces to engage a burly soldier who couldn't decide which of them presented the greatest danger. Scooping up a heavy bar caked with rust, I proceeded to bring it down on the helmet of the nearest guard. The material parted with a satisfying crack and the Linneaun fell to the ground. "Did you see where Iralcus went?" I panted to Duare as we turned to the next in line.

A few feet away, Duh-nee dodged blows and jabbed at the soldiers with his own thin blades. "I last saw him climbing the stairs inside the tower," he called out, then shouted in triumph as his dagger scored a hit and slipped to deadly effect between a Linneaun's armored bands.

"We have to stop him!" I gazed up at the enormous rocket, a titanic spire that pierced the gray clouded sky.

The others had gradually made their way to our side. At my signal, we ducked through the tower door and found ourselves at the foot of a spiral stairwell that must lead up to the rocket's control room. As the soldiers attempted to follow us through the narrow doorway, we maneuvered ourselves so that one or two of us could keep them at bay long enough for the rest to start the upward climb. Duare led the way, followed by Salde and then Breemak, who soon abandoned climbing the steps in his limping gait in favor of spreading his tattered wings to flap upward five or six at a time. Duh-nee was next and I went up last, stepping back from the door just in time to block the longsword of the nearest attacker at the expense of my makeshift weapon. A blow from the Linneaun cracked it in half and I dropped it. With a cry of satisfaction, the fellow leaped onto the stairs at my heels and charged up at me.

Duh-nee was climbing directly above me. He took in the onrushing warrior with a quick glance back over his shoulder. Then, squeezing past me on the narrow stairway, he darted out with his thin knife and scored a fatal blow between the soldier's bands. The massive corpse rolled down several steps, temporarily blocking any further pursuit from below.

We took advantage of the brief respite to race up the stairway toward the distant nose of the rocket. Above, heavy footsteps echoed on metal, suggesting that Iralcus was not far ahead of us. Steadying myself against the tower wall, I hurried up after the others. At one point, my palm slid through a patch of sticky dark blood. Perhaps Iralcus was more gravely injured than I had realized.

"How did the two of you get out here?" I called to Duare as we climbed. "And where are the others?"

We came looking for you," Duare told me. "We decided to split up in order to cover more ground and convene in an hour's time back near the elevators. Duh-nee and I were exploring down here and became trapped when Iralcus and his men came through the passage."

"Do you know what's become of the others?"

She shook her head. "They were fine, if exhausted, when we separated. I can only hope they remained so."

A hoarse shout above us heralded a sudden burst of pistol fire, as bright beams stabbed at the walls around us.

"They know we're here!" I cried. "Get as far away from the wall as you can." The spiraling stairs offered little cover. We had to hope the shooter would be unable to get a good angle on us while both parties continued to climb. "Duare, Duh-nee—do either of you have a gun?"

"I don't use those devices," Duh-nee said. "And sadly, I am down to only…" He took time to carefully count his weapons before he went on. "Three. Down to three of my own blades."

"They took everything I had when they initially caught us back in the building." Duare waved her sword around. "I'm afraid this is all that's left."

We pressed on, sizzling blasts punctuating our ascent. When we finally neared the top, we found ourselves virtually pinned in the center of the stairwell. Each time we made a move upward our assailants fired at us. Several shots narrowly missed our heads and we drew back to confer. "What should we do now?" Duare said. "We can't survive a direct assault on them. They would cut us down before we made it two steps."

"I don't know," I said. "If Iralcus decides to send a few of them back down to pick us off, we'll be sunk." We all knew that in that event we would have little choice but to retreat the way we had just come—not an attractive option, given the contingent of soldiers that must still await us below.

Duh-nee had been staring thoughtfully at the metal helix of stairs above us and the area from which most of the Linneauns' pistol fire seemed to originate. "I'm going to try something," he said. "Hold on to each other and lean against that wall."

With no other plan in place, we did not question the Samary. Duare, Salde, Breemak, and I all locked arms and dug in our heels as we put all our weight against the area Duh-nee had indicated.

Grabbing my belt with one hand, Duh-nee leaned out suddenly into the open space in the middle of the stairs, nearly pulling me out with him. I braced myself against the others as he threw one of his blades with his free hand, sending it flashing upward to where our tormentor stood. There was a shout of surprise and then a series of rapid clanking sounds as the pistol fell down several turns of the spiral, and then silence. Peering out to see where it had landed below, I was amazed when Duh-nee pulled himself back into the stairwell, large pistol in hand

"That was an unbelievable hit!" Duare exclaimed.

"And an even more remarkable catch!" I added.

"Thank you," Duh-nee said, handing the weapon gingerly to me as if it smelled bad. I passed it along to Duare, who tucked it into her belt.

We continued up the stairs, cautiously at first, but then more confidently as we encountered no fire from above.

Nor was there anyone waiting for us when we stepped out onto the top level. Presumably the Linneaun gunman, now deprived of his weapon, had gone on to rejoin his fellows through the great hatch in the rocket's hull.

Duare and I cranked the wheel in the center of the wide door and pulled it slowly back to peer inside.

I could see that the interior of the ship had been redesigned to allow for a vertical liftoff and landing. I assumed, however, that just as with my torpedo, the hatch would grant us egress to a large storage compartment directly below the main cabin.

I paused briefly at the entrance to the great hatch, pondering the wisdom of what we were about to do. But there was nothing for it but to take our chances and go inside.

The ship began to tremble ominously the moment we stepped in. "He wouldn't really try to launch this monstrous thing, would he?" Duare asked.

I wasn't sure how to answer her. True, Iralcus would be a fool to launch himself in the torpedo if he'd truly weaponized it with the destructive power of the Ancients, but at this point I was coming to believe his desperation and hubris might drive him to do anything. Perhaps he felt confident he could launch and land the ship without detonating it. If so, he could escape and reformulate his plans, and then all life on Amtor would still lie at risk.

"Let's just make sure we get to him before he can make that decision," I said.

We climbed quietly one by one up the rung ladder to gather on the small landing outside the control room. We had agreed that Salde, Breemak, and Duh-nee would hang back until we were sure the coast was clear. I stepped through the hatch alongside Duare, who held our only long-range weapon at the ready.

Inside, Iralcus and two of his white guards huddled with their backs toward us over the control panel on the opposite wall.

I took a deep breath. "Stop this, Iralcus," I said evenly. "You're playing with something far more dangerous than fire. But there's still time to salvage something for the people you claim to love."

Iralcus slammed his fists on the console and spun around to glare at me in fury. I shuddered, imagining the consequences should one of those massive hands connect with the wrong switch. "You!" he shouted. "Always you! Kill them!"

The guards stepped forward to face us, one with pistol drawn, and the other holding a knife. I noticed a steady flow of dark blood dripping from the latter's free hand, presumably the result of Duh-nee's expert blade work in the stairwell.

The first soldier's gun was quivering as he leveled it in our direction. Duare regarded him coolly, her own weapon aimed at his head. "Their nerves are shot," I whispered to her. "We'd better—"

Then he opened fire. Luckily his aim was as bad as his nerves, and we were able to duck back into the cargo hold. We huddled with the others to one side of the open hatch.

"We may have to charge them," I said as deadly rays continued to blaze through the open doorway.

"Why? We have them trapped," said Duare. "The charges in his pistol won't last forever and the other one has only a knife. They won't dare try to leave as long as they think we might have weapons. They don't even know how many of us are here. Ero Shan and the rest are bound to find us before long, and hopefully they'll come bearing arms.

At that moment, the ship began to rumble and shake about us as its mighty engines growled to life.

"That's why," I said. "All Iralcus needs is a little more time and he can get this crate airborne. Then we'll be the ones who are trapped!"

Duh-nee's bronzed face had turned pale with the commencement of the engine noise. "I am all for catching Iralcus and bringing him to justice," the little man said in a low voice. "But not if it involves flying through the skies in this metal tube!" Courageous enough to take out the sniper in the stairwell, he was now visibly shaken. "If this abomination is really going to leap into the air, then I need to get my feet back on solid ground first."

I rested my hand on his thin shoulder. "I understand," I told him. "Look, the guards at the base of the tower probably scattered the moment they heard the engines fire up, so you should be able to get out of here and back to the main building. You've been a great help to us. Now you need to go find Haln and help her. Go quickly!"

The little Samary patted my arm with a grateful smile. He turned with a small wave of farewell and began to climb rapidly down the ladder.

I could read in Salde's face that she had no more desire to

stay aboard a rocket that was preparing for liftoff than had Duh-nee. "Go," I said with a nod. "And take Breemak with you. You've both done more than enough and Duare and I need to finish this. Make sure nobody is in range if this thing happens to take off.

She leaned forward to enfold me in an awkward embrace. "I shall do so, Carson of Venus. Jodades!"

Duare was regarding me with a fond smile when I turned back to her. "Just the two of us now," she said. "Like fighting the Zanis so many years ago."

"You get nostalgic at the very worst times. Do you know that?"

She hefted the pistol with a grin. "I'll distract them with this, if you think you can manage to wrestle Iralcus away from those controls."

"You should know by now that I can do just about anything with you by my side." I leaned in to give her a brief kiss, then moved closer to the hatchway.

The guard with the gun had been firing a short burst every half minute or so, probably trying to keep us at bay while conserving his charges. As a new lull commenced, I made ready to rush into the control room. The sound of frantic footfalls on the stairway below caused me to swing around.

Duh-nee burst through the hatch from the stairwell and slammed it behind him. He climbed up the rungs and stood panting on the small platform.

"I got turned around at the bottom of the stairs," he gasped. "Directions have never been my strong suit! Salde called to me, but by then I was headed in just the wrong direction and ran right into a half dozen of those white guards. I think she and Breemak made it out. I raced back to the stairwell and back up here, but the soldiers are right—"

A heavy thudding on the outside of the metal hatch interrupted him. "—behind me!"

The door flew open and soldiers crowded into the cargo room.

"Duare!" I shouted. "The pistol!"

She turned and shot, knocking one of the attackers to the ground before he could start up the rung ladder to our platform. It was becoming apparent that the Linneauns were far more vulnerable to their own weapons than they had been to ours. I wondered if Iralcus and his scientists had managed to add a third deadly force to the flesh-destroying r-rays and the even more destructive t-rays.

As Duare cut down another Linneaun and then a third, Iralcus' two white-stained guards suddenly burst from the control room hatch and went barreling at full steam across the little platform toward her unprotected back. I shouted a warning and she turned just in time to nimbly dodge the first soldier's attack, smiling grimly as his momentum carried him out over the railing and sent him hurtling down to the deck below. Another sidestep enabled her to evade the thrust of the second guard's slashing blade, but his great fist knocked her heavily against the wall and jarred the pistol from her grasp. Duh-nee ran over to crouch protectively before Duare, his own thin blade weaving hypnotically in the face of the soldier, who already bore the evidence of their previous encounter on his bleeding hand. I snatched up the gun from the floor of the platform and dispatched the fellow with a quick shot.

Meanwhile, Iralcus had continued to work at the control panel. The sound of the engines had been fluctuating up and down the scale from a low rumble to a high whine while we fought. Suddenly the noise became a shriek so loud I thought my skull would split open. The torpedo itself had begun to rock in a sickening circular motion, teetering like nothing so much as a giant top that was about to pitch on its side. Duh-nee and I clung fiercely to the narrow railing that rimmed the platform, while the Linneauns below pitched drunkenly to the floor of the cargo hold. Something clanged outside, and with a screech of metal grinding against metal, the entire ship leaped convulsively upward. Two warriors were nearly inside the open hatch of the cargo room. A furious rush of wind sucked the two unlucky creatures out into empty air before a third managed to pull the door closed and secure it.

I gazed about in astonishment amid the chaos. Iralcus had done it. He had launched his deadly torpedo into the skies of Amtor!

We gained altitude rapidly. Through a glass-covered port set in the side of the tall cargo room walls, I watched the mountains spin by and disappear, to be replaced by a great swath of open sea. The Linneauns huddled together on the floor below us, rocking back and forth like terrified children.

As I turned back to the platform, I discovered that the first guard had lost his own pistol when he had pitched over the railing during his ill-fated attack on Duare. The gun had slid to the edge of the platform. I grabbed it just before it fell into the cargo hold.

"I have to stop this!" I shouted over the deafening thunder and whine. I handed Duare the pistol and pointed toward the control room door. She nodded once, then she and Duh-nee moved back to the railing to guard my back.

I took one last look at them. Then I turned and headed toward the cockpit to stop Iralcus once and for all.

18

BATTLE IN THE AIR

ISTEPPED CAUTIOUSLY OVER the threshold of the control room, only to find Iralcus waiting for me, his massive body pressed tight against the wall just to the side of the hatch. He slammed into me before I could get off a clean shot, and the unpredictable motion of the rocket sent the two of us tumbling together about the room. We struggled to gain control of the pistol as it fired repeatedly, sometimes by his hand and sometimes by mine, the wild blasts singeing the control panel and cutting dangerous-looking gouges into the metal walls. Whatever alterations Iralcus' scientists had made to the familiar Amtorian pistol, the beam it now fired acted like some sort of unholy amalgam of the original r-rays and t-rays, no longer seeming to discriminate between organic and inorganic matter in its destructive effects. Smoke and the stench of burning wires began to fill the tight space of the cockpit.

"This is futile!" I shouted above the awful din of the engines. "The way this ship is flying, we're going to crash into the sea or collide with one of those mountains."

Iralcus responded with an ugly grin. "I will welcome either death, Carson of Venus, as long as your life ends with mine!" He suddenly released the gun and struck out at me with his massive fist. The blow sent the pistol flying from my hand and knocked me flailing back into the controls, my elbow connecting with a painful thud with a small bank of metal switches. The torpedo began to roll alarmingly to starboard.

By the time I had scooped up the gun from the floor, Iralcus was out of the cockpit. Through the hatch I saw his broad back disappear as he staggered past Duare and Duh-nee and began to clamber down the rungs to the lower compartment.

Out on the platform, I found my companions busy holding their own against the Linneauns below, most of whom had overcome their initial fright and taken up their leader's cause again with pistol and dagger. Duare was exchanging fire with a group holed up behind a stack of crates who were covering a smaller contingent as the latter attempted to reach the upper level via the rung ladder. Meanwhile, Duh-nee had stretched out on the floor by the edge of the platform where he could slash with his thin knives at the helmets of any who managed to near the top.

Iralcus grabbed a pistol from one of his soldiers and fired up at us, but the rocket gave a sickening pitch and his shots went wild. Two of his own white guards fell to the floor dead. "Worthless!" he cried. "You are all worthless!" He steadied himself against the wall and fired again.

Duare dodged his first shot and Duh-nee scrabbled back from the edge at the second, which had nearly singed his hair. I stepped forward and aimed a blast at Iralcus' head, narrowly missing him and leaving a dark streak on the wall. With a furious howl, he fired repeatedly as the ship lurched and rolled, lighting up the hold with his volleys and cutting down another of his own soldiers.

Duare and I took turns firing our own weapons in an attempt to keep the maddened leader constantly off balance. From the corner of my eye, I saw Duh-nee creeping close to the edge of the platform once more. As he peered cautiously out at the room below, a great hand suddenly thrust up over the edge and yanked him forward. One of the guards had apparently taken advantage of the melee to stealthily scale the rungs. Their combined weight caused both the soldier and his diminutive prey to pitch backward off the ladder.

I shouted in dismay as I saw the little Samary plummet

out of sight. The torpedo listed farther to starboard, rolling until we'd turned nearly forty-five degrees.

I was torn between braving Iralcus' continued wild shots to go over the side and aid Duh-nee—assuming the little man had survived the fall to the floor of the cargo hold—and trying to make my way back to the cockpit. I decided with regret that the second choice made the most sense. I wasn't sure there was anything I could do to save the ship at this point, but I had to try. As if divining my intentions, Iralcus gestured to his surviving troops to concentrate all their fire on Duare, while he focused his own gun solely on me, the barrage of searing rays pinning me at the side of the platform farthest from the control room hatch. It was a standoff: I couldn't get to the control room, but neither could Iralcus reach me with his beams.

Suddenly he swerved, his face split in a terrible grimace of rage and determination as he trained the pistol's powerful rays a few feet from where he crouched and directly on the ship's outer hatch. Could he really be planning to blow a hole in the side of the torpedo?

"No!" I shouted, knowing it was no use. "You'll kill us all!"

He concentrated his fire on the nearer edge of the hatch, his blasts slowly carving a jagged tear through the thick metal. Abruptly, one of the hinges gave way, and then the other, and the hatch flew outward. A veritable tornado of howling wind swept into the compartment. As Iralcus secured himself by one enormous hand to a nearby stanchion, the unlucky soldiers closest to the opening were wrenched off their feet and flung screaming through the open hatch and into the gray clouds beyond.

I grabbed the railing of the platform and wrapped my arm around it as tightly as I could. Duare did the same a few feet from me, and then we clung on for dear life, shouting desperate words to one another that neither of us could hear over the roar of the engines and the mad shrieking wind.

As we clung there, I watched in horror as Iralcus began a

titanic struggle to raise his pistol against the wind. Slowly he brought it to bear in our direction and narrowed his eyes as he prepared to cut us down.

There was nothing for it. I swung up my own weapon and shot twice, grazing the side of his unprotected head with the first beam and striking him full in the chest with the second. Iralcus the mighty fell to the metal floor, mouth gaping in a silent howl of mingled pain and outrage. No longer gripping the stanchion, he started to slide slowly along the wall toward the open hatch. Fumbling in desperation at the lower remnant of the broken hinge, he managed to halt his progress at the very edge of the opening, blood streaming from his scalp and his chest cratered with deep burns.

A flicker of movement drew my eye away from Iralcus. A rectangular wooden cargo pallet piled high with heavy crates that had been positioned against the wall at the base of our platform came slowly into view, the straps that secured the various containers flapping like tattered sails as it was forced toward the hatch by the inexorable winds. Duare and I saw the small figure clinging to the topmost crate at the same moment.

Duare loosed one of her hands from the railing for a second and reached out in a useless gesture. Though her voice was lost in the maelstrom, I saw her lips form the words "Duh-nee! No!" We watched in helpless horror as the pallet reached the lip of the hatch. For a moment it stuck there, wedged lengthwise against the frame of the door. A strap gave way, then another, and a pair of long crates on either side of the little figure sailed outward. Duh-nee still clung fiercely to the side of the largest of the crates, which looked to be more securely fastened to the pallet than the others. If he could manage to make his way down the other side, I told myself, he might still stand a chance. Then the whole structure lifted up from the floor in a slow arc toward the hatch. The remaining straps parting like threads, the rest of the pallet's contents poured out through the hatch and the little Samary vanished with the broken boxes into the Amtorian sky.

I looked away. Duare's eyes were rimmed with tears when I met her gaze and I feel no shame in saying that she was not alone.

The pallet now covered two-thirds of the open hatch, reducing the gale-force winds, and we were able to move together at one end of the railing. Steadying my back against the wall, I took Duare in my arms as the whole rocket began to shake violently. It felt as if we were no longer climbing, but I couldn't tell whether we had leveled off or were starting to descend.

I stared down at the cargo hold in dull disbelief over Duare's quaking shoulder. Bloodied and bruised, Iralcus had begun to move again, groping around with one hand for his pistol. Unable to locate the weapon, he pounded the hull at his side and screamed in rage. The metal almost seemed to buckle under his furious blows and for a moment I thought it might actually crack open beneath his onslaught. In his wrath he abandoned his hold on the broken hinge and pulled himself erect to stand with back pressed against the pallet.

He lifted his head. For a long moment his dark eyes, still ablaze with loathing, locked with mine. Battered lips writhing around a string of words I could not understand, he raised his fist in trembling defiance. Then the pallet cracked in two behind him and the full force of the wind rushed howling back into the cargo hold. The erstwhile conqueror of Amtor hung for an instant in the air outside the hatch, his blood-streaked face a blazing beacon of unabated fury. A second later, he was gone.

The torpedo gave another convulsive roll. Duare and I clutched the railing with one hand and held on to each other with the other as we were pressed against the floor at the edge of the platform. With the further change in position, more of the larger cargo items began to slide across the floor and out the opening. The bodies of the warriors Iralcus had killed exited the hatch in a grim procession. Then the ship shifted again and a massive metal locker came tumbling end over end through the air to slam against the hatch, thus sealing it almost completely, and at the very least giving us a moment's respite till the rocket's next somersault.

The relative quiet, save for a whistle of air around the edges of the hatch, was almost eerie. Ears ringing, I heard Duare ask: "What now, Carson? How do we get out of this mad place?"

I looked around us as we clung dazedly to the platform railing. What had once been the juncture of wall and ceiling was now a corner of slanted floor. Taking Duare's hand in mine, I pointed to the upside-down hatch of the cockpit. "First we get to the controls."

We edged our way hand over hand along the railing till we were a few feet from the doorway. "Ready?" I asked. She nodded and I swung myself carefully through the door. A second later Duare landed nimbly by my side on what had been the cockpit ceiling. The broad control panel hung at an angle above us, before it a giant-sized chair obviously designed for a Linneaun and thankfully still bolted to the onetime floor.

It looked like there would be room for both of us in the capacious curve of the seat. Thankful that the cockpit had been constructed with very little headroom for the average Linneaun, I crouched low and jumped for the arm of the seat. I pulled myself up and slipped beneath the broad seat belt, then reached down to offer a hand to Duare. With a small chuckle, she executed her own leap, added a spin worthy of an Olympic gymnast, and was soon hanging upside down by my side.

I studied the dials, switches, and levers in growing frustration. Not unexpectedly, the hot rush of blood to my head did little to improve my comprehension as I tried to make sense of the mixture of strange and familiar instruments.

Duare looked from the panel to my frown of consternation.

"Carson, there has to be something you recognize," she said urgently. "What else might they have duplicated that you could put to use?

I shook my head, my eyes scanning an array of instruments that were at the same time baffling and uncannily familiar. The Linneauns had reshaped my creation to fit their own scientific framework, copying the basic look, but not the functionality. "I can't…" I began.

Duare placed her hand over mine and gave it a little shake. "Think back," she said. "Picture what it was like when you first arrived here in your own ship."

I pursed my lips, remembering. "Clouds, a sea of clouds as far as the eye could see. I couldn't make out much of anything after I entered the atmosphere. Bailing out seemed the only option for survival." I turned to stare at her, eyes wide. "So I put on my parachute and jumped out the hatch. Of course!"

"And where did you keep your parachutes?" Duare asked.

"Over there in the forward locker."

My relief began to fade as quickly as it had arisen. This torpedo was built to be a missile, not a spaceship for passengers. And yet…the spark of another idea began to grow. As Duare made her way over to the locker and worked at the door, I reached up to a squarish box set into the wall above—now below—the control panel.

"Nothing here," Duare reported with disappointment from the open locker.

"I'm trying something else," I told her, prying at a latch on the side of the box. "Bingo!" Inside sat the unmarked handle I was looking for. I said a prayer that the Linneauns had installed it with the same purpose in mind that I had had when I equipped my own torpedo with a similar device. Iralcus had told me that his people were a highly imitative race. Now our lives depended on the veracity of that comment, and on my gamble that Iralcus himself had wanted to stage a test flight and recovery with the torpedo before ultimately using it as a missile of destruction. If my hunch was correct, that would explain why he had been confident enough to launch himself in the rocket in his attempt to flee.

Somewhere beneath us, an engine suddenly groaned and sputtered. The forward motion of the ship diminished perceptibly, until it felt as if we were no longer being propelled by anything other than our own momentum.

As the ship began to fall in a swift arc, I pulled Duare back to my side and we secured ourselves together in the oversized pilot's seat. The safety harness was also too big, but we tightened it about us as best we could. The world spun around us as the nose of the torpedo gradually dipped until it pointed back down toward the surface of Amtor. We were still in the cloud layer, but I could dimly make out the outline of water and coast through the forward ports.

Once the nose was pointed downward, the ship began to swiftly accelerate in that direction. I reached past Duare and put my hand on the lever in the square box.

Duare and I exchanged smiles. Hers was brave and determined; I hoped that mine matched it. "I guess it's now or never," I said. I yanked the handle upward and gave it a sharp twist to the right.

Nothing happened.

Duare had been watching my face. Her own went pale at my expression. "Was that supposed to have accomplished something?" she asked.

"Maybe I'm not tall enough," I told her. "Maybe this was designed for those long, double-jointed Linneaun arms." I pulled myself free of the harness and braced my foot on the wall before giving the handle another, more powerful turn.

This time we heard a sharp click somewhere nearby.

The sound of a muffled explosion came from outside the room. The whole rocket gave a massive lurch a second later, throwing us back into the seat. Duare grabbed me and held on as the ship shook and twisted as if fighting against some new force.

I exhaled a long breath as we felt the torpedo slow its descent.

"What did you do?" Duare asked. "It sounded like an attack."

"I equipped my original torpedo with a series of built-in parachutes designed to trigger in the atmosphere during my descent to the surface—the surface of Mars, as I once thought. As a backup to the automatic relays, I installed individual manual releases, as well as this master switch that could release all of the chutes simultaneously." I gave her a broad smile. "I was a very thorough designer."

"And one whose design the Linneauns admired enough to imitate." Duare hugged me. "I am very glad of that."

I saw no need to tell Duare that it had been a fail-safe device for a desperate situation, as the parachutes had never been intended for a safe manned touchdown, but rather to slow the craft just enough to allow me to jump out the hatch with my own parachute strapped to my back. However, this torpedo was moving much more slowly than it would have been had it just come racing into the atmosphere from outer space. I hoped the chutes would not be torn off during the rest of our descent and that they might buoy us sufficiently that our impact with the surface did not kill us.

The rocket was still falling at a faster speed than I felt comfortable with. I could see through the port that we were rapidly approaching a broad stretch of water beneath us. That gave me a bit more hope, as the sea was definitely preferable to the land in terms of achieving a survivable impact. Then it would merely be a matter of extricating ourselves from a rapidly sinking metal box, avoiding being sucked under or drowned in some other fashion, and somehow making our way through monster-infested waters to the nearest shore. It was a lot to ask of providence.

The sea rushed toward the ports and we landed hard in the water, the ship rolling and bucking as it plunged down into the depths and then bobbed slowly back to the surface.

Our battered craft lolled on its side amid a tangle of cables and billowing parachutes.

Duare and I held onto each other as the water churned above the ports. Thankfully the safety harness had kept us from slamming into the control panel or the bulkhead beyond it. Once the craft had settled into the rhythm of the gentle waves, we freed ourselves from the great chair and made our way out of the cockpit and down—or slightly up, in this case—to the floor of the cargo hold, where the water was already a foot deep and rapidly rising.

Duare and I stood ankle deep in the water and smiled wearily at each other. We were wet and filthy and smeared with smoke, but it appeared that we had survived the landing otherwise intact. Duare reached out to rub a single small spot of soot from my forehead and we both started to laugh. I embraced her then, and we stood holding one another for a few more moments than we probably should have as the ocean poured in from the aft section of the rocket.

We had discarded our packs and weapons at the top of the platform when we first entered the cockpit. I wasn't sure if we'd be able to carry them with us during what promised to be a long swim back to the Linneaun settlement through waters teeming with the hungry leviathans of Amtor's oceans, but we strapped them on anyway and headed to the hatch. I had picked up a long shaft of metal from the floor of the hold, just in case we needed a pry bar to help us get past the bulky locker that now swung half-free over the opening. I hefted it experimentally as we slogged through the swirling waters, wondering how it would fare as a makeshift harpoon in the event of unwanted reptilian company up ahead.

The opening between the top of the locker and the hatch was just wide enough for us to slip through. I mounted the dented metal surface and extended a hand to Duare.

"Ready?" I asked when she crouched by my side. "We should try to climb up onto the top of the torpedo while it's still afloat rather than diving into the water before we absolutely have to. We can survey the scene from there and decide what to do next. Who knows what nasty and inquisitive creatures may have been attracted by our splashdown—or what enemies may see us out here and come for us."

"You sound just like Nalte," she replied with a smile and a brave lift of her chin. "She seems to revel in pointing out the worst possible outcome in any given situation."

"She's earned the right," I said with a grin. "After all, she's survived an awful lot of worst possible outcomes—as have we."

The locker shifted under us as we clambered out the top of the hatch, and more of the sea rushed into the cargo hold. The torpedo began to settle around us.

"Up!" I cried, following Duare as she found purchase on a metal rung on the side of the craft. There were more of them evenly spaced in a circle around the rocket.

We reached the upward-facing side of the now rapidly sinking torpedo and turned our gaze to the surrounding waters.

"Look over there!" Duare said, pointing to the horizon behind me. There was the Linneaun outpost, the base hazy through plumes of smoke, while a swarm of anotars still buzzed about its upper levels.

We were quite far from the shore. I got to my feet and paced the length of the rocket's body that was still above the water. My mind raced back over the plans I'd drawn up for my original spacefaring torpedo, hoping there was something in them that I'd forgotten that might help. The parachutes floating alongside the ship were of no immediate use, though it occurred to me that with enough time I might find a way to fill them with air and bind them into some sort of raft. Unfortunately, time was no longer our friend.

Duare had come to stand by my side. She put a hand on my arm. "Didn't you see it?" she asked.

I turned back to peruse the gray-green waters in the direction she'd pointed. For a few moments I saw nothing but the hypnotic swell and fall of the gradually subsiding waves generated by our splashdown. At last I noticed the dark dot bobbing some distance away: a Myposan bireme, heading our way.

We were saved.

EPILOGUE
INTO THE UNKNOWN

OUR TRIP BACK to the coast aboard the bireme gave us ample time to catch up on the events that had unfolded in the rest of the world while Duare and I had been occupied with the late Iralcus Iguiri. As rows of fish-men strained at the oars below us, we learned from the Myposan captain that both his own jong Yron and the ruling council of the Sanjong of Havatoo had independently come to the conclusion that the Linneaun strongman had dealt each of them a bad hand. In Yron's case, the last straw had been the ever-increasing number of workers Iralcus had demanded to support his plans to conquer the region, while the Sanjong had belatedly realized that despite his protestations to the contrary, Iralcus had never intended to share his military innovations with Havatoo. Both the Myposans and the Havatooans had at last recognized Linnea as a common threat and reached out to powerful Korva to broker a temporary truce and face down their mighty enemy together.

We arrived at the little bay where what was left of the giant complex Iralcus had constructed to serve as the command center of his campaign squatted in smoking ruins above the poor dead village that had been at the heart of the whole affair. Spreading out around it on both sides of the rocky shore was the onetime peaceful country of Linnea.

A small contingent of Myposan guards conducted us to a rambling wooden structure that appeared to have once served as a barn and was now the temporary headquarters for the reconstituted Linneaun government. There Salde received us warmly as head of the new Linneaun state, her bulky body looking almost regal in her formal blue-and-yellow sash. She led us out to a pleasant garden framed by a circle of tall hedges behind the long wooden building, where Ero Shan and Nalte rose to greet us with joyful cries from a table laden with refreshments.

"Hail the courageous conquerors of Iralcus Iguiri!" Ero Shan proclaimed grandly, while Nalte ran to give each of us a hug of what felt like bone-crushing proportions. Stepping back, she raised her hand to her forehead in a mock salute. "Your troops are delighted to be reunited with their commanders!" she said, her face wreathed in a wide smile.

"If only all of them were here with us," Duare said wistfully. "Salde told us that Breemak flew off to parts unknown after they escaped from the tower, while…" Her words trailed off into silence.

Nalte's expressive face fell and Ero Shan put his arm around her. "Duh-nee…?" he asked.

I shook my head.

Seated like a statue at the edge of the garden, on a jut of rock overlooking a little pond of ornamental fish, Haln turned her scarred and tattooed face at our approach, but did not get up. I felt my own heart sink like a stone in my chest.

The giant Samary looked up at me, her face expressionless.

"I'm sorry, Haln," I said simply. "What you told us all those days ago was true: your mate was a fierce warrior. He fought until his demise, and saved my life as well as Duare's. We could not have stopped the horrors Iralcus had planned for Amtor without him."

Haln squared her broad shoulders. "I expected as much," she said with a nod. Her great hands sat balled into fists in her lap. "The males of our tribe, you see, are not prepared for war as are the females. They are never taught that a death in combat is an honorable one."

"His death was an honorable one," said Duare at my side, her eyes moist. "I promise you that, Haln."

"Yet still I live," Haln said quietly, as if speaking to herself. "Do you understand the shame of outliving your mate, when all that you have been taught is the importance of a good death? Duh-nee helped save the world. But now what is left in it for me?"

"You would be more than welcome to return with us to Sanara," Duare said after a moment. "As royal emissary of Korva, I could use the help of someone I trusted in reaching out to the Samary. The time is long overdue for our two peoples to open formal relations, especially with Havatoo flexing its muscles at your doorstep. There is still much good to be done in the world, Haln, and much honor to be achieved in ways that do not involve killing or being killed."

"It is a thought," Haln replied. Her rigid jaw had begun to quiver and we turned to let her grieve her lost mate in solitude.

Just then a rustle of commotion came from outside the hedge ring and a bolt of red came sailing over into the garden to land on stumpy legs.

"Well, this is a fine show of hospitality!" The angan folded his leathery wings and ran his hand back over his scalp, scowling as the motion dislodged a single small feather. He turned a critical eye to the dishes of fruit and sweetmeats crowding the nearby table. "As always, others dine in style while Breemak the Brave must be content with the scraps." He looked around at our astonished faces. "Well?"

We did not stay speechless for long. Crowding around the bird-man, the four of us pelted him with questions, only Haln remaining by herself, hunched over the pool and staring down into the waters.

Breemak halted the babble of interrogation with a raised hand. "It is simple. I departed the underground tunnel in order to patrol the skies and be ready to defeat the enemy should he take to the air. In my travels I encountered something that I thought should be returned to you, and so here

I came." He drew himself up. "Of course, the boorish Linneauns wanted us to enter the garden by way of that crowded building which smells of many zaldars, but I am an angan warrior and the skies are mine to traverse, no matter the nation below!"

I could feel my spirits begin to lift as the bird-man prattled on. I clapped him on the shoulder with a laugh, careful not to ruffle any more feathers. "Breemak, my friend, we are delighted to see you again, whether in the sky or on the ground," I told him.

"But wait," said Duare, brows creased in puzzlement. "Breemak, you said 'us'..."

"I did," replied the bird-man. "But not everyone is so agile that he can leap tall hedges."

A small sound came from the direction of the fish pool. Haln had gotten to her feet. She stood looking past us, her broad face expressionless, her big hands working at her sides. We turned as one to face the building behind us, where a thin figure stood leaning on a makeshift crutch.

Nalte's hands flew to her open mouth with a gasp that was half sob. "How—"

Haln thundered past us, closing the distance between them in giant strides. She stood for a single moment as if at a loss, then clutched Duh-nee in her great arms and spun him high into the air.

"I told you," Breemak said with exaggerated patience. "I was heading as far from Linnea as I could fly when I saw that ugly metal tube hurtling through the air, belching smoke and fire. I was curious, but I could not fly that high. It turned out I didn't have to, for a moment later something came tumbling out of the clouds above me. It looked a little worse for wear, but I thought it might be of some value to someone—" here he allowed a sly smile to break his facade of nonchalance "—so I decided to bring it here." He gave a meaningful pause. "Here, where I am certain that someone will soon offer a very tired hero a taste of food and drink."

We went to join the continuing reunion of Duh-nee and his mate while Breemak helped himself to the refreshments.

Haln set Duh-nee down and wiped tears from her cheeks. She cleared her throat. "Do you think you might have use for *two* Samary representatives?" she asked Duare. "One of whom is very good at counting things?"

As the rejoicing continued among our little band, I noticed Salde standing off to one side. I crossed the grass to her.

"This is a good day," I told her.

"Yes," she agreed, "And I have no wish to interrupt your celebration, but I must ask what happened to Iralcus up there."

I filled her in on the events that had transpired since we had last seen her, before the launching of the great torpedo. "It is safe to say that he will no longer be leading an army against the peoples of Amtor," I concluded. "Speaking of which—what has become of the rest of that army?"

"Once Iralcus blasted off in his rocket, his forces believed he had deserted them, never to be seen again. In a way they were right, of course. Most of them dispersed and retreated toward the mountains. I have been assembling a new Council of Six Claws under the utmost secrecy over the past several months, with the ultimate aim of leading a resistance against Iralcus Iguiri. With the soldiers scattered and their leader gone, we have already begun to pull things back together for our people. The Council has issued orders to engage the troops and bring them back into the collective, with instructions to begin dismantling the torpedo-cars and the great lanjotars." She paused, her eyes scanning the far horizon beyond the hedge.

"We have been isolated for so very long here in Linnea," she continued. "It had always been our way, until Iralcus arose to change everything. Those whom he initiated into his new warrior caste were originally hunters, not soldiers. It was their duty to protect us from the beasts and the monsters, but under the decree of the previous Council they had always been forbidden to leave our territory. And so it shall be again." It was hard to imagine the Linneauns becoming isolated again, given the network of tunnels that radiated outward from this place to far distant corners of Amtor. I had been wondering about them for a while, since they seemed to be an engineering marvel that had nothing to do with any information Iralcus could have gleaned from my crashed ship. I posed the question to Salde. "How did Iralcus manage such a massive project in only two decades?"

"Iralcus did not make the tunnels!" Salde said. "From the beginning, his work was focused always on the torpedo-cars and the giant lanjotars." She chuckled. "Do you think the great conqueror would allow himself to be diverted from his war machines in order to construct some fanciful iron mistal, with which to go burrowing through the crust of Amtor itself?" A mistal was the Amtorian equivalent of a rat or mole. "No," she went on, "they are part of the ages-old legacy of the Ancients. It is true that there are many tunnel openings here in Linnea, which is how we first came to explore them. Some lead beneath the mountain to the Ancients' archives, others run off to span the world—though most all of the latter were blocked by debris over the ages to the point of being impenetrable. It was those that Iralcus ordered opened when he decided to conquer Amtor. It was indeed a mighty task, to clear out the rubble of millennia and lay tracks for the rocket-cars, but it was child's play compared to what the Ancients originally accomplished. Soon, however, we will have no more need of such means of travel."

"I hope you don't withdraw from the world entirely. I think that there is much that our peoples could teach each other," I told her. I gave my head a sorrowful shake. "I'll always regret that the crash of my ship all those years ago was the cause of such prolonged grief for Linnea. I wish that there was something I could do for its people."

Salde raised her hand before I could continue.

"We know that none of this was your doing, Carson

of Venus. The arrival of your vessel injured no one, for it dropped out of the sky on the edge of our settlement where no Linneaun resided. Iralcus simply used the crash to cover up the tragedy his own reckless experiments had inflicted upon our people. I suspected as much and was about to expose his treachery when the infectious gas was released and the members of the Council were among those who perished instantly. That opened the path for Iralcus' seizure of our government. After that he quickly became so powerful that by the time I was ready to act it had already been decreed high treason to question his rule."

"I still wish that there was something that could be done to improve the lot of your people," I said. "Name it and I and my friends will do our best to accomplish it."

"Your offer is appreciated, my friend," Salde replied. "Unfortunately, there is little you or anyone else can do. The task that lies before my people is enormous, for we are dying. For years I have been delving into the sacred archives of the Ancients, which we had begun to uncover on the outskirts of our lands just before the crash of your torpedo. Iralcus himself stole some of those timeworn records, and I believe that is how he was able to develop those devices to allow himself and a favored few to exist—at least for short intervals—without one of these." She tapped the faceplate of her helmet. "He destroyed that information once he had made use of it, but I have been searching through the remaining records, so far in vain, to find a final cure for the pestilence with which his carelessness and malice has cursed us all. In recent years, I found references that indicate that the Ancients had once accidentally released a similar affliction upon themselves, and not long ago I came across the description of what I believe must be a cure."

"But that's wonderful news!" I cried. "Have you been able to manufacture any yet?"

She shook her head sadly. "I and my fellows have worked to reconstruct the antidote, but despite our best efforts we

have not been able to obtain a single vital but missing ingredient, an extract of a substance which was said to lie only in the
mud beds of some remote mountainous land. Without it the
remedy is useless, and I fear that my people will finally perish
and be gone within but a few generations."

I stood in silence for a long moment, afraid to say anything
in case I was mistaken. "Salde, I may perhaps be of some
service, after all," I said at last, for what she had described was
surely the remarkable healing mixture employed by the Cloud
People in faraway Anlap. When I told Salde of the substance
and added the information that my companions and I had
brought a small supply of it with us, she became excited.

Within minutes the quiet barn had become a hive of
bustling activity and in less than an hour Salde's scientists
had conducted a series of simple tests that confirmed that it
was indeed the missing ingredient in the Ancients' antidote.
Mass-producing the treatment would take some time, but if
all went well there was a good chance the entire population
of Linnea would be cured and finally free of the breathing
devices that had kept them imprisoned in those helmets for
so many years.

That evening my companions and I celebrated our recent
strokes of good fortune down by the rocky shore, at the small
camp that had been established by the Korvan military force
that had led the strike on Iralcus' base. There we were joined
by Taman, who told me that he had received my mental
projection after all, after which he had insisted on command-
ing the Korvan fleet himself.

While I was regaling the jong with the strange tale of our
adventures, a man dressed in the plain loincloth and trappings
of a private in the Korvan army approached us and stood
waiting with head bowed to be acknowledged. When I turned
to him, the man said meekly, "Greetings, Tanjong. Would
you have any garments you wish to be laundered?"

I did an old-fashioned double-take when I recognized the
man as none other than Lisant Or, spoiled son of that rich

miner who had laid claim to the jong's ear, and the same fellow who had given me so much trouble at the outset of the whole affair. I stood there speechless until Taman dismissed Lisant Or with a wave and the man departed the tent with a low bow.

Taman chuckled at the look on my face once we were alone again.

"Fortunes change," he said. "During their attempted invasion of our country, the Linneauns managed to completely destroy the mining operations belonging to Lisant Or's father. After the loss of his fortunes, the former magnate notified his son that from here on out he would have to make his own way in the world, and then went a step further and enlisted him in the army! It turns out not everyone is cut out to use a sword or a gun. Some are much better suited for laundry detail."

The festivities ran long into the night and involved much food and more bottles of fine wine than even Duh-nee could count—on those rare occasions when his mate released him from her side. Nevertheless, the following morning found me standing in the wreckage of the Linneaun fortress shortly after dawn, staring thoughtfully at one of the several entrances to the colossal tunnels of the Ancients, some of which ran deep into the mountains while others spanned the globe.

I could not say precisely what had roused me from my bed and drawn me there, though I suspected it might have had something to do with my old friend Jason Gridley, whose inexplicable appearances and disappearances were never far from my thoughts. It had been near the opening of just such a gargantuan tunnel that we had been miraculously reunited across the yawning chasm of space and time.

I pondered my conversations with Jason, and what he had told me of the mysterious force that had plucked him and his friend Victory Harben from the very center of the Earth to send them hurtling through the trackless wastes from one extraordinary world to another. Why had he come to Amtor? His theory was that he and I were linked somehow, entangled by some as yet unknowable law of physics. But did that also explain why we had been drawn together to reunite there in the Myposan outpost before the tunnels of the Ancients? I recalled the weird spectacle of a fifteen-foot corpse with green skin and four arms lying in a cavern bathed by azure light. It was all too bizarre. If Salde's tales were to be believed, the tunnels were primordial, dating back to the dawn of life itself here on my adopted planet. Could there be some secret mystery that lay in wait for me deeper in the tunnels, something that had entangled me in its web as surely as Jason and I had somehow been connected? I shook my head. I had no idea—yet—but as I stood there gazing into the yawning darkness of the tunnel entrance I felt a strange compulsion to step inside.

I don't know how long I had been there when the feeling crept over me that I was no longer alone. Turning, I found Duare standing behind me, a quizzical expression on her exquisite features.

"What are you thinking about, my love?" she asked softly. "You looked like a statue standing there."

"Oh, this and that," I replied with a little laugh. "Nothing very profound this early in the morning.

But Duare knew me far too well for that.

"In fact you are thinking about exploring the great caverns of the Ancients," she said, "while I have been dreaming about nothing more adventurous than our comfortable bed back in Sanara." She took a step forward and clasped my hand. "We haven't spent a day in our own home since before the ridiculous fiasco with that telescope. Do you not think it would be nice to rest, relax, and enjoy the quiet back home in Korva for a while?"

I loved our life in Korva, but perhaps that was part of the problem. After a while the soft bed, the cracks in the kitchen wall, the arrangement of pebbles in the walkway had become too familiar. "It seems we've lived there forever," I began, then halted. That wasn't the real issue. I began again: "Diplomacy, negotiations. I've never been one for meetings and drawing up trade agreements. If this ordeal with the Linneauns has served any useful purpose at all, it's been to remind me that there are plenty of wonders still left to discover on Amtor. There'll always be that soft bed waiting for us back home, but for now..." I gestured to the path into the unknown that yawned before us and squeezed her hand. "What do you say?"

Duare's radiant smile was all the answer I needed.

EDGAR RICE BURROUGHS UNIVERSE

PELLUCIDAR

DARK OF THE SUN

INTRODUCING

VICTORY HARBEN

TRANSCRIBED BY CHRISTOPHER PAUL CAREY

FROM GRIDLEY WAVE TRANSMISSIONS RECEIVED AT THE OFFICES OF
EDGAR RICE BURROUGHS, INC.,
TARZANA, CALIFORNIA

ERB
INC.

EDITOR'S NOTE
SIGNALS FROM BEYOND

I N HIS FOREWORD TO THE NOVEL at hand, author Matt Betts has explained how Carson Napier related to him the events of *Carson of Venus: The Edge of All Worlds* via mental projection. The account that follows, however, came to our world by a different means—a strange form of transmission known as the Gridley Wave.

It was in his own prologue to the novel *Tanar of Pellucidar* that Edgar Rice Burroughs first recorded how inventor Jason Gridley discovered this "new and entirely unsuspected" means of communication at a distance. Interestingly, he paused in his narrative as he grasped for the right words to describe the uncanny phenomenon before finally landing upon, "...well, let us call it a wave." Readers of the following narrative will find there was a very good reason for this curious statement, unknown until now.

The Gridley Wave could pass through any known interference or radio static. Mr. Burroughs claimed it could instantly penetrate the Earth's crust to reach the hollow world of Pellucidar or cross the vast gulf of space between our planet and the other worlds. It was by means of the Gridley Wave that Mr. Burroughs received the real-life narratives of several of the tales of wonder and adventure he later published under the guise of fiction.

For many years after the distinguished author passed from this world, no further stories came from these distant worlds for one simple reason: no one knew where his

Gridley Wave receiver-transmitter was to be found. But the recent discovery of a curious apparatus in a locked drawer in Mr. Burroughs' old desk has changed all that, and I am pleased to announce that new tales from distant worlds are again being received at the offices of Edgar Rice Burroughs, Inc., in Tarzana, California.

"Pellucidar: Dark of the Sun" is one such tale, which I have transcribed from a transmission sent by Jason Gridley himself. The story, which precedes the events told in *Carson of Venus: The Edge of All Worlds*, will go a long way toward enlightening the reader as to the mysterious appearances of Jason Gridley and Victory Harben in that novel.

Christopher Paul Carey
Director of Publishing
Edgar Rice Burroughs, Inc.

PROLOGUE

FROM THE LIDI PLAINS OF THURIA in the Land of Awful Shadow, to the Mountains of the Clouds that span the vast peninsula stretching between the Sojar Az and the Lural Az, to the great settlements of Sari and Amoz upon the continent's eastern shores—there reigns the mighty Empire of Pellucidar under the wise and beneficent guidance of its emperor, David Innes.

It was David Innes who, more than a generation before the tale I am about to tell, bored through the Earth's crust in the digging machine known as the iron mole. It was he also who, along with his companion, the erudite Abner Perry, discovered Pellucidar—a world within a world, its Stone Age inhabitants and monstrous primeval beasts abiding upon the surface of the Earth's hollow interior, with a tiny but glorious sun hanging stationary in the precise center of the enormous orbicular cavity. It was he, too, who united the savage human tribes of the region of Pellucidar in which he and Abner Perry found themselves. And it was he who at last cast off the yoke of slavery placed upon the tribes for eons by their hideous, reptilian overlords, that strange race of intelligent pterosaurs called the Mahars, and their apish servants, the giant Sagoths.

But no matter how mighty the hegemony carved out under his banner nor profound the changes he brought to the peoples of the inner world, David Innes has long made one thing clear—that he regards the terms "empire" and "emperor" with the deepest sense of irony as they apply to his own realm and rule. David, who has sacrificed blood, sweat, and tears, and borne the loss of so many of his friends and allies to repel the constant threats to his land, knows all too well that his "vast" empire is anything but. No—when compared to the truly mind-bogglingly enormous expanses of unexplored continents and oceans comprising the millions of square miles that stretch across Pellucidar's concave surface, his "empire" is no grander than an insignificant mote floating in the infinite reaches of the cosmos. So he has stated to me upon many occasions, and I am wont to agree with him.

As I have told you, my name is Jason Gridley. You are doubtless aware of at least some details of my biography, as they were laid down by Mr. Burroughs in the accounts he went on to publish as works of fiction. Of course, you already know of the Gridley Wave—the means by which I transmit this message—the existence of which I discovered in 1926. It was this discovery, made at my old ranch house in Tarzana with Mr. Burroughs at my side, that first awakened me to the realization that my friend's seemingly fantastical tales of other worlds were in truth based on fact.

Having made contact with Abner Perry at the Earth's core, I proceeded to travel to Pellucidar myself. But I need not bore you by recounting the events of that bygone adventure, and how, accompanied by Lord Greystoke, I traveled to the inner world through the north polar opening aboard the vacuum airship O-220, and thereby met my future mate, Jana, the Red Flower of Zoram. That is already a matter of record.* Neither shall I relate the multiple times I ferried an airship back and forth through the polar opening, each time in secret, for all of us in the know agreed the outside world was not yet ready to learn of the great mystery that lay five hundred miles beneath the foundations of her

---

* See the novel *Tarzan at the Earth's Core* by Edgar Rice Burroughs.

great cities. Nor is this the proper time to relate all the details of how, after settling for a period on the outer crust, Jana and I later journeyed back to Pellucidar and made it our home. I have it on good authority that in due time you will hear the full account of the latter adventure, at which time I will also give you the facts as I know them.** Some details of that tale are, however, pertinent to the present narrative, and I shall make reference to them here as needed.

I feel it necessary to impress upon you the gravity of the story I now relate. It is the beginning of a saga that will doubtless span several volumes when you have transcribed it from the accounts of those who will be contacting you in the days and months ahead. It is a strange epic, perhaps one better suited for a bard like Homer to tell rather than a simple radio bug like me. Moreover, do not be surprised when, by saga's end, you commence to regard the great globe upon which you reside much as David Innes regards his great empire when viewed against the backdrop of the seemingly measureless expanses of Pellucidar—that is, as nothing but a speck of dust floating amid boundless eternity.

My tale begins, by the reckoning of the outer world, during the first half of 1950. It was then that the Gridley Wave failed. But I get ahead of myself.

** See the novel *Tarzan: Battle for Pellucidar* by Win Scott Eckert, releasing Summer 2020 from Edgar Rice Burroughs, Inc.

PELLUCIDAR: DARK OF THE SUN
A Tale of the Swords of Eternity Super-Arc

VICTORY HARBEN GAZED UP through narrowed eyelids at Pellucidar's eternal noonday sun. Even before she spoke, I knew her squinting had as much to do with her skeptical nature as it did the brightness of the tiny star forever hanging miraculously at zenith in the hollow world's sky. My goddaughter is a scientist, after all.

"This world is impossible, old man," she said finally, confirming my intuition as well as bruising my fragile ego with the epithet to which she had unfortunately taken a liking. "You know that, right?"

"And yet you were born here," I said. "Does that make *you* impossible?"

Victory looked away from the fiery orb and flashed me a smile. "Only before breakfast," she said, alluding to what the Queen had told Alice on the other side of the looking glass.

"We're missing something," she went on. "I know it. For millennia, the people of the outer world believed the Sun, the Moon, and the stars revolved around the flat disk of the Earth, that the seas poured off the world's edge in an unimaginably titanic waterfall that fell into oblivion. It took just one person to change our viewpoint and allow us to understand what was really going on. I think it's the same with Pellucidar."

Her point made, Victory left behind the mystery of the hollow Earth and its impossible sun and strode across the

223

verdant meadow. Behind her loomed a dark opening in the ground that led down into the subterranean ruins from which we had just emerged.

After all these years, I was filled with joy to see my goddaughter again. In some ways, she had changed but little since I had last seen her six years before, when she had been an eleven-year-old girl leaving Pellucidar for the first time. Her smile was still brighter than the sun that shone down upon us and her mind sharper than a velociraptor's teeth. She was still blunt in the manner in which she expressed her opinions, and she was still usually infuriatingly right on the other end of whatever intellectual argument in which we found ourselves engaged.

But now she was an eighteen-year-old, university-educated woman who had lived in two worlds—literally. Little Victory von Harben had been born into a savage world within a world. There, in Pellucidar, she had spent the first few years of her life engaged in pursuits such as learning how to flintknap spearheads to defend herself against the great lizards and other frightful predators of a primeval age. Bones sticking out of her coiffure, young Victory had sat around the cook fire tearing off bits of thag steak with her strong teeth, her lips smeared with grease, every bit a member of the inner world's Paleolithic society as her Sarian peers.

But no simple Stone Age savage was Victory Harben. For though Victory's father was a fierce warrior named Nadok who hailed from the distant Voraki tribe, her mother was Gretchen von Harben, sister of my good friend Erich von Harben, both of whom hailed from the outer world. Almost two decades before the present tale, I had escorted young Gretchen, an anthropologist, on an expedition to Pellucidar, where she had an adventure of her own in far-flung lands and fell in love with the brave Nadok. Thereafter, the couple returned to Sari, the capital of the empire, where Victory was born.

From her mother, Victory had inherited a healthy curiosity about science and the universe. This was bolstered under the influence of Abner Perry, whom the girl loved and revered, as well as under the tutelage of her godfather during his visits to Pellucidar—that is, me.

But Victory was not destined to be garbed in animal skins and wear bones in her hair forever, for at the tender age of eleven she underwent a life-changing experience. It was then that her innate curiosity got the better of her and she ran away from her parents seeking adventure. Soon she found herself with more excitement than she had bargained for, standing face to face with a Mahar queen deep in the bowels of the underground city of Mintra, far to the northeast of David Innes' empire. That she survived the encounter and lived to tell the tale is a testimony to her tenacity and resilience.

Be that as it may, what she learned from the queen left Victory forever changed. When she returned from her unruly escapade, it was with the utter conviction that she must travel to the outer world and broaden her knowledge. She demanded to study at university, as her mother had. But Victory was not interested in anthropology—no, she wanted to study physics and mathematics, which, she firmly stated, the Mahar queen of Mintra had told her wove the very fabric of existence into being.

Seeing her young self in Victory, Gretchen could not refuse her daughter's wishes. And so Victory made the journey to the outer crust. There she found quite a different world from the land of her birth. At first, she made her home in America, under the custody of Captain Heinrich Hines of the O-220 and his wife, Anna. As the United States was then at war with Germany, she dropped the preposition "von" from her noble surname; her heritage was already more complicated than she cared to discuss. Ultimately, Victory Harben traveled to England, where she pursued accelerated studies in her chosen fields, graduating from university with a degree in theoretical physics at the age of only eighteen.

I have long wondered whether the weird timelessness of Pellucidar in some way explained how Victory, by the time she was eleven, was able to learn, comprehend, and converse with Abner Perry and myself upon topics of advanced science and mathematics. Often her understanding of these concepts went so deep that she wounded our pride by rightly pointing out our errors.

Thus it was of Victory I first thought when the Gridley Wave failed. But without the Gridley Wave at my disposal, I had no means of contacting her, for she still resided in the outer world, the crust of which no standard radio wave could penetrate. I had no choice but to return to the surface and fetch her.

That Victory would be willing to come I had no doubt, for only weeks previous to my journey I had contacted her via the Gridley Wave apparatus set up at the Greystokes' Chamston-Hedding estate, where she was wintering. At that time, we had discussed her wish to see once again her family and friends in Pellucidar. Moreover, I knew she could not resist a mystery, especially if it were a scientific one involving the Gridley Wave, which had always intrigued her. I hoped what she had learned at university might prove useful, for I could desperately use her help.

My trip to the outer world was brief and Victory was as keen as I to return to the world of her birth and solve the riddle of the missing wave. So it was that only two months later we had moored our dirigible in Sari and journeyed far to the northeast to the ruins of Mintra, where we now found ourselves.

"There," Victory exclaimed, "I was right!"

I stood over my goddaughter as she kneeled in the wild grass before a clay tablet, which we had just retrieved from an archival chamber deep within the subterranean fastness of the deserted Mahar city. Her graceful umber fingers ran swiftly across the strange glyphs carved into the tablet's fire-hardened surface.

"You can read Mahar that easily?" I remarked skeptically.

"Learned at the knee of Abner Perry himself," she said. "The Mahars once reigned over a territory that spanned the entire empire of federated tribes. Who knows how much of Pellucidar they still rule, and yet you never bothered to learn how to read their language?"

I laughed. "You haven't changed much, *Professor* Harben."

Victory's large violet eyes remained fixed on the tablet. "I'm *not* a professor," she said, and for a moment I thought my lighthearted rib might have struck a nerve. Then I saw the corner of her mouth pull up into a half smile, and she added, "Not yet, anyway."

Her fingers continued tracing the glyphs. "The ancient Mahars *did* know about the Gridley Wave, just as I'd told you. And apparently it failed in the past, for they knew how to jump-start it, too. Here's the frequency we need."

"How could they know about the Gridley Wave? They don't even have machines."

Victory stood up and walked over to the portable Gridley Wave apparatus we had brought with us from Sari, having transported it in a cart drawn by a small lidi, or diplodocus, who stood at the edge of our camp munching leaves off of what must have been a particularly delicious tree. I followed Victory to the apparatus, gazing up at the forty-foot-tall, latticework radio tower we had assembled at the site. Behind the tower the breathtaking, horizonless panorama of Pellucidar curved upward until it was lost in the distant haze.

"You know Abner's theory, right?" she asked. "That the Mahars project their thoughts into the fourth dimension, where they can access the thoughts of a fellow conversant via a sixth sense? Scientific understanding isn't limited to being able to build machines and fancy apparatus. Sometimes it's the result of simple biology. The Mahars have abilities we humans haven't evolved. And apparently one of them is a faculty that allows them to 'hear' oscillations in the frequencies of energy and subatomic particles. Of course, I don't really mean they hear them. Mahars don't have ears."

"Victory, don't touch that!" I cried as my goddaughter turned the apparatus' frequency dial. It was a sensitive control, and one I had very good reason to believe could cause the apparatus to emit a potentially hazardous signal if dialed too high. For that very reason I had never tried it. Victory knew all this only too well, as I had often cautioned her as such.

"Your calculations are all wrong, old man," she said. "Here…this should do it according to the tablet." With her final adjustment, the indicator needle crept up into the meter's red "warning" area.

As the radio box began to emit a serene humming in response to her adjustment, the girl took in my exasperated look and smiled. "You're stuck on Niels Bohr when you should be reading Dyson and Feynman. No wonder you haven't been able to figure out why the Gridley Wave's stopped working."

When I stated earlier that the Gridley Wave had failed, I did not mean to say that any of the several transmitter-receivers Abner Perry and myself had built in Pellucidar had in any manner broken down. That was not it at all. Rather, I meant that, as a universal law of nature, the Gridley Wave simply ceased to be.

Imagine, if you will, that some other universal law, such as gravity, suddenly no longer functioned, and no trace of its influence could be detected by any means, whether scientific or sensory. That is, envision that, as if with a flip of a switch, some absentminded god had accidentally turned off the very principle that holds our bodies to the ground. Then, I think, you will understand the effect the absence of the Gridley Wave had upon Abner's and my nerves, and

upon all those who reside in the Empire of Pellucidar and
had come to rely upon it for communication and navigation.

At the time of this story, Gridley Wave sets were
located in both the city of Sari and the base that David
Innes had named Greenwich many miles almost due east
of the empire's capital. Furthermore, battery-powered
Gridley Wave "pinging" stations lay at various sites within
the empire, each of which was designed to send out a
simple, repetitive signal that could be detected by a portable device and triangulated with the other stations'
signals, thereby aiding in navigation. Of course, these
stations were useful only to those of us who hailed from
the outer world, as David Innes, Abner Perry, and I did.
Native-born Pellucidarians—Victory included—had little
need for either such stations or ordinary magnetic com-
passes, as they were blessed with an inborn homing instinct akin to that of carrier pigeons, allowing them to
find their way home from any given point within the
inner world.

My biographer and I have both described this unique
signal, this effect, that in my youth I rather proudly
dubbed the Gridley Wave, using terms such as wave and
frequency. In truth, it was much more complicated than
that. So complicated, in fact, that I admit I did not truly
comprehend the principle's fundamental nature when I
first discovered it. Mr. Burroughs and I discussed this at
great length upon more than a few occasions. Even Abner
Perry was left baffled to explain the "wave" that we had
each independently stumbled upon, which lurked like a
phantom worm burrowed deep beneath the static of
standard radio frequencies.

Moreover, when I returned to the outer crust, I had
discussed the phenomenon with some of the greatest minds
our civilization has ever produced. Most scoffed at the
new type of frequency I proposed, which I always made
sure to couch in theoretical terms, the better to keep it a

secret; just as I could not abide the idea of pristine Pellucidar being despoiled by outerworlders, neither did I wish to see the Gridley Wave exploited for foolhardy or maleficent purposes. But my attempt to find an answer on the Earth's surface failed. Nor could the scientists of the Red Planet of Barsoom, with whom I had also made contact, provide an adequate hypothesis to explain the effect.

Victory stood up, hands on her hips. "You do know the Gridley Wave is both a wave *and* a particle, right? Just like the principle behind my uncertainty gun prototype." She drew a strange-looking pistol from the holster on her hip, its copper and gold fittings glistening under the bright rays of Pellucidar's eternal noonday sun.

When I say pistol, I use the term loosely, for no one besides Victory and me had ever looked upon the like of its one-of-a-kind design. Was it truly a gun, a weapon? It was hard to say, but regardless, it looked like one. But that had not been its purpose, which was to test the very principles Victory believed to be intrinsic to the Gridley Wave.

I eyed the uncertainty gun warily. "You're eighteen years old. Shouldn't you be at the prom or something instead of making guns? Put that thing away until we've tested it. For all you know, it might blast a hole in the wall of our universe." And from what I knew about Victory's theories, I understood all too well that I might not be exaggerating.

"And shouldn't you be in a rocking chair?" Victory quipped. "You're what...a hundred and *two*?"

Now, a stranger eavesdropping on our conversation might jump to the conclusion that Victory was something of a disrespectful little brat toward her patient and ever suffering godfather. Let me assure you that nothing could be further from the truth. Though we had been teasing each other since Victory was a young child, we loved each other dearly, and neither of us would hesitate to meet death if it meant saving the other's life.

As if Victory had sensed my thoughts, her tone softened and she placed a hand on my shoulder. "But thanks to Pellucidar's timelessness," she said, "not a gray hair on your head and as scandalously handsome as ever."

Then her voice lowered. "I'm sorry to hear about Mr. Burroughs. I know you two were close."

I paused, not knowing how to reply. I had only recently learned about the passing of my friend—the Admiral, as I had affectionately called him because of an old yachting cap he was wont to wear—when I had returned to the surface to retrieve Victory. I had hoped to consult with him about the mystery of the Gridley Wave's failure, and his sudden absence in my life had left me shaken.

"Thank you," I said at last. "Things just aren't the same without him."

But I had little time to meditate upon my feelings, for at that very moment the apparatus beside which we stood began howling with a loud, shrill whine, accompanied by an eerie luminance that shone down upon us from above. I gazed up to see a beam of intense white-violet light shooting straight upward from the parabolic antenna atop the latticework tower. Or perhaps it would be more accurate to say a corkscrew of light, for indeed the radiance took the form of an oscillating sine wave. Whatever the appearance of the strange emission, it was aimed directly at the noonday sun.

That in itself would have been enough of a surprise, for in all our extensive experience with the type of apparatus that generated the Gridley Wave, we had never suspected it might emit anything other than an invisible signal. But what happened next made us freeze in horror, as it likely similarly paralyzed all life in the entirety of Pellucidar, excepting perhaps that which resided far away in the Land of Awful Shadow.

The central sun grew suddenly as black as pitch, as if it had been instantly snuffed out. And yet around the sun's darkened disk manifested a reddish-violet corona, casting a weird, faint glow over the landscape of the inner world.

We could see plainly that the strange emission from the tower struck the precise center of the darkened orb of the sun. I cannot speak for Victory, but I for one stood in stunned dismay at the only conviction I could reach—that somehow our apparatus had extinguished the once-eternal noonday sun of Pellucidar!

In what was perhaps just as telling an omen to the severity of the moment as the sickening dim light that fell upon us, an unnerving hush fell over the whole scene. Gone were the ever-present growls and moans and roars of the great saurians and ferocious mammalian predators of this primeval world. Missing too were the screechings and musical songs of the exotic birds and terrible flying lizards. Even the hum of the apparatus had gone quiet. I turned to see our lidi on the edge of our camp cowed by what it saw, its long neck craned in a most peculiar fashion as it looked up at the darkened sun, its jaw hanging open and beady eyes filled with terror.

Then, as if all the fauna in Pellucidar suddenly woke up at once, a cacophony of ear-splitting cries erupted across the land, and everywhere I heard beasts great and small charging in a panic through the dense foliage of the surrounding jungle. I felt a wind at my back and turned to see a frightfully fanged and taloned dromaeosaurid emerge from the violet gloom. I gasped in horror when the great reptile almost bowled over Victory as it tore through our encampment in mindless fear before the jungle once again swallowed it.

A fluttering as if that made by great wings arose from the direction of the opening leading down into the ruins of dead Mintra. Victory and I whirled together at the sound and found ourselves standing face to face with the dreadful abomination that had just emerged from the hole—a frightful Mahar!

Though it was a small specimen, not much taller than Victory herself, that did not in any way diminish its fearsome terribleness. There, standing on the topmost step leading up from the abandoned subterranean city, it arrayed its great wings as if proud to display its appalling splendor. I felt as if its fierce fore-talons, raised along with its reptilian wings, beckoned us to bow before it. Moreover, it was clear from the way it raked its imperious gaze over us that it considered itself the superior creature. We were but puny, mindless animals of a lesser order to it.

Upon seeing the Mahar, Victory had whipped her uncertainty gun from its holster, though I noted she did not aim the strange-looking barrel at our monstrous guest but rather held the pistol high. For myself, I eyed the spear I had earlier in the day thrust into the ground, which stood halfway between the Mahar and us.

Without considering that the Mahar might tear me to shreds with its merciless talons, I leaped for the spear and snatched it up, intent on thrusting it into the heart of the dread menace that confronted us. Only Victory's forceful shout stopped me.

"Don't hurt her!" she cried. "We don't know what she wants."

"It's a *Mahar*, Victory," I retorted. "It wants to enslave humanity." But I did as my goddaughter had implored and withdrew to her side.

"That's an assumption, old man," Victory went on. "The Mahars think differently from us."

"It's not an assumption," I said. "It's demonstrable history."

Victory made a noise of dissatisfaction. "History is written by the victors. Our two races have *never* understood one another."

"They've never given us a chance to understand them."

Now one might think Victory quite naïve to have believed an understanding might arise between the Mahars and the gilaks, as humans are called in the predominant tongue of this region of Pellucidar. But consider for a moment that Victory had not yet been born during the age in which the Mahars held all of the empire's human-ity in thralldom. She had never known a time when gilaks were forcibly removed from their villages by the Mahars' Sagoth armies and marched in chains across the fierce, primordial landscape, only to be led deep down into the suffocating, underground cities of their reptilian overlords. There they would serve their hideous masters until death overtook them, perishing from exertion or devoured in secret, bloodthirsty rituals, never having seen their homes or families again.

Consider, too, that she had been born on the eve of a great battle against an incursion of Mahars, years after they had been originally defeated and driven from the empire by David Innes and Abner Perry. Though Victory's mother had said she named her daughter in part because of a strange dream-vision she had had during childbirth of a barbaric queen of the same name, Gretchen had made it clear she had also been inspired to name her child in the hope of triumph in the coming confrontation with the winged menace. The name Victory, it turned out, was well chosen, for indeed the people of Sari and the united tribes of the empire overcame the Mahars and their fierce ape-men during the next morning's battle. But when Victory grew older, she took bitterly to the fact that she had been christened after the desired outcome of a conflict in which numerous members of an intelligent species had been slaughtered.

"You and Abner," I said. "Always inventing things like uncertainty guns and cannons, only then to act as gentle-hearted as swans."

"A swan will bite your fingers off," Victory said tersely.

But now was not the time for debate, so I argued no more. We stood before a member of the archenemy of the human race, a scourge that meant to wipe our species from the face of Pellucidar now that we had raised its ire. I am not ashamed to say that fear coursed through me, but it was not for myself that I felt afraid, but for my goddaughter. She was entrusted in my care, and should anything happen to her and I managed to survive, I would never forgive myself.

Beside me, Victory inhaled sharply as if in surprise.

"What is it?" I asked.

"I can't explain how I know," she replied, "but I've met this Mahar queen before. I just *feel* it's her. The Sagoths call her Tu-al-sa, one of the most ancient Mahars—and the very same whom David Innes once carried to the surface in his iron mole and later returned safely to Pellucidar. It's what made me go to the surface world and study math and physics."

An ominous feeling of dread crept over me upon hearing her words. "You're scaring me, Victory," I said. "This is starting to sound like a setup."

Victory shushed me and said, "She thinks we're rude for chattering in front of her. Well, for moving our lips, anyway… Mahars can't hear. But she knows we're communicating between ourselves."

It was then that I heard the voice in my mind. A voice that was at the same time not a voice. Though I knew full well the phenomenon that I was now experiencing, I marveled over it just the same. At one time, the Mahars believed humans were brainless cattle, and so they did not bother communicating with us. But now, more than a generation after David Innes led the gilaks of the region against their reptilian overlords and drove them from the empire, the Mahars knew differently. Now they were well aware they could access our thoughts via what Abner Perry calls our sixth sense and "speak" with us directly in our minds. But that did not mean the Mahars had lost their arrogance.

"Your limited mind conceives not that your fluilation teteculates with another angle."

Those were the words the soundless voice formed in my head. As it "spoke," I heard the words echo in both past and future tenses as my mind sought to translate the Mahar's intent into my native English, and then, again, into the Pellucidarian tongue. The Mahar language knows only present tense, and therefore, the human mind attempts to compensate, sometimes rendering the mental communication in the tense it finds most natural.

It is a strange, disconcerting experience to be directly fed meaningful bites of information without words to back them. It is stranger still to hear one's mind render words that one does not understand, such as "fluilation" and "teteculates." Where did those words come from? Had my mind merely filled in the blanks where information was given to it that it did not understand? Surely not from the Mahar, who lived in a world of complete deafness and therefore could not know, let along impart, any sense of phonetics. It was a mystery.

Confused, I said aloud, "My *fluilation...teteculates?* I'm sorry, I don't know those words."

Again, soundless words formed in my head.

"Just as you are oblivious, perhaps all within Pellucidar must soon pass into oblivion...and so, too, all who lie at the angles beyond."

"Lying at angles beyond?" I pointed down at the ground. "You mean those inhabiting the surface of the sphere of dirt and rock that surrounds Pellucidar? The people of the outer crust?" I could think of no other meaning for the Mahar's words.

"This communication becomes ineffective."

With its words still echoing against the walls of my cranium, the Mahar swept one of its great wings as if it were whirling a cape before itself so that it might turn and make a grand exit.

Victory had also clearly heard the queen's words in her mind, for she threw herself down on one knee before the Mahar and raised her hands over her head as if in supplication.

"Wait!" she cried. "Hear my thoughts, O Mighty and Sagacious Queen! We are not your enemy." Then Victory bowed her head as the strange corona surrounding the dark disk of the sun cast down its dim, surreal reddish-violet light upon her.

The Mahar lowered its cape-like wing and turned back to gaze down upon Victory as a monarch might upon its lowly subject. Victory, sensing she had achieved her royal audience, raised her head and continued with her desperate plea.

"Your people have essential knowledge about the principle with which we...*teteculate*...with those beyond Pellucidar. We seek your help! Why has the principle failed? And what have our adjustments to our transmitter using the ancient tablet done to Pellucidar's sun?"

"I remember you, daughter of Nadok the Voraki," the queen said, as I also could "hear" the words intended for my goddaughter. *"'Victory'...a repellent appellation signifying the Sarians' triumph over and mass slaughter of my people."*

Victory now rose and, standing tall and determined, reached out an arm in an unmistakable gesture of peace. At least unmistakable to humans, I thought. She stood only inches from the queen's long maw of razor-sharp teeth.

"I didn't get to choose my name or what happened between our peoples in the past," Victory said. "But together we can choose our future. Let's put our differences behind us and work together in peace. Will you help us?"

"Don't trust it, Victory!" I cried.

She motioned me to stay back. "Put down your spear, old man. If you can't trust her, then at least trust me. I know what I'm doing."

The Mahar turned its head and craned its neck so that one of its sinister eyes—each of which was positioned on either side of the head like a bird's—seemed to be examining the ritual tattoo on the upturned anterior side of Victory's extended forearm.

"Your flesh is marked, Victory Harben."

"My tattoo?" Victory said. "I got it as a little girl. It was decreed by the Krataklak elders who guide the Voraki, my father's tribe. A sort of coming-of-age ritual."

"So Nadok tells you."

Without warning, the ancient Mahar flapped its majestic wings and soared over our heads. Victory and I both ducked, fearing an attack, as the wind from its wings whooshed over us, but she came to rest near the control mechanism of the Gridley Wave apparatus.

We both watched as if mesmerized as the queen reached out with a scaled claw and placed its talons around the frequency dial.

"I now reveal to you its true meaning…and help you, as you request."

Tu-al-sa turned the dial, moving the indicator needle in the gauge above it to the extreme end of the red "danger" zone.

Before I could even cry out a warning, the apparatus began to whine like a banshee. In but an instant, the oscillating sine wave emitting from the tower's parabolic antenna transformed into a solid violet-white ray—a true beam of light, this time. The powerful ray shot up at the black disk of the sun and appeared to mirror off the solar surface, beaming back a second ray that ended only a few feet from where Victory stood. There, at the end of the ray, a vortex of swirling, bluish-purple energy irised out of thin air, funneled like a tornado on its side.

Victory, standing half turned before the mouth of the maelstrom, looked at me, her violet eyes wide with surprise. Her reddish-brown hair blew toward the vortex, as if the great mouth of the maelstrom were drawing all the air around her into its spiraling gullet.

I made to throw my spear, thinking to impale the devilish reptilian queen that had generated the turbulent funnel of energy, but found I had dropped the weapon in my shock.

Then the unthinkable happened. The furious winds of the maelstrom lifted Victory clear off her feet into the air and drew her into the raging mouth of energy. I heard a thud as her gun fell onto the grass. Then she disappeared into the funnel and I saw her no more.

It was all over in but a second or two, with no time for me to think, let alone to act. One moment, Victory was there; the next, she was gone as if she had never existed.

As soon as it had swallowed her, the vortex slowly began to shrink, its mouth irising smaller and smaller.

Consumed by rage, I confronted the Mahar queen, who still stood beside the Gridley Wave apparatus.

"What have you done?" I cried.

"Does she not ask for help, warm-blood?"

"This is how you *help* my goddaughter?" I asked bitterly. "By making her vanish into thin air? You tricked us, you sly lizard!"

Tu-al-sa again grasped the frequency dial with a claw, turning back the knob so that the gauge's needle returned to the "zero" mark. Instantly, the intense beam of light disappeared and the sun was dark no longer, now shining down as brightly as it always had from its perpetual zenith. Eerily, however, the unearthly maelstrom still swirled like a horizontal tornado of energy, though its mouth was now one quarter smaller than when it had swallowed Victory.

"Does not the sun again radiate?" said the voice in my mind. *"Can you not now use your apparatus to teteculate with other angles? Is this not 'helping'?"*

Anger, spurred on by fear for Victory, swept over me and my whole being shook in fury. Then the thin veneer

of civilization fell away like a useless husk and I lost all
sense in my utter rage. I was now but a simple Stone Age
savage thirsting for the kill.

I leaped upon my prey and squeezed its cold, reptilian
throat beneath my strong, warm-blooded hands.

"Tell me where she is…you hideous…*ugly*…bird!" And
with each word I spoke, I throttled the queen harder. The
stench of the carnivorous Mahar's breath nearly suffocated
me as the monster's long snout opened and its skinny lizard
tongue stuck out stiffly. I knew that within but moments
I would succeed in crushing its throat and putting it out
of its misery for all eternity.

It was then that the queen reared back and struck me
full on with one of its powerful wings. I flew through the
air and came to my senses when I struck the ground to
one side of the Gridley Wave apparatus. There I lay prone
until I reached out my arm and accidentally placed my
hand upon the shaft of the spear I had dropped earlier in
my shock. The presence of the weapon bolstered me and
I stood up, grasping it in both hands.

Again Tu-al-sa's words formed soundlessly in my mind.
*"I do not know where Victory Harben's fluilation draws her.
Perhaps, if she is lucky, she goes straight to Halos."*

"I don't know where or what 'Halos' is," I cried, "but I'll
send you straight to Hell!"

I raised my spear, only to see stars as a massive, hairy
fist struck me hard in the face.

"Meet my faithful servant, impudent warm-blood!" sounded
the disembodied voice in my aching skull.

I lay in the grass, blood streaming from my mouth. The
entire side of my face throbbed with pain and my vision
had blurred. And yet my eyes had not dimmed so much
that I had not failed to notice something golden and
glimmering beside me in the verdant sward. I reached out
and my fingers wrapped around the butt of the uncertainty
gun Victory had dropped in the grass.

With perhaps the greatest effort of my life, I lifted myself shakily to my feet and stood to face the towering mass of muscle and dark fur that had struck me. It was a Sagoth, one of the brutish gorilloid servants of the Mahars. The mountain of flesh and bone must have been eight feet tall if he was an inch. He glared at me, his red-rimmed eyes narrowing in bestial rage, and charged.

Now my friend Clayton, who is better known as Tarzan of the Apes, has told me his view that the Sagoths were just innocent victims of the Mahars. But time was running out and I had lost my patience. I had but one recourse if I were to survive, and yet it was a gamble, a pull of the roulette wheel—an uncertainty.

I raised Victory's gun, aimed its sight at my target, and pulled the trigger.

The charge that blasted from the gun surprised me as much as its effect, for within its wide beam I swore I saw stars and nebulae and galaxies. If I was surprised, the Sagoth was even more so, for as the beam hit him squarely in the chest, his dark eyes, which had been narrowed with grim purpose, widened into perfectly round orbs.

I blinked, and in the next moment I saw nothing but swirling wisps of luminance dissipating upon the breeze where the Sagoth had stood.

The breeze made me turn, for it was caused by the maelstrom, which, when I bore my gaze upon it, I saw had shrunken greatly, the mouth of its funnel now but the size of a manhole cover.

In desperation, I ran to the Gridley Wave apparatus, flipped a series of switches to activate the normal transmission mode, and adjusted the frequency dial.

"Jason Gridley calling Greenwich and Sari Stations," I said into the microphone. "Please relay this message to David Innes. The Mahar queen of Mintra is responsible for what happened to the sun. She's hurled Victory Harben through a portal…I believe into another world…"

I stood up, pulling the microphone's cord to its fullest extent so that I might get closer to the swirling maelstrom, the mouth of which was now just a foot in diameter. With my other hand, I raised the uncertainty gun and, not knowing whether it might fire a dud or destroy the universe, pressed the trigger and shot its weird, unearthly beam into the center of the vortex.

The mouth of whirling bluish-purple energy widened by about three feet, which was enough for my purposes.

"And I'm going after her!" I cried into the microphone, and then let it go.

By the time I had leaped headfirst into the maelstrom, its hungering mouth had widened to a diameter of six feet. Whether it kept widening after I made my leap I did not know, for I had left the world of Pellucidar behind. The last trace I caught of the inner world as I was sucked into the void was the soundless voice of the Mahar matriarch in my mind.

"A grave error, warm-blood! Your fluilations are—" And then I heard old Tu-al-sa no more.

Almost as soon as I had entered the vortex, I found myself tumbling out of it into a turquoise-hued field. I stood up amid an expansive prairie, its blue, waist-high grass stretching from one horizon to another. I thought to myself that those horizons looked strange, for everywhere the land met the sky in a flat line. Gone was the breathtaking, horizonless panorama of Pellucidar, where the ground curved upward into the mists.

I gazed up at a sky as brilliantly turquoise as the grass. There hung two suns, one larger than the other, glaring down at me like a pair of bloody red eyes. If I had harbored any doubt that I had left Pellucidar behind, it now evaporated.

I was on another world.

In the distance I saw a cyclopean city carved out of

white stone, a massive dome rising from its towering walls. Just beyond the great metropolis loomed what appeared to be an impossibly huge rocket ship pointing straight into the sky.

"Where am I?" I said aloud. "And more importantly… where is Victory Harben?"

It would be a long time and I would experience many harrowing adventures on countless worlds before learning the answer. If only I knew then what I know now—that my advent upon that strange world of brilliant blue would soon be but the first in a succession of worlds on which I would find myself. For when I had passed through the vortex, some mysterious force seemed to have permeated my being. After spending what I estimated to have been five earthly weeks on the turquoise world, I heard a sound that resembled that of a steel cable snapping. Suddenly the world around me disappeared. I experienced a rushing sensation as if I were hurtling through the cold void of space, and then I found myself standing stark naked upon an even stranger world.

But my unprompted and unexpected teleportations did not stop there. After several days on the planet Caloomna, ringed like Saturn and with many moons in the sky, again I heard the steel cable snap. And again I was hurled to yet a different world. Then, after a seemingly random interval, I found myself upon yet another. And then another, and yet another, and another. And on and on, remaining on some worlds for only a matter of seconds, while residing on others for what seemed to be many months. I wondered what the Mahar queen had done to me—and for what arcane, maleficent purpose?

All the while I thought of Victory, out there in the unknown. Was she being hurled from world to world the same as I? I did not know, until at last I appeared on a planet called Amtor. There, by either a quirk of fate or some unfathomable law of attraction, I encountered a man whom I had known on Earth. Carson Napier was his name, and from him I learned that Victory had recently appeared on his adopted world, manifesting in the same perplexing, dizzying fashion as I. Then she had disappeared just as quickly.

Ah, but it gave me hope! We were in some manner connected, entangled in the web of fate. And somehow… somehow, I would find her.

ERB UNIVERSE™

The Swords of Eternity super-arc continues in
Tarzan: Battle for Pellucidar
by Win Scott Eckert

ABOUT THE AUTHORS

THE EDGE OF ALL WORLDS
CARSON OF VENUS®

MATT BETTS is the author of such science fiction novels as the critically recognized adventure *Odd Men Out* and its sequel *Red Gear Nine*, the urban fantasy *Indelible Ink*, the giant monster vs. giant robot book *The Shadow beneath the Waves*, and the cryptid horror tale *White Anvil: Sasquatch Onslaught*. He is also an accomplished speculative poet, and lives in Ohio with his wife and children.

PELLUCIDAR®
DARK OF THE SUN

CHRISTOPHER PAUL CAREY is the author of several books, including *Swords Against the Moon Men*—an authorized sequel to Edgar Rice Burroughs' *The Moon Maid*—and the forthcoming ERB Universe novel *Victory Harben: Fires of Halos*. He has also scripted comic books featuring Burroughs' characters such as Tarzan, Dejah Thoris, and Carson of Venus. He is Director of Publishing at Edgar Rice Burroughs, Inc., and the creative director of the Edgar Rice Burroughs Universe series.

Edgar Rice Burroughs: Master of Adventure

The creator of the immortal characters Tarzan of the Apes and John Carter of Mars, EDGAR RICE BURROUGHS is one of the world's most popular authors. Mr. Burroughs' timeless tales of heroes and heroines transport readers from the jungles of Africa and the dead sea bottoms of Barsoom to the miles-high forests of Amtor and the savage inner world of Pellucidar, and even to alien civilizations beyond the farthest star. Mr. Burroughs' books are estimated to have sold hundreds of millions of copies, and they have spawned 60 films and 250 television episodes.

About Edgar Rice Burroughs, Inc.

Founded in 1923 by Edgar Rice Burroughs, one of the first authors to incorporate himself, EDGAR RICE BURROUGHS, INC., holds numerous trademarks and the rights to all literary works of the author still protected by copyright, including stories of Tarzan of the Apes and John Carter of Mars. The company oversees authorized adaptations of his literary works in film, television, radio, publishing, theatrical stage productions, licensing, and merchandising. Edgar Rice Burroughs, Inc., continues to manage and license the vast archive of Mr. Burroughs' literary works, fictional characters, and corresponding artworks that has grown for over a century. The company is still owned by the Burroughs family and remains headquartered in Tarzana, California, the town named after the Tarzana Ranch Mr. Burroughs purchased there in 1919 that led to the town's future development.

In 2015, under the leadership of President James Sullos, Jr., the company relaunched its publishing division, which was founded by Mr. Burroughs in 1931. With the publication of new authorized editions of Mr. Burroughs' works and brand-new novels and stories by today's talented authors, the company continues its long tradition of bringing tales of wonder and imagination featuring the Master of Adventure's many iconic characters and exotic worlds to an eager reading public.

Visit **EdgarRiceBurroughs.com** for more information.

QUANTUM INTERLUDE
One Small Leap for Victory

I FELT THE HOT WIND of Pellucidar against my back gusting out of Tu-al-sa's maelstrom, from which I had just emerged. Above me in the crystal-clear night sky, a wide planetary ring arced across a backdrop of nebulae and stars more brilliant than any visible from Earth on the clearest desert night. I stood upon a spire of orangish rock speckled with patches of a strange teal growth that resembled moss. Below me, a little stream cut through the craggy terrain.

A creature unlike any I had encountered before watered at the stream. Its body and legs were shaped like a giraffe's, but its neck was a long flexible, snakelike tube. Two serpentine ancillary appendages with mouths at the ends emerged from the creature's forebody, snaking downward and lapping up water with their narrow tongues.

The thing must have heard my sharp intake of breath, for it whipped its neck around and glared at me with its single eye, which resided at the end of the stalk. One of its two ophidian appendages turned toward me, its lips pulled back to reveal sharp, triangular teeth.

I heard a gentle wafting sound. I looked up to see a horse-sized creature in the sky, its body and wings as translucent and thin as wax paper. It phosphoresced with a soft green luminescence as it fluttered across the cosmic tapestry above.

A little thrill that was part fear and part exhilaration ran through my entire frame.

Well, Earth *was* getting a little boring…

JOIN
EDGAR RICE
BURROUGHS®
FANDOM!

The only fan organization to be personally approved by Edgar Rice Burroughs, The Burroughs Bibliophiles is the largest ERB fan club in the world, with members spanning the globe and maintaining local chapters across the United States and in England.

Also endorsed by Burroughs, *The Burroughs Bulletin*, the organization's official publication, features fascinating articles, essays, interviews, and more centered on the rich history and continuing legacy of the Master of Adventure. The Bibliophiles also annually sponsors the premier ERB fan convention.

Regular membership dues include:

● *Four issues of* The Burroughs Bulletin

● The Gridley Wave *newsletter in PDF*

● *The latest news in ERB fandom*

● *Information about the annual ERB fan convention*

For more information about the society and membership, visit **BurroughsBibliophiles.com** or The Burroughs Bibliophiles Facebook page, or email the Editor at BurroughsBibliophiles@gmail.com.

Call (573) 647-0225
or mail
318 Patriot Way,
Yorktown, Virginia
23693-4639, USA.

EDGAR RICE BURROUGHS UNIVERSE™

THE EYE OF AMTOR™

CARSON

OF VENUS®

THE FIRST ERB COMIC
[BO]OK IN HISTORY TO BE
[D]ECLARED CANONICAL
BY EDGAR RICE
BURROUGHS, INC.!

[W]RITTEN BY MIKE WOLFER,
FROM A PLOT BY AUTHOR
MATT BETTS

● ILLUSTRATED BY
VINCENZO CARRATU

INCLUDES "PELLUCIDAR®:
[H]ARK OF THE SUN" BY
[A]UTHOR CHRISTOPHER
[P]AUL CAREY & ARTIST
[M]IKE WOLFER, FEATURING
[J]ASON GRIDLEY™ AND
[T]HE DEBUT OF NEW
[E]RB UNIVERSE HEROINE
[V]ICTORY HARBEN™!

THE OFFICIAL, CANONICAL PREQUEL TO THE ALL-NEW ERB UNIVERSE NOVEL
CARSON OF VENUS: THE EDGE OF ALL WORLDS BY AUTHOR MATT BETTS!

AMERICAN MYTHOLOGY PRODUCTIONS™

ENTER THE
EDGAR RICE BURROUGHS
UNIVERSE ™

When a mysterious force catapults inventor Jason Gridley and his protégé Victory Harben from their home in Pellucidar, separating them and flinging them across space and time, they embark on a grand tour of strange, wondrous worlds. As their search for one another leads them to the realms of Amtor, Barsoom, and other worlds even more distant and outlandish, Jason and Victory will meet heroes and heroines of unparalleled courage and ability: Carson Napier, Tarzan, John Carter, and more. With the help of their intrepid allies, Jason and Victory will uncover a plot both insidious and unthinkable—one that threatens to tear apart the very fabric of the universe!

CARSON OF VENUS ®
THE EDGE OF ALL WORLDS
by Matt Betts

TARZAN ®
BATTLE FOR PELLUCIDAR ®
by Win Scott Eckert

JOHN CARTER OF MARS ®
GODS OF THE FORGOTTEN
by Geary Gravel

VICTORY HARBEN ™
FIRES OF HALOS
by Christopher Paul Carey

THE FIRST UNIVERSE OF ITS KIND

A century before the term "crossover" became a buzzword in popular culture, Edgar Rice Burroughs created the first expansive, fully cohesive literary universe. Coexisting in this vast cosmos was a pantheon of immortal heroes and heroines—Tarzan of the Apes®, Jane Clayton™, John Carter®, Dejah Thoris®, Carson Napier™, and David Innes™ being only the best known among them. In Burroughs' 80-plus novels, their epic adventures transported them to the strange and exotic worlds of Barsoom®, Amtor™, Pellucidar®, Caspak™, and Va-nah™, as well as the lost civilizations of Earth and even realms beyond the farthest star. Now the Edgar Rice Burroughs Universe expands in an all-new series of canonical novels written by today's talented authors!

JOIN THE ADVENTURE AT ERBUNIVERSE.COM

ERB INC.

EDGAR RICE BURROUGHS
AUTHORIZED LIBRARY™

COLLECT EVERY VOLUME!

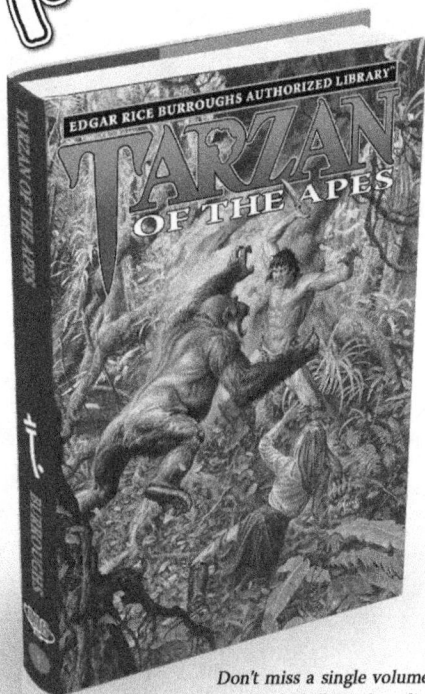

For the first time ever, the Edgar Rice Burroughs Authorized Library presents the complete literary works of the Master of Adventure in handsome uniform editions. Published by the company founded by Burroughs himself in 1923, each volume of the Authorized Library is packed with extras and rarities not to be found in any other edition. From cover art and frontispieces by legendary artist Joe Jusko to forewords and afterwords by today's authorities and luminaries to a treasure trove of bonus materials mined from the company's extensive archives in Tarzana, California, the Edgar Rice Burroughs Authorized Library will take you on a journey of wonder and imagination you will never forget.

Don't miss a single volume! Sign up for email updates at ERBurroughs.com to keep apprised of all 80-plus editions of the Authorized Library as they become available.

TARZAN OF THE APES — BURROUGHS — 1
THE RETURN OF TARZAN — BURROUGHS — 2
THE BEASTS OF TARZAN — BURROUGHS — 3
THE SON OF TARZAN — BURROUGHS — 4
TARZAN AND THE JEWELS OF OPAR — BURROUGHS — 5
JUNGLE TALES OF TARZAN — BURROUGHS — 6
TARZAN THE UNTAMED — BURROUGHS — 7
TARZAN THE TERRIBLE — BURROUGHS — 8
TARZAN AND THE GOLDEN LION — BURROUGHS — 9
TARZAN AND THE ANT MEN — BURROUGHS — 10
TARZAN, LORD OF THE JUNGLE — BURROUGHS — 11
TARZAN AND THE LOST EMPIRE — BURROUGHS — 12
TARZAN AT THE EARTH'S CORE — BURROUGHS — 13
TARZAN THE INVINCIBLE — BURROUGHS — 14
TARZAN TRIUMPHANT — BURROUGHS — 15
TARZAN AND THE CITY OF GOLD — BURROUGHS — 16
TARZAN AND THE LION MEN — BURROUGHS — 17
TARZAN AND THE LEOPARD MEN — BURROUGHS — 18
TARZAN'S QUEST — BURROUGHS — 19
TARZAN THE MAGNIFICENT — BURROUGHS — 20
TARZAN AND THE FORBIDDEN CITY — BURROUGHS — 21
TARZAN AND THE FOREIGN LEGION — BURROUGHS — 22
TARZAN AND THE MADMAN — BURROUGHS — 23
TARZAN AND THE CASTAWAYS — BURROUGHS — 24

THE JOURNEY BEGINS AT ERBURROUGHS.COM

ERB INC.™

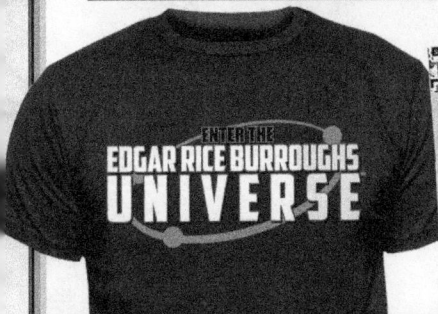

CPSIA information can be obtained
at www.ICGtesting.com
Printed in the USA
FSHW012152230420
69355FS

9 781945 462238